Sar

DAPHNE'S QUESTIONABLE BET

To all you quirky girls out there, I SEE YOU, and I think you're AWESOME.

CHAPTER ONE

*O*nesie pajamas were basically the greatest creation of all time. Nothing beat lying down on the couch, snuggly in a onesie, and reading a blood-curdling horror novel by the warm fire. The hood of the onesie had to be up, of course, my sea of dirty-blonde wavy hair tucked in the back so I wouldn't twirl it.

Scratch that. Reaching back, I secured a thin length of hair in my hand, twirling it around my finger and thumb, really working the strands as I got sucked into the chapter.

I'd pulled the coffee table close to me, sliding the rug over the wood floor, so my hot chocolate could be within arms' reach.

My night was looking optimistic.

Two hair-raising chapters in, "Psycho" by Post Malone rang out from my phone. I hurried to snatch it from the coffee table—knowing it was my best friend Veronica video calling—my hand smacking into the mug in the process. Hot chocolate cascaded down my hand, searing my skin.

I was too busy shaking out my hand to really appreciate Veronica dancing on the screen, knowing what song would be playing on my end. I pressed the answer button as I wiped my other hand on my pink Cheer Care Bear onesie.

"Why do you look like you just found sour cream on your plate?" Veronica asked, her dance coming to a halt. Judging from the confined space and dresses hanging on the hooks behind her, she was in a dressing room.

I held up my hand, even though the evidence was already gone. "Spilled hot chocolate on myself."

"Oof, that's gotta hurt." Veronica's long, black hair hung down around her face, smooth and shiny. Her thick lips were covered in loose skin since she bit her lip so much.

I stuck out my tongue in disgust. "And now I'm thinking about sour cream."

"Cherry Coke."

Sighing in relief, I sunk back into the couch, holding my phone out in front of me. "Much better."

She narrowed her brown eyes, trying to take in the hood of my onesie. "What's the mood today?"

I angled the phone so she could see the rainbow covering my stomach. "Happy."

"Good. I need your help." She changed the view on her phone so I could see her through the mirror. "A?" The short navy-blue chiffon dress was cut low, the sequins glittering in the store light. She set the phone on a chair, darkness filling up the screen.

As she shuffled around—changing into another dress—I took a sip of my hot chocolate. I frowned at the top of it. It should have been covered in melty marshmallow goodness, but we were out.

"Or B?" Veronica asked. She'd changed into a burgundy dress with a high neck and lace cap sleeves, the skirt hanging just above her knees.

"B." I sipped the hot chocolate, the mug warming my hand.

She pursed her lips. "You didn't even ask what I need it for. That could change your answer."

"Doesn't matter. Your mom will kill you if you wear A, and B is a better color on you."

Tilting her head to the side, she stared at herself in the mirror. "That's what I was thinking, but DeShawn likes the color blue."

I almost dropped the phone. "I'm sorry, did you just say DeShawn?"

Her grin practically split her face in two. "We have a date tomorrow night!"

"DeShawn." I set the mug on the coffee table so I wouldn't spill any more liquid on myself. My heart was hammering in shock.

She hopped up and down a few times, letting out a squeal. "Yes!" She cringed when she remembered she was in a dressing room, checking over her shoulder like someone would actually be standing there.

"The same DeShawn you've hated since elementary school? The one you added to your "hit list" in middle school?"

Veronica waved her hand. "That's old news. He's totally changed." She wiggled her eyebrows. "He's all buffed up now."

"The same DeShawn that's a running back on the football team, and you told me a few weeks ago after a game that he should 'run himself on back to Loserville where he belongs'?"

She placed her hand on her hip. "You really need to get past all that and focus here."

I pulled back the hood of my onesie, running my fingers

through my messy hair. "I'm sorry, I just don't know how to process this. In third grade, you told him the two of you were sworn enemies, and you'd rather take a thousand daggers to the heart than be in a reading group with him." I smiled. "I knew in that moment that I'd picked the perfect best friend."

Veronica threw out a hand. "How do you remember all of this?"

I slapped on my best "duh" expression. "It was a monumental moment in my life."

She blew out a deep breath, sending some hair that had fallen in front of her face billowing. "I swear, you remember the most random things."

The rumble of the garage door echoed down the hall, letting me know Mom was home. I checked the time on my rose-gold smartwatch.

"Mom's home early," I mumbled.

Veronica leaned closer to the phone, her fake eyelashes and penciled-on eyebrows taking up most of the screen. "I can't understand you when you mumble."

The back door slammed open, and I spun around in time to see Mom running down the hall, peeling off her high heels in the process and throwing them on the ground.

"I'm in a Hurry" by Alabama played in my mind, reminding me of my dad. One of his favorite bands.

"Get packed!" Mom rounded the corner and tossed her purse on the kitchen table. The leather slid effortlessly across the wood, thankfully stopping short before it could fall off the table. "We're moving."

The song in my head came to a screeching halt, like records being scratched, making me cringe. Worst. Sound. Ever.

Wait. What?

Moving?

Shaking the screeching record from my head, I stared after Mom in shock, my mind frantically trying to piece together what was happening. I must have heard her wrong.

"What?" I yelled at the same time Veronica did.

"Turn the phone around so I can see her!" Veronica snapped.

I did as I was told.

"Mom, call me silly, but I swear it sounded like you said we were moving." I sat up, watching my words settle in her eyes, and the determined nod that followed caused a whimper to crawl up my throat. I *had* heard her right. Reaching up, I tucked my hood back over my head, feeling the darkness looming. Something bad was about to happen.

Mom started undoing the buttons on her blouse as she moved toward the stairs. "You heard me right. I want to be out by tonight."

"Let's keep this PG, Mrs. Richards," Veronica said.

Mom paused her unbuttoning and squinted at the phone. "Oh, hey, Veronica. How are you doing?" She waved her hand. "Sorry, I don't have time for small talk right now. Daphne, get upstairs and pack up everything worth keeping." She bounded up the stairs two at a time, moving quite deftly for wearing a pencil skirt.

I watched her ascend the stairs, confused. We were moving? Why? Where?

"Why are we still sitting here?" Veronica shrieked. "Follow her!"

"Oh, yeah." I ran up the stairs, stumbling halfway up. I regained my footing and sprinted to Mom's room.

Her blouse and skirt were on the bed as she shimmied into a pair of sweats, only wearing a bra on top.

"This just went way past PG. So never wanted to see that side of your mom, Daphne."

I turned the phone so she could see me. "You're the one who told me to face her."

Veronica rolled her eyes. "Clothes coming off should automatically assume I don't want to watch." Her thick lips turned into a smile. "Unless it involves Asher Angel."

I twisted my lips to the side and tapped my chin. "I just don't get the hype."

"Daphne!" Mom yelled, making me look at her. She was finally fully dressed. She yanked a suitcase down from the top shelf in the closet and tossed it on her bed. "Focus. Just essentials. I'll have Shannon take care of the rest." She opened her dresser drawer with so much force, it rolled off the tracks. Shrugging, she set the entire drawer on the bed and transferred the items to her suitcase.

We had officially switched to a code red Mom breakdown.

"Veronica, I'll call you back," I said, the words spaced out. I threw out the next words as an afterthought. "Get the maroon dress."

"Don't you dare hang—"

I ended the call and slipped the phone into the pocket I'd sewn on the side of my onesie—seriously, manufacturers should know that pockets are a given for every piece of clothing—before holding my hands out in front of me like I was trying to calm the crazy Judson twins I used to babysit. "Okay, let's breathe for a second." I sat down on her bed, patting the spot next to me. "What's going on?"

"Nothing." Mom moved to another drawer, taking that one out from the dresser as well and turning it upside down over the suitcase, all the contents haphazardly pouring in. "I felt like a change."

"Which meant up and leaving in the middle of the night from the house we've spent the last eight years in?" I leaned forward and grabbed her hands before she could move toward another drawer. "The same house where you made me help repaint the entire downstairs just a couple of months ago."

Mom forced a smile, tucking her short blonde hair behind her ear. "It will make it easier to sell."

I guided her to the bed until she was sitting next to me. "Talk."

With a sigh, Mom fell back onto the bed, sinking into the mattress. "Patrick showed up at work again today."

I lay down next to her, staring up at the ceiling fan. Dust hung from the sides of the blades from lack of use—thanks, freezing cold Utah winter—and our busy schedule. "This is like the tenth time."

"I know." She rubbed her forehead. "The guy just won't take no for an answer."

I turned onto my side so I could face her. "Yes, it's creepy, but it's not a 'get up and move' situation. Can't you file a restraining order or something?"

She looked at me, her face scrunching like it always did when she had to tell me something she really didn't want to. "I did. A couple of weeks ago. Nothing changed."

"Why didn't you tell me?"

"I didn't want to worry you."

I gestured to her suitcase. "And coming home, declaring we're moving, and rushing to pack *isn't* going to worry me?"

Mom propped herself up on her elbow, facing me. Dark puffs of skin sat under her green eyes. The last time I'd seen her this tired was at Dad's funeral. But through it all, a smile formed on her lips. "Grams and Gramps want to retire."

"It's about time." They owned an antique shop down in

Southern California and were at least five years past retirement.

"They want to travel for the next few years." Mom placed her hand on mine. "They've offered to sell me the shop and their home in Yorba Linda."

"I always knew you were their favorite child."

"I'm the only one in a spot where I could possibly uproot my life right now."

My mind spun. "Move back to California?"

I'd grown up in my grandparents' home, back when Mom and Dad were barely scraping by. They searched for jobs everywhere, including Utah, where Mom's sister, Shannon, and her family lived. Dad ended up getting offered a lucrative job in Utah, so they up and moved us when I was nine. We'd really enjoyed our time here, but Dad passed away a couple of years ago, leaving Mom and me alone in this huge house filled with reminders of happier days.

Mom glanced around the room like she was replaying memories. "I think a change would be good for us. We'd be back near the beach, Disneyland—"

"Veronica." A grin burst out on my face, way bigger than Veronica's had been. "I could actually hang out with her instead of taking her places via video chat."

Mom scratched above her lip. "So weird that the two of you do that." She lowered her hand. "Like, really weird."

I got so many strange looks from people when I'd call Veronica at nearby events, like festivals, and we'd just video call the whole time so we could "experience" it together.

"The weather is nicer," I said, easing into the idea of moving. "We'd be able to escape the Utah winter early."

Mom twisted her lips to the side. "But it's more expensive."

"And more crowded," I put in.

Mom sat all the way up. "No Six Sisters' Deli."

I sat up next to her, thinking about our favorite local restaurant down the road. "I'll miss their egg salad sandwich."

"You think we should do this?" She stared at her hands, eyes unfocused.

I lightly pushed her shoulder. "You were just shouting that we were."

She twisted a hand. "Not really shouting—"

"Total shouting. Neighbors probably heard." I placed a hand on my cheek. "Mrs. Weaver is going to be ticked if we move." She was our elderly next-door neighbor that we'd grown very attached to. I considered her another grandma.

Mom put her arm around my shoulder and pulled me close to her. I rested my head on her shoulder, breathing in her peach scent.

"We need a fresh start." She rubbed her hand on my arm. "And I think it will be good for you to be back with Veronica. You two need each other."

We'd both been dealing with a lot. Veronica's dad walking out on their family. Her taking care of her younger brother and sister so their mom could work more hours. My ever-building anxiety, which had recently led to panic attacks. Things hadn't been right since Dad passed away.

I stood, straightening out my onesie. "I'll go pack."

CHAPTER TWO

*T*hick palm trees greeted us as we pulled into my grandparents' subdivision, immediately washing me with a comfort of home, and I knew we'd made the right choice.

Mom reached over from the driver's seat and took my hand. "I feel good about this."

"Me, too," I said, squeezing her hand.

Veronica hadn't stopped squealing since I'd told her we were coming back to California. She wanted to throw a block party and basically invite everyone we went to elementary school with, but I talked her down from that. I wanted to ease into the change, especially since it was in the middle of my junior year.

Grams and Gramps were waiting outside of the house when we pulled into the driveway, both of them waving so excitedly, their wrinkly skin flapped on their arms. Gramps had on his typical Hawaiian shirt, cargo shorts, and flip flops, even though it was fifty degrees outside. His shaggy hair and beard had gone full gray. Grams' eyeglasses were perched in her dyed-blonde hair. Her top and cardigan were both blue, same as her flats and the necklace dangling around her neck. Always put together, Grams.

Unlike my mom—who had me at the ripe age of twenty-one—Grams and Gramps had Mom when they were in their late thirties. Mom was the youngest child and unplanned. They always say she was one of their greatest blessings.

Veronica was on the grass, jumping up and down and holding a humongous sign that said, *Welcome home, Daphne and Laura!* in a glittery magenta ink. Best. Color. Ever.

As soon as I opened the passenger side door of my mom's white BMW, Veronica hit play on her phone, and "Sucker" by the Jonas Brothers blared out. She danced around on the grass, spinning in circles and shaking the sign, her tunic shirt billowing with the movement.

I joined her on the grass, letting the upbeat tune fill my soul, immediately finding my groove and singing very off-key at the top of my lungs.

Even Mom got in on the action, busting out her Zumba moves to the music.

As soon as the song ended, Veronica threw down the sign and went to wrap her arms around me. I was already heading toward her, moving with way too much force, so we collided with one another, both falling to the ground. Some-how, we kept our arms around each other in the process, and we hugged each other tight as we lay there on the lawn.

Veronica kissed my cheek about five times before she spoke. "I've missed you so much."

I squeezed her cheek against mine. "Let's never part again."

"Deal."

Gramps cleared his throat, and I looked up to see him

staring down at us with an amused smile. "Do we get hugs, too? Or are you only excited to see Veronica?" His rumbly voice was music to my ears.

Smiling, I scrambled to my feet and threw my arms around Gramps' neck, burying my head into his neck and breathing in his woodsy cologne.

"I've missed you, too, Gramps."

His cool lips found my forehead, giving me a kiss. "Oh, my sweet Daphne girl." He pulled back and looked over at Grams. "That's it. We're staying."

Grams rolled her eyes at him before she gave me a tight hug, swaying me side to side. "You look absolutely beautiful, young lady." Kissing my cheek—and for sure leaving behind a pink lips mark—she put her arm around my shoulder. "And as much as I'd love to, we're not staying." She smelled like lipstick, hairspray, and floral perfume all wrapped into one. How I'd always remembered her.

Veronica bounded up from the grass and brushed off the back of her jeans. "Where's the first stop?"

"London," Grams said with a grin.

"Then on to Scotland, Paris, Italy, Spain, and anywhere else we can go." Gramps popped a lozenge into his mouth. "I'm personally looking forward to Croatia and Greece."

"Sweden for me," Grams put in. "That's where my family is from. Can't wait to do some family history while we're there."

"Sounds exciting," Veronica said with obvious sarcasm.

Mom bounced on her toes. "As lovely as this is, I really gotta pee. How about we go inside?" She hurried in before any of us could answer.

"I made lasagna," Grams said as we walked toward the house.

Veronica and I both did a fist pump. Grams and

Gramps were basically the greatest cooks ever, and I wanted them to stay for that reason alone. But they really wanted to travel, and they deserved to. They'd never left the United States. All their focus had been on their shop and family, making sure everyone was well provided for.

As Gramps and Veronica went to unloading our suitcases from the car, Grams showed me to my room. It had been a few years since we'd come back to visit. Mom was so busy with work, and me with my online shop. I sold handmade sling bags, trying to save up to buy my own car.

I stopped short in the entryway to my room, surprised. "You redecorated."

Grams cautiously watched my face, her lips pursing in concern the longer the silence spaced out. She fiddled with her long necklace, clearly uncomfortable. She opened her mouth to say something, but I ran into the room and shook my hips in a dance. "Happy" by Pharrell Williams blasted in my head, so I shimmied back and forth, humming along.

"This. Is. Amazing!"

Grams had taken all my favorite things—Care Bears, Captain America, the color magenta, and Cherry Coke—and created a hodgepodge of decoration. It was all mismatched and so random—like the vintage Captain America figurine on the nightstand. There was even a hammock chair hanging from the ceiling, and I knew I'd spend a lot of time there.

"I love it, Grams." I threw my arms around her, and she sagged under me in relief. "I can't believe you did this for me."

She pulled back and glanced around the room, the corners of her eyes tightening. "Trust me, it killed me to decorate it this way. I mean, there's no flow or theme." She ran her wrinkly hand down my wavy hair. "But I knew it was perfectly Daphne."

I sat down on the full-sized bed, taking one of the stuffed Care Bears lining the Captain America headboard into my arms. I squeezed it close. "Hey, Grams?"

She sat next to me on the bed. "Yes?"

Glancing around, I took in every detail. So much time had to have been put into this room. "Mom's been planning this move for a while, hasn't she?"

She smiled sheepishly. "She knew that the more time you had to think about it, the more the anxiety would build inside you, and you'd completely stress yourself out." She put her arm around me. "Besides, you always loved an adventure."

True. There had been something really exciting about a spur-of-the-moment move, rushing to only grab the essentials. It was like prepping for the zombie apocalypse, only without the stupid flesh-eating zombies.

I leaned my head against her shoulder. "Do you really have to leave tomorrow? Can't you at least stay a couple of weeks?"

"We got a great deal on the airfare that we couldn't pass up. Besides, Gramps and I got an international phone plan. We can video chat all you want."

"But the time difference."

"We'll figure it out." She stood and tugged me up with her. "We've got the whole evening to party. Let's make the most of it." She winked at me. "I made cherry pie as well."

My favorite. She always did it just right. Plus, the homemade whipped cream? To die for.

I let go of her hand, ran out of the room, and sprinted down the hall, my arms flailing. "I'm coming, pie!"

CHAPTER THREE

*W*e dropped Grams and Gramps off at the airport the next morning. We were almost home when I got a video call from Gramps.

"Miss me already?" I asked.

Gramps smiled at me from his seat on the airplane. "Of course. Had to hear your voice one last time before we left." He moved the camera, so Grams was also in view.

I did the same, so they could see Mom in the driver's seat. She waved at the phone without taking her eyes off the road.

I'd pulled the screen back enough that my shirt was showing.

"Why are you wearing that shirt?" Gramps asked with a frown.

After we got back in the car, I'd taken off my sweater, so they hadn't seen what shirt I was wearing when we were at the airport.

I motioned to the Grumpy Care Bear on my shirt. He was frowning, matching with the clouds and raindrops on his stomach. "It's a reflection of my mood. This is how I feel about you leaving."

"In a couple of weeks, you won't even notice we're gone," Grams said, shifting closer to Gramps.

"Not true," I said. "You kids have fun on your trip. Take tons of pictures and send them to me."

"And have some gelato for me when you get to Italy!" Mom talked way louder than she needed to. She wasn't *that* far away from the phone.

Mom and Dad had gone to Italy on their honeymoon, and then returned for a second trip on their ten-year anniversary. It was definitely on my bucket list.

Gramps shook his finger at the screen. "Don't you two girls go ruining the house. No wild parties."

Mom frowned. "Guess I'll have to cancel the kegger I was planning for tonight."

I patted her arm, fake-consoling her. "I'll cancel the strippers for you as well."

Grams busted out laughing, but Gramps just continued to scowl at us.

Mom rolled her eyes. "When have I ever had a kegger?"

Gramps scratched his beard. "Let's see. When was that? Nineteen eighty-something."

"That was Shannon!" Mom said. "Wrong kid, Dad."

He narrowed his eyes, his bushy gray eyebrows coming together. "Oh, that's right. Sorry. I always get you two confused."

"Yes, I can see why the different hair color and height, plus the eight-year age difference, would confuse you." Mom's words oozed sarcasm.

Grams and I both laughed.

We pulled into our subdivision.

Mom waved her fingers at the phone. "Love you guys! Have so much fun!"

"Love you, too, sweetie," Grams said through her chuckles. "We'll text you when we land."

Gramps blew us a kiss. "Love you, my favorite girls."

"Tell the pilot to fly safe!" I got in before he hung up the phone.

Mom glanced sideways at me. "Yes, I'm sure the pilot would love your Gramps knocking on the cockpit door with that piece of advice."

I shrugged. "Could be helpful." I opened the door and got out, stretching my arms over my head after I shut the door. I adjusted my magenta handmade bag slung around my body. "We should have stopped for breakfast."

Mom paused on the driver's side. "We should have." She checked her watch. "We could go back out. The only thing planned today is to unpack." She grinned at me. "Tomorrow, the true fun begins."

I tapped the top of the car with my knuckles. "Yeah, about that. I was thinking homeschool."

Mom tilted her head to the side. "You'll get to see Veronica at school."

"Yes, but there will also be other people attending said school."

"Cute boys."

I twisted my lips to the side. "Tempting."

"Laura Fletcher?" A woman shouted from behind me. I whipped around to see a middle-aged woman in the driveway next to us. She had her hand on her chest, her jaw dropped in shock.

Mom came out from around the car. "Kimber?" Her whole body had gone rigid, an irritation painted on her face that even I hadn't ever conjured up, and I drove her crazy all the time.

Kimber sauntered closer, her high heels clicking on the pavement. She swept her curly, brown hair behind her shoulder. "Laura. Fletcher. Here in the flesh."

"Richards." Mom's voice was as tight as the lines on her face. "It's Laura *Richards* now."

I took a step back so I could get a better view of the stare-down, clutching the strap of my bag against my chest. I had no idea who this lady was, but I did know Mom hated her with a fiery passion, and Mom didn't hate anyone.

"Mama Said Knock You Out" by LL Cool J started up in my head, and I found myself bopping my head to the beat, my foot tapping against the pavement. Music had always been my emotional outlet. My way to help deal with anxiety. So, songs randomly popped into my mind, creating the soundtrack my mood needed.

Kimber clucked her tongue. Even from where I stood, I could see her nostrils flaring. If it weren't for the row of bushes separating the driveways, I had a feeling there would be a throw-down going on right now.

"Right." Kimber wiped below her lip like she was trying to highlight her thick, red lips. "How's Ian?"

The anger from Mom's face melted a little, replaced by the sorrow that always resided in her eyes when Dad was brought up. "He passed away a few years ago. Cancer."

The fire faded from Kimber's eyes as well. "I'm sorry to hear that. He was a good man."

"Yes, he was," Mom said.

Well, at least they agreed on that much.

"Mom, have you seen my black ..." A girl my age jogged onto the driveway, trailing off when she saw Mom and me. "Hey."

Releasing the death-grip on my bag strap, I waved at her. "Hey."

The girl had her dyed-black hair up in a high ponytail, her lipstick as red as her mom's. She wore a conservative red cotton dress, and her feet were bare.

"Sierra," Kimber said. "Back inside."

"We're going to be late for church," Sierra said, snapping out of her trance.

Mom's fingers twitched, and I could tell she was doing everything in her power not to rub her forehead, something she did when she was upset. "So, I guess we're neighbors now."

Kimber's eyes flared, all the fire rushing back. "You live here?"

"I'm assuming you met my parents," Mom said, taking a step closer to her, and, boy, was I thankful for that row of bushes separating them. "You had to have put two and two together."

Kimber tilted her chin up ever so slightly. "Just because their last name is Fletcher doesn't automatically make them your parents. Besides, we've only been here about nine months. We're still getting to know the neighborhood."

Sierra tugged on the sleeve of her mom's dress. "Mom, what's going on?"

Kimber swept out a hand. "Meet our new neighbors. Laura *Richards*, and ..." Her gaze wandered over to me, and a whole new look crossed her face—disgust.

Ouch. No one had ever looked at me like they wanted to puke before. Well, except Jake from middle school, but the guy was a complete moron, so he didn't count.

I almost reached back so I could grab some hair and twirl it around my finger—nervous habit—but Mom wouldn't like that, and I had this overwhelming sensation not to do anything to embarrass her at the moment.

Mom wrapped a protective arm around my shoulder, making me come closer to her. "This is my daughter, Daphne."

"She looks just like you did," Kimber said.

Ah. So that was why she hated the sight of me.

"I'm taking it you've met?" Sierra asked, curiosity written all over her.

"We went to high school together," Kimber said.

I waved again at Sierra. "Daphne."

"Sierra. What grade are you in?"

"Eleventh."

A natural smile found its way to her thick lips. "Me, too. I can come by later today, and we can talk about school and stuff if you want."

I opened my mouth to agree, but both Mom and Kimber spoke at the same time. "No!"

Sierra and I both whipped our heads toward our moms.

"Uh, why not?" I asked.

"You have Veronica," Mom said, her smile strained. "You don't need a second opinion."

Kimber spoke loudly to her daughter, so Mom and I could hear. "You must be careful who you acquaint yourself with, Sierra. It would be best to leave the *Richards* family alone."

So much disdain dripped from her voice.

Sierra looked as confused as I felt. She licked her lips. "Well, we have to go. Church, remember?"

"Right." Kimber lifted her chin again, pride in her eyes, like going to church made her better than my mom.

We went to church, too, lady. Not that it mattered.

Kimber did an about-face and marched to her SUV, snapping at Sierra to go get her father and brother.

Sierra flinched—I think at the mention of her dad. I wondered what that was all about.

Mom steered me toward the house.

"I thought we were getting breakfast," I mumbled.

"I've lost my appetite," Mom said.

As I glanced over my shoulder to Kimber, staring us down from the driver's seat of her SUV, I suddenly wondered if we'd made a mistake by moving back to California.

CHAPTER FOUR

*M*om immediately went to the beige couch in the living room and plopped down, scrolling through her phone.

Tossing my bag on the coffee table, I took a hesitant seat next to her, waiting for her to cool down before I spoke. Reaching over, I grabbed the seashell on the end table, turning it over in my hand.

Grams and Gramps had recently remodeled, going with a beachy theme that looked like something out of an HGTV show. While I loved the look, a part of me was afraid to touch anything and mess up the glam. I gently placed the seashell back on the table, not wanting to break it.

"There's a church not too far from here," Mom said, still scrolling through her phone. "Service starts in an hour."

"Are we going to talk about what just happened out there?" I turned toward her, tucking my leg underneath me.

She stood, slipping her phone into her back pocket. "I have to go get ready."

Taking her by the arm, I yanked her back down on the couch next to me. "We can't ignore this. That was totally crazy. I was seconds away from getting front rows seats to a WWE SmackDown."

I mean, I had to know what was going on. Mom and Kimber hated each other, that much was obvious. There were different levels of hatred. First, there was frenemies, the "let's do our best to be civil to each other in public, but deep down inside, we hate each other, and everyone knows it." Then there was the snarky-jab level, the "let's be open-book enemies, always taking jabs at each other online and trying to put the other down with as much snark as possible." Then there was the loathe level, the "we don't speak to each other in real life or online, but we cyber-stalk the crap out of each other, making sure my life is better than yours, and if anyone mentions your name, I will take the opportunity to spit upon your very existence."

Mom and Kimber went *beyond* that. They had gone to the uber-hate level, the "I pretend like you don't even exist, never think about you, never talk about you, and if someone mentions your name, I act like I've never heard of it before because you aren't even worth the tiniest speck of acknowledgment, and I will do everything in my power to protect my daughter from the vileness you exude." I mean, Kimber didn't even know Dad had died.

Mom sighed, sinking back into the couch. "I met Kimber in middle school. We got along just fine but didn't really run with the same crowd." She took the phone out of her back pocket and tossed it on the coffee table. "Sophomore year, we had a class together. Your dad sat between us."

"I'm not going to like where this is going, am I?"

"Nope."

I pointed to the Grumpy Care Bear on my shirt. "Well,

I'm already in the right mood. Hit me. Preferably not SmackDown style."

Mom's lips twitched into a small smile. "Your dad was so charming. I fell for him instantly. But, so did Kimber."

I rubbed my hands together. "Oh, a love triangle! Love that trope." I scrunched my face, the giddiness falling away. "Wait, Dad didn't like, kiss her or anything, did he?"

Mom smiled sheepishly, her face apologetic.

I threw my hands up and moved to stand. "I'm out."

She yanked me down before I could get too far. "It was only a couple of times."

"Not making this better."

"We ended up in this huge war between the two of us. Who could win your dad."

Thanks to Mom constantly playing nineties music around me, "The Boy Is Mine" by Brandy and Monica intruded my thoughts, adding to the drama.

I folded my arms. "You didn't marry Dad out of spite, did you?"

Mom reached forward, gently placing her hand on my arm, loosening my tight muscles. "Of course not. I love your dad more than anything. I knew from the moment we met that he was the one for me."

"He always said he felt the same way about you. Sparks flying and everything. Why would he give Kimber a chance?"

Mom tilted her head to the side, her eyebrows quirked. "He was fifteen and had two girls fighting over him. What guy wouldn't love that?"

"True. Gross, but true."

"What Dad and Kimber had was superficial. It never really went anywhere." She sighed, the gooey kind. "What we had, though, was special. We ended up falling in love, and Kimber got left in the wind. She's hated me ever since."

I rested my arm on the back of the couch. "I can see why she would hate you, but why do you hate her? You won."

"She wouldn't give up. Even after Dad told her that he loved me. She did everything she could to break us up. Spread rumors. Made up stories about us spending the night at each other's house and telling our parents about it in hopes they'd break us apart." She fidgeted in her seat like she was reliving the event. "We even made this stupid bet on who could win Prom Queen. She ended up winning, with your dad as Prom King. Everyone loved that man."

"How did I not know this?"

She lifted one shoulder in a shrug. "We don't like bringing it up. Dad always felt bad about giving Kimber the time of day, and I hated to be reminded that he did."

The doorbell rang, and Mom and I exchanged a glance.

"Do you think it's *them*?" I asked.

Mom shook her head. "I doubt it. My parents really should have installed a camera doorbell system."

The person knocked, quick and eager.

Hopping up from the couch, I tiptoed over to the door. "Luckily, there's this thing call a peephole. Let's see who's on the other side!" I peered through the hole, a grin breaking out on my face. "No. Freaking. Way!"

Suddenly, "Best Day of My Life" by the American Authors blared in my head, reflecting my mood.

I threw open the door and yelled, "Tay-Tay!" before jumping up and down, screaming.

My friend, Taylor, stood on the other side, doing the same. A guy stood behind her, fingers jammed into his ears, his face scrunched like he was in pain.

Taylor's wavy brown hair bounced while her hazel eyes lit up in excitement. She was wearing black booties, a maroon velvet skirt, and her favorite black leather jacket. Just like I remembered from her bazillion Instagram posts. The next thing I knew, her arms were around my neck, squeezing me fiercely. She smelled strongly of a musky perfume, matching her sultry personality.

When she finally pulled back, she squealed. "You're really here!" Her tone was throaty and scratchy, but in a sexy way.

"I told you I was coming," I said, smiling widely.

She took my hands in hers. "I know. But just to see you in the flesh is amazing!"

The guy cleared his throat, and Taylor dropped my hands. She looked over her shoulder at him. "This is my boyfriend, Zander."

Zander had his brown hair slicked to the side, his narrow eyes somehow mixed with amusement and angst at the same time. His baby blue shirt was buttoned all the way to the top, the short sleeves rolled up a few times. Skinny slacks and loafers topped off his look. He reached a thin hand out to me. "Nice to finally meet you in person." He pointed at Taylor. "She never shuts up about you."

"We need to celebrate!" Taylor said. "Let's go do something."

Mom came up next to me and put an arm around my shoulder. "It's so good to see you, Taylor."

"You, too, Mrs. Richards!" Taylor flinched, the smile falling from her face as she balled her hands into fists and held them in front of her chin. "Is it still Mrs. or did I totally screw that up?"

Mom chuckled. "Mrs. is perfect." She brushed some hair from my eyes. "How about you girls do something tomorrow after school?" She turned her smile to Taylor. "In fact, why don't you and Veronica come over for dinner? We'll order take-out and catch up."

Taylor nodded. "That's right. I forgot. Sundays are for family and church. Tomorrow will be great." She gave me a quick hug. "It's seriously so good to see you. I'll be there tomorrow morning at the entrance so you can have Veronica and me at your side."

"Thanks, that means a lot," I said.

Starting new situations sometimes gave me anxiety, and I loved that my friends knew that and always kept it in mind. It might help me survive the day.

CHAPTER FIVE

*V*eronica rolled into the parking lot, Post Malone blaring from the speakers in her Toyota Prius and vibrating the seat beneath me. I bounced along with the music, the top half of my body swaying, my arms swinging back and forth in the air.

When she pulled into a spot, I reluctantly quit dancing and unbuckled my seatbelt. "How did you score this car again?"

Veronica turned off the engine. "Good grades." She shrugged. "Plus, Mom feels bad about *him* leaving." She scoffed. "Like a car's going to fill the void."

I rubbed my hand along the center console. "Certainly helps."

Her phone chimed, so she reached into her bag and pulled it out. As she shook her head, her fingers flew across the phone. "Seriously, Javy is so lucky to have me."

Javier was Veronica's fourteen-year-old brother. The kid was always forgetting everything, like his lunch or homework. Since their dad left, their mom had been working a ton, mostly to keep herself distracted. But that left Veronica in charge of her brother and ten-year-old sister, Luciana.

"I put your homework in the bag, dorkface," Veronica muttered as she typed. "Just like I told you when I dropped you off at school." She stuffed her phone back in her bag. "You're so lucky you don't have siblings."

"Come on, you know you love them."

She smiled. "Of course, I do. They just drive me crazy at times." Glancing in the rearview mirror, she fixed her bangs. "I made a mistake, didn't I? Why did I go with bangs?"

I reached over and yanked her hand down from her forehead. "You look amazing."

A huge grin burst across her face. "Ready for this?"

I stared out the window at the high school. I hadn't really been nervous until this moment. "Sure?"

Opening the door, she glared at me. "Don't do this to yourself."

"Do what?" I hopped out of the car and shut the door.

Veronica rested her clasped hands on the top of the car, staring at me. "Psych yourself out. It's going to be fine. You have me, Taylor, and Zander. Not to mention so many people we went to elementary school with."

Adjusting the strap of my backpack, I hurried around the car until I was at her side, linking my arm through hers. "A lot has changed since then. I've changed. They've changed."

"Your endless worry certainly hasn't."

I pushed my arm into hers, making her grin. "I'm so glad you're here."

She motioned to my shirt. "Besides, I'll be with you all day via tee."

She'd gotten me a T-shirt that had two Care Bears roller skating and the phrase, *Rollin' with my homie* on it.

"And I wore my Wonder Woman belt in your honor," Veronica said. I'd given it to her for her last birthday. She reached up and swept back some of my hair that had fallen over my eyes. "Don't cover up those green beauties."

I would have smiled, but all I could think about was all the people inside the school, swarming around, talking, and judging everyone around them. I didn't want to be on the end of their judging.

She tried to pull me away from the car, but my feet were cemented to the ground. Everything around me shut off, the world suddenly zooming in on me. Pain radiated through my chest, squeezing tight. My breathing quickened, chest heaving in and out with the movement.

Veronica's calm face appeared before me as she placed her hands on my cheeks. "Breathe, Daphne. In and out."

Each breath was a rapid fire, like an oxygen machine gun with unlimited ammo.

"In," Veronica sweetly said.

Fire practically seared my lungs as I breathed in.

"Hold."

Closing my eyes, I held my breath, trying to picture my happy place.

"Out."

Cherry Coke. Watermelon Sour Patch Kids. Mom. Veronica. Taylor.

"In and hold."

Kittens. Puzzles. Captain America.

"Out."

Grams and Gramps.

"In and hold."

Dad, taking me to a Kelly Clarkson concert, singing

along to the songs louder than me and buying himself a shirt that was a smidge too tight. Mom tried to throw away the shirt, but Dad dug it out of the trash, opting to wear it when he did chores around the house.

"Out."

Slowly, my breathing evened, falling into rhythm at a reasonable pace. I opened my eyes just in time to see Veronica throw her arms around me, holding me close.

"I promise it's going to be okay," she whispered. "Shut out the noise." With a rub of my back, she pulled away. "We've got this."

I nodded, a smile slowly creeping onto my face. "We've got this."

Taking my hand, she gently tugged me toward the school, steering me between the cars. Shut out the noise. Not just the world around me, but everything attacking my brain, trying to convince it of things that weren't true.

"Hey, Veronica!" a bouncing voice said from behind us.

We stopped and spun around to see a guy jogging toward us in all his gorgeous glory. "Dibs" by Kelsea Ballerini played in my mind, cranked up to ten, practically vibrating every inch of me. The whole perfect cuteness of the song reflected everything swarming inside me.

"Did you finish our math ..." The guy trailed off when his eyes landed on me. His mouth twisted into a crooked smile, his nose inching up at the movement. "Hey."

Heat trickled up my neck to my cheeks. I wanted to say hi, but my mouth went dry. Out in the sun, his brown hair had the slightest tint of red. Freckles canvased his face like a priceless painting. My fingers twitched, wanting to brush along his cheeks.

Veronica elbowed me, which made me pause my singing. Wait. I'd been singing out loud?

"Heeeyyyy." My voice cracked, going up a few octaves.

Veronica sighed next to me. She linked her arm through mine. "Weston, this is my best friend, Daphne. She just moved here from Utah."

He ran his trembling fingers through his hair, his shirt riding up at the movement, showing off a retro Captain America belt. "Cool." At the crack of his voice, I suddenly felt better for my blunder.

"I have one, too!" I yelled way too loud, pointing at his waist.

Veronica cringed next to me, shrinking into herself and letting go of my arm.

His gaze slid down to his belt. "A Cap belt?"

I lifted my shirt just high enough to show it off. Mine had the shield repeated all the way around and on the buckle. "Got it for my sixteenth birthday!"

"Awesome!" Weston's toothy grin was contagious.

I tucked the bottom of my shirt into the front of my jeans, so the belt could be seen all day. "I tried to wear it like this, but Veronica said I couldn't because it didn't match with my shirt."

"It definitely looks better with it showing," Weston said.

I slapped Veronica's arm. "See!"

"Well," Veronica said, "as fun as this is, we need to get Daphne to the front office." She took my hand. "Weston, I can meet you in the library at break to go over our math homework."

His eyes lingered on mine, his one-sided grin adorable. "Sounds good."

Veronica tugged on my hand, trying to get me to move, but I wanted to stare at Weston a little while longer. She finally yanked me so hard, I stumbled toward her, tripping over my own foot and falling toward the ground. Placing my hand out, I slammed into the asphalt. Searing pain shot through my wrist and jolted up my arm.

I scrambled to my feet, straightening out my shirt and shaking out my wrist. "I'm fine. Totally fine."

Veronica linked her arm through mine and moved toward the school. "Sorry about that."

"It's fine." My voice cracked, so I cleared my throat. "He's not staring, is he?"

Veronica looked over her shoulder and opened her mouth to speak, but I cut her off. "Never mind. Don't tell me. I'm going to pretend that never happened."

I walked into the school without looking back, "Dibs" starting back up in my mind.

CHAPTER SIX

*V*eronica and Taylor helped me figure out a schedule that even if I didn't have a class with one of them, there was someone to walk me between classes. They didn't want me to have a second alone where I could stop and analyze everything I'd said that day and break it down on the awkward scale. Followed by me beating myself for saying it.

Zander had English with me, so we left the group at lunch and made our way to the English building toward the back of the school.

I glanced up at the blue sky as we wound through the sea of students. "This is amazing. Being outside as I walk to class."

Zander tugged on the front of his floral tee, so it wasn't so tight against his neck. "What do you mean?"

"In Utah, the schools are indoors. Like, I could go the whole day without stepping outside if I didn't want to." I rolled my eyes. "Except for the times my P.E. teacher made us go outside."

"That's crazy." Zander stepped closer to me as a girl shoved past him. "What else was different?"

I held up a finger. "We had lockers. Like with combinations and decorations inside and everything."

Zander opened the door to the building. "Wow."

I shuffled in, doing a little salsa move before continuing my walk down the hall.

"Is this the dancing Taylor warned me about?" Zander asked.

"Better get used to it."

Zander stopped in front of the classroom and swept out his arm. "Welcome to Mr. Buckley's class. You're going to either love or hate him."

I shook my fists in the air. "Yay!" One whiff when I walked in the door, and I placed a hand to my nose. "Why does it smell like my Grams' pickle pasta salad in here?"

A deep chuckle sounded behind me, definitely too deep to belong to Zander. "Mr. Buckley loves his pickle juice."

Pickle juice? Um, eww!

When I turned around, the tall guy stopped laughing, his blue eyes wide with shock. "Daphne?"

I took the beefy guy in, digging the flannel shirt and ripped jeans. He'd grown a lot since elementary school. He had sun-kissed skin and wavy black hair. "Bentley Anderson."

With a wide grin, he pulled me in for a hug. "My old tetherball rival."

We rocked back and forth before he let me go. I straightened out my shirt. "Pretty sure creaming me every time doesn't make me a rival. Makes me a guinea pig."

He ran his fingers through his hair, sweeping it away from his humored eyes. "You were so bad."

"You were like a head taller than me! You hit the ball so high, I couldn't reach it."

"What's with the traffic jam?" Sierra's voice came from behind Bentley. He scooched over so I could see her. She was dressed all in black except for her red lipstick and the red flannel tied around her waist. The smile on her face faltered when she saw me standing there.

I wasn't sure where we stood. Our moms hated each other, but that didn't mean we had to. I wondered if her mom told her about what happened in high school. Her thick lips twitched in annoyance, the irritation reaching up to her eyes. Yep. Her mom told her, and she was not happy about it.

I'd raised my hand to wave at her, but I slowly lowered it to my side as I drowned in the awkward silence.

"Where's a red flag when you need one?" I mumbled under my breath.

"What?" Zander asked, his eyebrows pinched in confusion.

"The flag boaters use to signal someone is in the water," I said.

They all stared at me, not sure what I was talking about.

"Cuz, I'm drowning, and I need to be rescued here." When the confusion didn't leave their faces, I waved my hand. "Never mind."

"I'm a terrible water skier." Weston's shaky voice came from behind Sierra and Bentley.

I grinned at him. "Same. Coordination and balance? My body doesn't know those two words." At least someone followed my random train of thought. Veronica was the only one who was really good at it.

The bell rang overhead, but none of us moved. I kept glancing at Weston, noticing him looking at me. Then I realized they were all staring at me. It was suddenly hot in the room, and I needed a fan. Tiny spots appeared in my vision, and, oh boy, was I dizzy.

There were some papers sitting on the desk next to me, so I snatched them up and used them to fan myself. Sweat beaded on my forehead and the back of my neck. Oh, and the small of my back. Pretty soon, it would be cascading down my body like a river.

"That's my assignment," a guy sitting at the desk said.

"What?" I stopped fanning myself long enough to look at the papers. "Oh, sorry." I handed them back.

"You must be the new student," a deep voice said from behind me. I spun around to see a muscular bald man, his thick arms folded, every piece of him intimidating. The one thing that really threw me off, though, was his lime-green suit.

"And you must be pickle man." My eyes widened in shock. "I just said that out loud, didn't I?"

"Yep," Zander chuckled next to me. When the teacher's eyes narrowed at me, Zander stopped laughing and rushed to his seat.

Bentley, Sierra, and Weston were hot at his heels.

"You can call me Mr. Buckley," he said, his voice stern.

I swear his pecs were moving under his suit. Laughing at me like they could rip me to shreds in point two seconds and then dance in my remnants. They'd better at least pick a good song for the memorial.

"There's a seat available in the back." He pointed a thick finger toward the back of the class.

I wanted to move, but another part of me worried that if I eased the muscles in my legs—wow, I was squeezing them tight—I might pee.

He took a step forward, towering over me. "Do you need assistance?"

"No, sir," I managed to choke out. Man, I was sweating so bad. I needed that fan back. Or an ice-cold Cherry Coke.

A wide grin broke out on his face, revealing a set of bright-white teeth. "I'm just playing with you. Welcome to my class. It's good to have you."

My breath came out loud over my dry lips, almost sounding like a dying bird. "Thanks."

The smile evaporated. "Now, have a seat."

Prying my legs apart—thankfully, no pee escaped—I hurried down the aisle, taking the empty seat in the back. A couple of papers appeared in front of my face, and I looked to my right to see Weston holding them out to me. I snatched them up and went to fanning my face.

"You'll get used to it," Bentley said from the left of me.

The smallest amount of relief washed through me, knowing I had the two of them on either side of me. Like guard rails for my spastic thoughts.

Then I looked past Bentley to see Sierra sitting on the other side of him, her hardened gaze passing between the two of us. When her narrowed eyes finally settled on me, a look of competition filled them.

Her black eyebrow quirked, her eyes flashing to Bentley for a second. Oh, she couldn't mean what I thought she meant, could she?

She tilted her head, as if asking if I accepted her challenge. I wasn't sure exactly what the challenge was, but it had something to do with Bentley and what our moms went through all those years ago. Which made Bentley my dad, and thinking about it that way made me squirm.

But then I looked at Bentley, taking his casual, friendly

self in, and he was really cute. Sweet. Great tetherball player, which was key to any great relationship. Wonderful smile. Charming. I could do worse.

With a wicked grin, I nodded at Sierra.

CHAPTER SEVEN

P.E. was a class created by the devil himself. I mean, staying in shape was important. Mom and I took Zumba classes all the time. I could dance. Not well, but it was fun enough that I didn't care that I looked like a wet seal flopping around when I did.

But P.E. made me do all the things I was not good at—sports. Those required hand-eye coordination and balance, which were the two words my body rejected.

I failed P.E my freshman year. Mostly because I ditched a lot. The only rebellious thing I'd ever done in my entire life. Which was why I was in my junior year, standing outside in the cool breeze on the partly sunny day surrounded by a bunch of freshmen. Apparently, there were no openings with the sophomores.

Mom made me promise to attend every class. She said she'd contribute to my car fund, so I agreed.

Ms. Hernandez was basically a walking Asics ad from her hairband all the way to her red and yellow tennis shoes. She had her dark, curly hair pulled back in a high ponytail, which raised her already high cheekbones even more.

"Welcome," she said, sizing me up, her tone firm and commanding. "I'm going to do everything in my power to make sure you pass this class. I talked to your teacher back in Utah and—"

"You talked with Mr. Faletutulu?" I asked in shock.

She quirked a sculpted eyebrow. "You say his name quite well. Took me a few tries."

"He made us practice every day until we got it right." I held up my hand. "You really talked to him?"

She nodded. "I take my job very seriously, Ms. Richards. He said he was pleased with your progress. He did say you could be quite salty at times."

I grimaced. "Sarcastic, maybe. Salty? Dunno about that."

She held up the whistle that was wrapped around her neck. "I like salt." She blew the whistle so loud I took a step back.

All the freshmen swarmed to her, standing tall and straight.

"Listen up," Ms. Hernandez said. "We have a new recruit. Daphne Richards. Treat her with respect and show her the ropes."

"There aren't actual ropes, are there?" I asked with my arm raised. "That's just a disaster waiting to happen."

Ms. Hernandez's lips twitched with the smallest smile. "No."

I wiped my hand across my forehead. "Whew. Thank goodness."

"Let's warm-up. Two laps around the track." She turned to a group of boys clustered together. "Trent, Dax, Sebastian. You're on babysitting duty."

Everyone else took off, jogging toward the track like

they were in the military, all in sync, and in two straight lines.

Three freshmen suddenly surrounded me, giving me three different looks. The first guy, average height and weight, brown hair and eyes, had a stern look that told me he took P.E. *very* seriously.

The second, a bleached-blond scrawny thing, looked like he was either high or thinking about getting high.

The third, with curly black hair and an eager smile, shifted uncomfortably where he stood, like he didn't know what to do with his hands. Or the rest of his body.

"I'm Trent Dawson," the first guy said. "Call me Dawson."

"*I don't want to wait for our lives to be over,*" I sang under my breath before I cursed my mom for making me watch the entire *Dawson's Creek* series a couple of months ago. Also, for the record, I was team Pacey.

"What?" Trent asked. I was so not calling him Dawson. This wasn't the military.

"Nothing," I said.

He nodded at blondie. "This is Dax Powers, and he'll stay by your side." His eyes narrowed on the eager beaver. "Sebastian Lopez. Stay by me. And don't look back at Richards. We need you focused."

Sebastian stared at the asphalt, looking embarrassed.

Trent clapped his hands together. "Let's head out. We're already behind the others."

The three quickly got into formation, jogging toward the track. I hurried to catch up, falling behind Sebastian and next to Dax.

Trent counted, making sure our steps were exact.

Oh, this was going to be fun.

The thing I hated about running was, well, everything.

My knees, ankles, hips, shoulders, none of them appreciated all the jarring movement.

I breathed in, taking in all the air. "Wow. You guys have an abundance of air down here. You should send some on up to Utah."

"Quiet, Richards!" Trent yelled from the front of the pack. We were quickly catching up to the others on the track. "Talking ruins focus."

"Not for me," I said, trotting easier than I usually did. "I mean, this is amazing." I took a deep breath. "Back home, I'd be out of breath by now. Wheezing. But this." Another deep breath. "It's beautiful, is what it is." Maybe running wouldn't be so bad. Except for all the jarring.

"So, you have less air in Utah?" Dax asked from my side. The low sea level wasn't helping with his breathing. I bet this was the only exercise the guy ever got.

"Higher altitude," I said. "Makes you run out of breath a whole lot faster."

Sebastian turned around to say something to me, losing his footing. He stumbled forward, flailing his arms, trying not to fall. I hurried forward and grabbed the back of his shirt, holding him up until he could regain his footing.

"Nice save, Richards!" Ms. Hernandez yelled from the center of the track.

"I told you not to turn around, Lopez!" Trent said with a growl. Well, kind of a wheezy growl.

"I wanted to ask her something!" Sebastian snapped. His curly hair bounced as he ran. The strain in his face told me he was working hard to keep up with Trent's brisk pace.

Even with all the extra air, running still sucked. Dancing would make it so much better. So, I did a little hip swing move with my steps like I was at Zumba.

"No dancing while running, Richards!" Ms. Hernandez said.

I went back to normal, boring, running.

We ran the rest of the way in silence. As soon as we finished, Sebastian flopped onto the grass in the center of the field.

"I'm going to die," he mumbled.

"Maybe if you laid off the Cheetos," Trent said, glowering down at him, "it wouldn't be so difficult."

I stepped up to Trent, folding my arms and tilting my chin high. "Maybe you should lay off douchebaggery. This is P.E., not the freaking Olympics."

A loud whistle blew near my ear, making me slam my palms against my ears.

"We don't use that word here," Ms. Hernandez said.

I slowly lowered my hands. "Like, the entire state of California, or just during this class?"

"During this class," Ms. Hernandez said. She turned to the others. "Everyone sit on the grass. We're going to work on our core."

I sat down next to Sebastian and smiled.

He smiled shyly back. "Thanks."

"He reminds me of this kid back in Utah." I clasped my hands behind my head, ready to do crunches. "He has no idea what an 'at ease' stance even is. Always ready for war."

The phone tucked in the band of my pants buzzed. I normally didn't have it with me during P.E., but I was waiting to hear from Grams and Gramps.

I shifted my body away from Ms. Hernandez and pulled out my phone. Gramps stared back at me, tired, but smiling.

"Hey, Gramps," I said as quietly as I could.

He leaned forward. "Why are we whispering?"

"I'm in P.E."

"Ah. Just wanted to let you know we are safe and sound in London." He took a drink of Dr Pepper from a bottle. "Even found one of these beauties at a local store."

Grams snatched the phone from him and waved at me. "Hey, Daphne!"

"Shhh!" I glanced over my shoulder, but Ms. Hernandez was busy helping a girl with her form.

Grams flinched. "Oops. Sorry." Her grin came back. "You look great. I think being in California is doing you good."

"It's only been like a couple of days," I said.

"Which confirms my hypothesis," she said.

Suddenly, a head popped over my shoulder, and both Grams and I let out a yelp.

"Richards!" Trent yelled. "Phones are not allowed here!"

"Yeesh," I said. "Calm down, drill sergeant."

"Phone?" Ms. Hernandez said. She came over to us, shaking her head in disappointment when she saw the phone in my hand.

Not the way I wanted to start off.

"I'm so sorry, Ms. Hernandez," I said, standing. "It's just—"

"It's my fault," Grams yelled from the phone.

By now, everyone had stopped their crunches and were watching the scene unfold. Heat climbed from my neck up to my cheeks from all the attention.

Ms. Hernandez turned her focus to my phone.

Grams looked sullen. "You see, we had to go out of the country for surgery for her grandpa."

What? Thank goodness I stopped myself before I said that out loud.

Tears glistened in Grams' eyes. "This place has the best surgeons for his condition, and it's basically our last resort. Daphne has been so worried about the outcome. The time distance threw everything off. I just had to call and let her know the surgery went well before we went to bed."

I put a hand on my chest, letting out a fake breath of relief. "I'm so glad to hear that." With all the nerves of having people looking at me, my voice shook, which added a nice touch.

"I'll force myself to stay up later tomorrow so I can catch you after school." Grams wiped a tear from her eye. "Wish you could be here, Daphne girl. But Gramps is fighting for you." She snatched up a tissue from the desk next to her and dabbed under her nose. "I hope I didn't get you in too much trouble."

I chanced a glance at Ms. Hernandez. I hadn't wanted to pull my gaze from the phone, worried I'd ruin Grams' spectacular performance. All those years she spent in community theater were paying off.

Ms. Hernandez's eyes had softened. "I think we can let it slide this one time."

"Oh, thank you," Grams said. "Love you, Daphne."

"Love you, too, Grams." I turned the phone away from everyone so only I could see Grams. "Give Gramps my love."

With a sly smile and a wink, she ended the call. I immediately calmed just from having that moment with Grams. My family always brought me back to my safe place. I relished the peace.

Ms. Hernandez clapped her hands. "Back to work!"

And, it was gone.

Dax leaned over once Ms. Hernandez was far enough

away from us. "You need to learn how to be sneaky about it. Having your phone in class."

"I was trying." I nodded at Trent. "But Stonewall Jackson over there ruined everything."

"There's an art to it," Dax continued. "While everything was going down with your grandparents—" He pulled a balled-up Subway wrapper from his pocket. "—I ate a sub. Not one person noticed."

"So, it's about creating a distraction," I said.

Smiling, he nodded. "Exactly."

"Um, question," I said. "Why did you have a sub in your pocket?"

Dax looked at me like my question was more absurd than the act itself. "Why *wouldn't* I?"

"Cuz it's weird," I mumbled under my breath.

I mean, yeah, I carried around a bottle of cherry flavoring in my bag—totally normal—but I didn't bring it with me to P.E.

Although, the more I thought about it, the more I was craving a sub sandwich, so I guess Dax won this round.

CHAPTER EIGHT

*V*eronica and Taylor ended up bringing Mom and me some carne asada tacos from a local joint for dinner.

Mom and I both moved toward the family room, where we usually liked to eat back home, but with the house renovation, it was way too pretty to eat in. With an identical sigh, we went into the kitchen and sat down.

"I want to hear all about your day," Mom said, unwrapping her taco. "Don't leave anything out. I sat alone in the antique shop all day, and I need some excitement."

My teeth sunk into the taco, and the perfectly seasoned meat brought me to my happy place. "This is so good," I said through my chewing.

Mom's eyes went crossed. "It's heaven."

Veronica grinned across the table. "Told you they had the best carne asada tacos." She started to say something else but cut off, her smile fading. She used to frequent the place with her dad.

"They sure don't make them like this in Utah," I said before I took another bite.

Mom wiped her mouth with a napkin. "School. Details."

Taylor threw out her arms. "She survived! Minimal battle wounds."

I pointed to the Care Bears on my shirt. "That's because I had my homies with me."

"*Rollin' with my homies*," Mom sang. "*Sippin' on yak all night*."

We all stared at her.

She stuffed some meat back into her taco that had fallen out, then licked the remnants off her finger. "Coolio."

When we continued to stare at her, confused, she sighed. "I've failed as a mother. We can watch Clueless later."

"Which is exactly how I feel right now," I said, making her laugh.

A weird look crossed over Veronica's eyes like she had a secret. She opened her mouth to say something, but then took a bite of her taco instead.

"What?" I asked, wiping my mouth with a napkin.

She grinned through her chewing and cast a knowing glance at Taylor.

Taylor's eyes lit up. "Oh, that's right."

"What?" Mom asked, leaning forward in intrigue.

Veronica finished off the bite in her mouth. "Daphne already has a secret admirer."

Mom's jaw dropped. "Already?" She reached out and placed a hand on Veronica's arm. "Is he hot?"

"He's cute," Taylor said. "Totally perfect for Daphne."

I sat back, snatching up some of my hair and twirling it around my finger. "Cute? Why don't I get hot? I deserve hot."

"Oh, I know *you* think he's hot," Veronica said. "He's Daphne level hot."

I frowned. "What does that mean?"

Taylor waved her hand nonchalantly. "Everyone has their own idea of hot. I mean, Veronica and I have extremely different taste in guys."

Veronica took a diced tomato that had fallen out of her taco and threw it at Taylor, barely missing her face. "DeShawn is gorgeous!"

"To you." Taylor picked up the tomato that had landed on her shoulder and tossed it on her plate. "I think Zander is hot."

"Eh." Veronica twisted her hand side to side. "He's okay."

Taylor looked at me. "Hence the different versions of hot."

There was only one guy that had caught my eye at school, and that was Weston. Had he said something to them?

What if it was Sebastian from P.E.? He kept looking all googly-eyed at me. But he was way too young. A sophomore I could possibly do, but not a freshman. I hadn't given any indication that I liked him, did I? I did stand up for him, but I would have done that for anybody.

"Who?" Mom pointed to Veronica's phone that sat on the table. "Show me his picture."

"Why would she have a picture of him?" I asked.

Rolling her eyes, Veronica picked up her phone and started scrolling through it. "There's this thing called Instagram. It's where people post pictures of themselves. You should look into it."

I stuck out my tongue at her. "I have an Instagram account."

"That you use solely for your business," Taylor said. "I mean, your handbags are amazing, don't get me wrong." She reached over and squeezed my cheeks together. "But sometimes we wanna see this cute face of yours."

I slapped her hand away, laughing.

Veronica turned her phone to Mom, and Mom grinned ear to ear. "Totally Daphne hot."

"Let me see," I said, reaching forward.

Veronica snatched the phone away from me. "But this is so much more fun."

I turned to Taylor, but she just shrugged and stuffed her face with a taco.

"Is he at least in our grade?" I asked.

Veronica popped a diced tomato into her mouth. "Maybe. Maybe not."

I could straight out ask if it was Weston, but what if I jinxed it? Or what if he *wasn't* interested in me and then I'd be all sad, and I'd have to go switch my Care Bear shirt to Grumpy.

I casually picked up my taco. "Whatever. I don't care."

"Uh-huh," Veronica said.

I needed to change the subject before I got too caught up in all things Weston. I mean, I'd only known the guy for a few hours. I looked at Veronica. "What do you think of Bentley Anderson?"

"So hot," Taylor said, pointing her taco at me.

Veronica nodded. "I agree." She scrolled through her phone and showed Mom his picture. "He's on the dive and swim teams, plus plays water polo. Loves being in the water. Totally fit."

"Friendly," Taylor put in. "Nice to everyone, including people he *shouldn't* be nice to."

Mom sat back in her seat. "Why can't guys like that

be on the dating sites I use? Except, you know, twenty years older." There was a weird inflection on the last few words.

"Don't give up, Mrs. Richards," Taylor said with her husky voice. "My grandma found love on one of those sites. I've never seen her so happy."

Mom rubbed her forehead. "Great. So, I need to wait about thirty years to find someone."

"You don't need a man," Veronica said. She motioned to Mom. "Look at you. You're thriving on your own."

Mom twirled her wedding ring that she kept on a necklace. "Doesn't mean I don't want companionship. I mean, I like making out as much as the next girl."

"Mom!"

She shrugged. "What? Kissing is fun. You can't deny that."

She was right, but I really didn't like thinking about my mom making out. Especially with someone who wasn't Dad. Honestly, I'd give anything to see my parents making out again. It meant Dad would be alive.

Taylor balled up the foil wrapper from her taco. "Oh! I could set you up with my oldest brother. He just turned thirty-four, so, like, close-ish to your age, Mrs. Richards." She batted her eyelashes at me. "Then, we could forever be related."

Taylor had six older brothers who constantly teased her, hence her need to always dress in skirts that were usually a hair too short. She loved to drive them crazy.

"Wait," Taylor said. "That would make Mrs. Richards my sister-in-law." She grinned wildly at me. "You could be my niece!"

"Yeah, so not happening," I said. How weird would that be?

Veronica's eyes lit up. "We're going to find you a man, Mrs. Richards. Show me what sites you use."

Mom slipped her phone out of her back pocket and opened an app. "This is my favorite to use. I tried a bunch of others, and they just didn't work out."

Veronica and Taylor crowded around Mom, looking at the screen.

Taylor pointed at the phone. "Oh, what about that guy? He's got a mysterious vibe."

Both Mom and I laughed at the same time. She found out the hard way that those guys were the worst. Mystery was fine until you wanted an open and honest relationship. Then their secrets would come pouring out, and she'd find out why they were still single.

"Not too mysterious," Mom said.

Taylor and Veronica shared a funny look, but they both shrugged and went back to perusing the pictures.

My phone pinged. I glanced down to see I had new followers. Bentley, Sebastian, Dax, and Zander. I blushed when I saw Weston's follow. It wasn't like it meant anything. But why was I all of the sudden sweating? Maybe it was the tacos. There had been some peppers in them.

Or it could be the fact that Weston was undeniably hot.

With all the new followers, maybe Taylor and Veronica were right, and I needed to post pictures of my life, not just the bags I made.

Bentley had tagged me in a photo. Apparently, he'd snapped a picture of me in class, laughing at something Weston had said. Below it was the caption, *Welcome back to Cali, Daphne! We need a tetherball rematch. Maybe I'll let you win this time!*

I quickly responded. *How about a dance-off?*

Bentley's reply came seconds later. *I have two left feet.*

Me: *So do I. It'll be an even match.*

Bentley: *Maybe we just need to hang out and catch up.* :)

Me: *I have been wanting to do a bonfire at the beach.*

Bentley: *It's January!*

Me: *That's what onesies are for.*

Bentley: *I do look good in a onesie.*

I was smiling big until I saw that Sierra 'liked' all the posts. Then she commented. *This sounds like so much fun! I'll put something together.*

I wanted to reply, *You weren't invited*, but Bentley had to say, *YES!! Let's get as many people as we can!*

"Daphne?"

I looked up to see Mom staring at me. Taylor and Veronica had both moved to the couch, still scrolling through Mom's phone.

"What's going on?" Mom asked.

I debated whether to mention anything to her, seeing as it would probably bring up a lot of bad memories, but Mom and I had made a pact to always tell each other everything after Dad died. It helped to talk through our emotions instead of leaving them bottled up.

"Sierra Winters," I said, watching her face.

Anger filled her eyes as her hand wrapped tightly around her napkin, balling it up. "Did she do something to you?"

"No. Not really. I think she's not really happy with me."

My phone pinged with a private message from Sierra. I opened it and read it to myself. *I think we should make a little wager.*

"What does she have in mind?" Mom asked from over my shoulder.

I jumped a little in my seat. "Yeesh. Don't creep up on a girl like that."

I typed my response: *What do you have in mind?*

Mom rubbed my shoulders, her voice coming out soft. "Whatever it is, you don't have to do it. This is her mother talking through her."

Sierra: *Bentley Anderson.*

Mom's hands froze on my shoulders as she leaned down to look at the screen. "What does she mean by that?"

Me: *???*

Sierra: *We have a few months until prom, and I know one of us could score a date with him.*

"He's that hot guy Veronica showed me a picture of, right?" Mom asked. "The diver?"

"That would be the one," I said.

Mom took a seat in a chair next to me. "Would you even want to go to prom with Bentley?"

"He'd be a great date. He's a really nice guy, and I'm sure we'd have fun together."

Sierra: *Whoever can get him to ask them to prom is the winner. But HE has to be the one to ask.*

I looked over at Mom. "What do you think?"

She sighed. "I think Kimber's the one behind it. She probably wants to prove that her daughter is better than mine."

"Uh, Mrs. Richards," Veronica said from the couch, "you just got a private message from someone named Kimber."

Mom and I exchanged a glance before we hurried over to the couch. Mom snatched the phone from Veronica and read the message out loud. *I'll understand if Daphne doesn't want to take the bet.*

"What bet?" Taylor and Veronica asked at the same time.

"Shhh!" I turned to Mom. "Keep reading."

Kimber: *We both know that Sierra is the most polished of the two and has already established a relationship with Bentley. Daphne would be the underdog, and of course, you wouldn't want her to be humiliated.*

Mom's eyes turned to ice. "Underdog? Please. You're way better looking than Sierra. Bentley would be lucky to go to prom with you."

"What is—" Taylor started.

Mom held up a hand to cut her off, keeping her eyes on me. "I'm positive we can get Bentley to ask you." Her eyes softened. "Only if you want to, of course."

She knew I wouldn't turn down a challenge. I couldn't. My DNA wasn't wired with the ability. I'd gotten that from her.

With a grin, I typed my response to Sierra. *Deal.*

CHAPTER NINE

*M*om, Veronica, and Taylor tried to pick out my outfit for the next morning, but I wouldn't let them. If I was going to get Bentley Anderson to ask me to prom, it was going to be the real me, not some fake version. It wouldn't feel like a victory that way.

Bentley's dad, Whitaker Anderson, was on the city council. Their family was Yorba Linda's version of the Kennedys. Which made Sierra tough competition, since she was the junior class president and star of the girls' basketball team.

But I had sweet dance moves.

I slipped into my jeans and then buckled my Captain America belt. I always liked the sound it made, like I was securing myself in place, protected from any bad vibes out there in the world.

My pink Cherry Coke sweatshirt rested on the back of the chair in front of my desk. I snatched it up, about to put it on, only to notice the bottom half had been cut off. Rushing over to the full-length mirror on my closet door, I quickly put it on, then grabbed the end of my sweater and examined it. The cut was perfect, like it had been done with care. The sweatshirt stopped at the top of my jeans, showing off my belt. That part I liked.

Then I raised my arms, and my stomach was exposed. Nope. Not happening.

I called Veronica, putting her on speakerphone while I rummaged my closet for a plain white tee. I'd organized the shirts hanging in my closet by brand in alphabetical order: Captain America, Care Bears, Cherry Coke, ending with plain tees needed for boring reasons.

"I'm just about to leave," Veronica said as soon as she answered. "Javy overslept. I'll be there in about ten."

"Why is my sweatshirt cut?" I ripped it off, snatched a white tee from a hanger, put it on, then put the sweatshirt back on.

"It's called fashion," Veronica said. "Don't freak out."

"You ruined my sweatshirt." I examined myself in the mirror again, happy when my white shirt showed when I lifted my arms, not my stomach.

"I *improved* it. You'll thank me later."

"Whatever, I took care of it."

"What do you mean?"

"See you soon!" I hung up the phone and hurried down the hall to catch breakfast.

Mom smiled wide when I came into the kitchen. "Morning! Have a seat. I made breakfast." She was dressed for the day, floral blouse loosely tucked into her white cropped jeans. As soon as I sat down, she hurried toward me, her pale pink high heels clinking on the wood floor. She set a couple of chocolate chip waffles in front of me, piled high with whipped cream.

I arched an eyebrow at her as I hesitantly grabbed the fork next to the plate. "What did you do?"

Mom sat down in the chair next to me, her smile so overly done. "I didn't do anything. I just wanted to make sure you had a good start to your morning. We need you happy if you plan to win Berkeley's heart."

"Bentley."

Mom snapped her fingers. "Right. Bentley."

I used my fork to cut a piece of the waffle. "And I don't want to win his heart. Just want him to ask me to prom."

Remembering I needed to up my social media game, I snapped a picture of me taking my first bite of waffle, then posted it.

Mom checked her watch. "Hurry and eat. Veronica will be here soon." She shuffled back into the kitchen and went to cleaning everything up.

She must have really wanted me to win the bet to wake up early and make me a big breakfast. But as the gooey chocolate, fluffy waffles, and whipped cream melted in my mouth, I didn't mind.

The dishes clanked around in the sink as Mom cleaned them. "Oh, and I won't be home for dinner tonight. I can leave you some money, or maybe you could go over to Veronica's house. I know you love her mom's cooking."

"I'll ask her at school." I quickly stuffed another bite in my mouth. I just needed a Cherry Coke to top it off, and I'd be the happiest girl in the world.

As if the heavens were answering my prayers, Mom set a bottle of Cherry Coke in front of me.

"Okay, what's going on?" Grabbing the Cherry Coke, I sat back in my chair. "This is more than just the Bentley bet."

Mom nervously tucked her hair behind her ear. "I have a date tonight."

I'd twisted the lid off and paused with the bottle on my lips. "You've gone on dates before."

It had been weird at first, but I'd gotten used to it. Maybe because it never worked out in the end.

"I know." She pulled out her phone from her back pocket and grinned at the screen. "We've actually been talking for a few months. An old high school friend of mine introduced us via text. But with the living in different states, nothing happened. Plus, he's ... different ... than most guys I date." She was rambling. "He texted last night when Veronica and Taylor had my phone and asked if we could finally meet. I was hesitant, but the girls talked me into it. He's a really great guy."

I took a swig of my drink. "These all sound like good things."

"His name is Cody, and he's a mortgage broker." Mom continued to smile at the screen as her fingers flew across the phone, probably writing a message to this Cody guy.

"Again, good things. I mean, if you hit it off, you hit it off. Might as well find out if he's a creeper in real life right away so you won't waste any more time on the guy."

Mom wiped above her lip and stepped away from me. "He's just a few years younger than me. Younger than you're probably used to, since I mostly stick to guys my age."

I held the Cherry Coke close to my chest. "How much younger?"

"Just a few years."

"Dating a guy who's thirty-four or thirty-five isn't that big of a deal."

"It's not." She coughed, and her next words came out so low and mumbled, it took me a second to process them. "Just take another ten years off that."

As I let it sink in, I drank my soda, letting the bubbly

goodness try and drown my confusion. I just kept drinking, swallowing, gulping, like I'd just spent the day in the Sahara Desert with no water in sight.

"Daphne?" Mom sounded concerned.

I held up a finger, downing my drink.

"It's just a date. It might not even work out. And like you said, he could be a creeper, so he could be out of the picture in no time."

That was definitely *not* reassuring. If he really was a creeper, *she* could also be out of the picture soon. I'd be an orphan. Sentenced to live a parentless life without anyone to introduce me to weird things from the nineties.

But maybe that meant I could travel the world with Grams and Gramps. Go to Italy. Try gelato. Meet some hunky guy on a gondola and have a whirlwind romance.

The drink ran out, so I set the bottle back on the table and wiped my mouth with the back of my hand.

Mom knelt in front of me. "Talk to me."

"He's twenty-five?"

"Twenty-four."

"You're thirty-eight."

Mom pinched her lips. "Yes, I'm aware."

"That's a fourteen-year age difference."

Mom rubbed her forehead, the irritation setting in. "Again, I'm aware."

I pushed my finger into my chest. "That's a couple of years shy of the difference between you and ME!"

Sighing, she stood back up. "One date."

"You guys weren't even born in the same decade. I mean, that's like the *NSYNC era versus the One Direction era."

"Bye, Bye, Bye" came into my mind, which was exactly what I wanted to say to this conversation.

"I was actually a Backstreet Boys fan. Team A.J." She winked at me. "Kind of liked the bad boy vibe, you know?"

I grimaced. Then a thought crossed my mind. "Wait, Veronica and Taylor talked you into it?" What on earth were they thinking? They were supposed to pick for my mom, not *them*.

"Yep. So, get mad at them."

A horn blared outside.

"Veronica's here." Mom leaned down and quickly kissed my cheek. "Have a good day at school, sweetie."

"Not sure if that's possible," I mumbled.

I got up with a little too much force, making my chair slide out behind me, skidding across the wood floor and falling on its back. I probably should have put it back in place, but with all the weirdness dancing inside me, I rushed over to the front door and plucked my backpack from the hook, slamming the door behind me.

CHAPTER TEN

"*Y*ou told my mom to date a twenty-four-year-old guy?" I asked Veronica as soon as I slid into the passenger seat.

She stuck out her bottom lip in a pout. "Did the waffles and Cherry Coke not do the trick?"

I glanced in the backseat and waved at Javier, but he was intent on his phone, earbuds stuffed in his ears, not paying even the slightest bit of attention.

A drawing of a dragon on his arm caught my eye. Reaching back, I took his arm, looking over the image. "Did you do this, Javy?"

Popping out an earbud, he grinned at me. "Yep. Just a prototype. One day I'll get the real thing tattooed on."

"It's amazing," I said, checking out the scales.

Veronica clucked her tongue. "You're not getting a tattoo, Javy."

Javier glared at her. "It's my body, V. I can do what I want." He pulled a piece of paper from his backpack and handed it to me. "Those are all my other designs. I'm going to be a tattoo artist once I graduate."

I wasn't sure how to react. I mean, the boy had pure talent. His drawings blew me away. But Veronica was not having any of it, so I guess I had to side with my friend. Or, I could just keep my mouth shut. I handed back the paper with a soft smile.

"Well, good luck getting Mom to sign off on that," Veronica said.

Javier scoffed. "I don't need Mom's permission. I can get Dad's."

Veronica's hands tightened around the wheel, and, oh, dear, she was about to blow. Couldn't have that happen, especially when she was the one driving.

I motioned for Javier to put his earbuds back in, then turned my attention to Veronica. "Back to my mom. You do realize there's a smaller age difference between him and me than my mom and him, right?"

Her hands slowly loosened their death grip, and, honestly, the steering wheel owed me a thank you. It had been about to get demolished. "I wasn't really thinking about that. I was thinking he was hot, had some fun interests, and would be good for your mom." She flipped on her blinker and came to a stop at a stop sign, waiting for the oncoming traffic to pass. "Which means he would be good for you, too."

I snorted, taking some of the hair hanging over my shoulder and twirling it around my finger. "I don't need a twenty-four-year-old dad."

"It's *one* date. No one said anything about marriage."

I stared out the window, watching the palm trees pass by. I hoped I never took the sight for granted. It was one of my favorites.

"It's just weird," I said.

Veronica reached over and patted my leg. "You

shouldn't even be worrying about that. We need to focus on Bentley. Do you have a game plan?"

"Yep. Not make a fool out of myself."

Veronica scoffed. "Let's not pretend that's not going to happen. We both know you'll end up doing something stupid. The important thing is to come out the winner."

I gave her a thumbs-up. "Thanks for the encouragement."

"Listen, Sierra's nice, but I think Bentley would have a better time with you. You're more fun to be around."

"He may not feel the same."

"Uh-uh." She waggled her finger. "None of that attitude. You can win, Daphne."

I pumped my fists in the air. "I can win!"

She slammed her palm against the steering wheel. "That's my girl!"

Since my first and only class with Bentley was after lunch, I had all day to think about my approach. Did I want to be subtle? Slowly work my way into his life? Or did I want to dive right in? I mean, he was a diver. Although, I wouldn't be as nearly a graceful diver as he was. I had a good chance at belly-flopping.

Zander and I ran into Bentley before we got to the English building.

"I'm excited about the bonfire," Bentley said with a grin. "Even if it's in January."

I did a little shuffle with my steps. "There will be dancing, and we'll be in onesies. We'll be fine."

He chuckled, highlighting a dimple on his cheek. He

really was gorgeous. "It will definitely make for an interesting night, that's for sure."

"It was a little weird that Sierra invited herself, wasn't it?" I asked, glancing over at Zander. We'd practiced this during lunch.

Zander nodded a little too vigorously. The guy was definitely not an actor. "So weird. Someone's needing some attention, am I right?" He elbowed Bentley on the arm.

I held in a sigh. Way to be subtle.

Bentley scratched the side of his head. "I didn't see it that way. She probably just thought it sounded really fun."

I shot a glare at Zander behind Bentley's back. Zander threw out his arms and mouthed, "*What?*"

I answered with an eye-roll.

Shock ran through me when I entered the classroom. Sierra was already in her seat, which wasn't all that surprising. It was *what* she was wearing. Pastel. No black to be found. She'd even replaced her red lipstick with a light pink. It so didn't suit her personality. Or her complexion, if we were being completely honest here.

Bentley sat down in his seat, looking over at Sierra, his eyebrows pinched in confusion. "New clothes?"

Sierra's smile faltered. "Just thought I'd try something new."

"Huh," Bentley said, still staring.

"Was that a good or bad, huh?" Sierra asked.

"Neither," Bentley said. "Just different."

"It's a weird different," Weston muttered on the other side of me.

I turned to him, keeping my voice low. "I was thinking the same thing. It's just not ... her."

Weston nodded in agreement.

"So, Bentley," Sierra said purposefully loud to catch my

attention. "I could use some help in history. Could you come over tonight and help me? I swear you get the best grades in our class."

"Sure!" Bentley said. "I love history."

When I glanced over at Sierra, she shot me a smug smile. It was one study session, but it also gave her the chance to make the first move. I would need to keep a close eye on them and make sure nothing happened.

Thank goodness I lived next door.

What had Dax said about being sneaky? The art of distraction.

"So, Sierra, what are your plans for the bonfire?" I asked.

Her eyes lit up as she pulled a binder out from her backpack. She flipped it open quickly, tearing a page, before showing us the list she created. "It's going to be so much fun!"

Man, I loved that she was so organized and took the whole thing seriously. For a fraction of a second, I forgot she was my enemy.

As she rattled off her plans, Bentley focused on the binder along with Sierra, I took out my phone and texted Veronica and Taylor.

Me: *First spy mission tonight. Be at my house at six. Wear something comfortable.*

Taylor: *Shouldn't we wear black?*

Me: *I'd rather be comfortable.*

Veronica: *You can have both, ladies. Black sweats ftw.*

Me: *Ftw?*

Even though I only received a text back, I could hear the sigh from Taylor coming through.

Taylor: *For the win. You're hopeless.*

Veronica: *She's sportsless, is what she is. We gotta start taking her to some games. It's basketball season. Good one to start with since it's only two hours.*

I turned to Weston. "Do you know what 'ftw' means?"

Weston scratched the back of his head. "Uh, fix the weather? Fill the water? Friends that wander." His eyes lit up. "Fashionista turned water-skier!"

I twirled a piece of my hair, thinking. "Fix the waffles!"

"Ms. Richards?" Mr. Buckley's voice cut through my excitement. "Whenever you're ready, we'll start class."

I shrank in my seat, but not before sharing a smile with Weston.

So much for being discreet.

CHAPTER ELEVEN

I was sitting down in the kitchen, catching up on sling bag orders. My sewing machine was still in Utah, ready to be packed up and shipped down to us by a moving company, my Aunt Shannon overseeing it all.

Thankfully, Grams had an awesome sewing machine. She was an amazing seamstress, all her costumes from her community theater days filling up their attic as proof. Even when mine arrived from Utah, I'd still probably use Grams'. It was that awesome. It included a digital screen and everything.

The doorbell chimed, and I jumped in my seat. I needed to get used to the new sound with the system we just installed. It wasn't that different from a normal bell, it was just way loud, and Mom and I couldn't figure out how to turn it down.

The camera feed popped up on my screen, letting me know who stood on the porch. Confusion swept over me when I saw the man standing there. The *Pirates of the Caribbean* theme song came into my mind, and for a second,

I flung out my hands, conducting an imaginary orchestra in the kitchen.

"Uh, Mom?" I yelled out, setting my current bag—the pink cotton covered in cute llamas—on the table. "Why is Jack Sparrow standing on our porch?"

The man was dressed just like the pirate, makeup done perfectly, and even his long beard had been braided, beads attached.

Mom hustled into the kitchen wearing a wench costume, and I about had a heart attack. She quickly tightened the red and black striped sash tied around her waist, which was holding the fake sword at her side. A matching sash was wrapped around her hair, tied in a bun at the side. Her tall boots laced all the way up to her knees, the heels at least four inches off the ground. Gold hoop earrings dangled from her ears, so big I wondered if I could get my fist through the hole.

She lifted the top of her silk blouse to cover up most of her cleavage. "How do I look?"

"Like a wench."

She frowned. "Don't use that word. I hate that word."

I lifted an eyebrow, still trying to process everything I was seeing. "How about a pirate hooker? Pirate escort? Whichever you prefer."

The doorbell rang again.

With a grin, Mom hurried toward the front door, fixing her blouse again before she opened it.

"Wow." The guy's caramelly sweet voice added to his pirate swagger.

Standing, I crept toward the door, maneuvering myself so I could see the guy. He wore a brown vest and trousers, a white pirate's shirt, boots, a sword tied at his waist, and a replica Jack Sparrow hat.

And he was totally checking my mom out.

Gross.

"I'm hoping you're Cody," Mom said, a slight nervous quiver to her voice.

He held out a hand. "Aye! Where are me manners? I am the one and only Cody Brooks." He winced. "I need a better pirate name."

Mom quickly shook his hand, their clasped hands holding on tight. "Laura Richards. Don't worry, I don't have a pirate name, either."

His mouth quirked up into a devilish smile, revealing a gold tooth that I was pretty sure was fake. Hopefully.

"We can work on that," he drawled.

They were still "shaking" hands. Eww.

I hurried forward, skidding to a stop next to Mom. "Hello. Daphne Richards." I pointed to Mom. "Her daughter. Teenage daughter. Sixteen, to be exact. Almost seventeen, actually. No one told me we needed pirate names."

Mom chuckled, putting her arm around my waist and *finally* letting go of the pirate's hand. "Cody, this is my very beautiful and unique daughter, Daphne."

He reached his hand out to me, giving me a nice, solid shake that lasted a normal amount of time. "Nice to meet you, Daphne. Your mom has told me all about you." He tugged on one of the braids dangling from his beard. "She said you're a huge Cherry Coke fan. Even carry cherry syrup around with you in case of an emergency."

I turned wide eyes to Mom. "Holy crap. Have you been telling this guy everything about me? Does he already have my menstrual cycle down?"

Mom's eyes went wide in return, her lips pursing in her way of telling me to watch myself.

Cody just laughed and pulled out a small bottle he had

tucked in his trousers. "Vanilla for me. You always gotta be prepared, right?"

"Right." I looked at the bottle. "Hey! That's the same brand I use!"

"That's because it's the best." He tucked it back into his pants' pocket. "It's the perfect blend of sweetness and flavoring without going overboard."

I found myself smiling, then quickly stopped when I realized this was the twenty-four-year-old guy taking my mom out on a date. I wasn't supposed to like him.

"So, why are you dressed like pirates?" I asked.

Mom dropped her arm from around me. "Costume party."

"Costume party," I said dryly. "In January."

Cody didn't miss a beat, his smile staying fully intact. "My friend loves them. Throws one every month. Theme and everything."

I actually liked the sound of that and wanted to meet this said friend. But I wasn't about to admit that out loud. "Huh. Weird."

Mom slapped my arm, her pursed lips scolding me again.

Cody looked at his empty wrist. "Oh, I forgot. Left my watch at home. No smartwatches for pirates." His gaze swept to Mom, taking her in again. "We should probably get going."

Mom blushed. Like, actual cheeks and neck turning pink, even under all the makeup. Though it was beyond weird for me, it was probably nice for her to get checked out. I mean, Cody wasn't hiding his attraction for her at all.

Wait, neither was Mom. Her eyes practically zoomed in on his lips.

I clapped my hands, breaking both of them from their trance. "Have her home by nine."

"Nine?" Mom asked.

"It's a school night." I mean, who even has a costume party in the middle of the week? Was it with his frat brothers or something?

Mom rolled her eyes. "For you, not me." She kissed my cheek. "Don't wait up."

Ha. Like that was going to happen.

Cody turned down the walkway, so I grabbed Mom's arm and shook my phone at her. "Remember, I have an app that can track you."

Mom's jaw dropped. "You wouldn't do that."

I folded my arms. "This is a two-way street, Mom. If you're going to track me when I'm out with friends or on dates, you better believe I'm tracking you on your little rendezvous."

Mom tugged up the top of her blouse again. "I guess that's only fair." She pointed a finger at me. "Do not follow me." She nodded at the Winters' home. "You have your own scouting to do, remember?"

I loved that Mom was totally down for me spying on Sierra. Her love of winning was sometimes out of hand.

CHAPTER TWELVE

*a*fter Mom left, I changed into my green Good Luck Bear onesie, hoping to soak myself in all the good luck vibes.

"Alexa, play 'Girl on Fire' by Alicia Keys," I said.

Letting the music fill my soul, I twirled around the room, singing along and getting myself pumped for the night. I could do this. I could win the bet. Sierra Winters had nothing on me.

My phone vibrated in my side pocket, ending my magical moment. Right as I turned down the music, a lady's voice rang through my phone. *Taylor Thomas is at the door.*

I opened the app to see Taylor standing on the porch, bouncing a little like she was preparing for a fight.

Grinning, I ran out of my room, down the hall, and swung the door open.

Taylor immediately threw her arms into a low circle, flexing, like she was about to enter the WWE ring. She growled, showing off her teeth. "Who's ready to devour the competition?"

I threw my arms in the air, pumping my fists. "I am!"

She made a show of punching my stomach—barely tapping it—and I hunched over, grunting.

She put her hands on her hips. "You're so not ready."

I stood up, smoothing out my onesie. "You punched me."

"Fake punched you. You should have fake slammed me to the ground or something." That was the thing with Taylor growing up with all brothers. They taught her how to wrestle. She pushed past me, coming inside the house. "Please tell me you have food. I'm starving." She'd also gotten her lack of tact from them.

I shut the door and followed her into the kitchen. "I thought you were having dinner with Zander?"

She opened the pantry, scanning for something she liked. "His work was short-handed and called him in. He's saving for prom, so he's taking all the hours he can get." Pulling out a bag of potato chips, she unrolled it and sniffed. Apparently satisfied it wouldn't kill her, she shrugged and popped a chip into her mouth.

"Prom is months away." I sat down on the stool in front of the island and opened a delivery app on my phone.

She took the stool next to me. "He wants to go somewhere nice for dinner since it will be our one-year anniversary."

"It's been that long?" I scrolled through all the options, not sure what I wanted to eat. Everything looked and sounded good.

"Crazy, right?" Crunching on some chips, she leaned over my shoulder to check the list with me. "No Indian. Had that last night."

"We just had Mexican, so we can cross that out."

"Italian?" Taylor pointed at a restaurant listed on the screen.

I shook my head. "My stomach hates Italian. I need to be fully functioning for tonight, not having an intimate relationship with the toilet."

"TMI, Daphne. A 'no' would have sufficed." She laughed when I glared at her. "Oh!" She pointed at a burger joint. "Best burgers and shakes."

Opening their menu, I scanned the options. "How are we going to spy on Sierra? Her room is on the second floor. This is a one-story house."

"You have trees outside." She leaned toward me, a very convincing monkey noise leaving her mouth.

I made my selections from the menu and handed the phone over to Taylor for her to choose. "Why isn't Veronica here yet? She should have been here by now."

"Isn't she studying with Weston?" Taylor asked.

For some weird reason, my cheeks heated at the sound of his name. I liked it. Weston. So fun and charming.

"She said they'd be done before dinner."

Taylor handed the phone back to me. "Text her."

I ordered the food and then shot Veronica a message. She responded within seconds. *Sorry. Stuck on a stupid math problem. Be there ASAP.*

"So, what's the game plan for Bentley?" Taylor asked, turning her body to face me. "Have you invited him to do anything with you?"

"We only have the bonfire scheduled as of now."

Taylor's eyebrows drew together. "In January?"

I shrugged. "I felt like a bonfire."

"Sounds like fun." She didn't hold back the sarcasm in her tone.

"Tell me all your bright ideas, all-mighty one!" I tried to use a powerful tone, but it came out cracking worse than a boy going through puberty.

"Do you need a cough drop there, Daph?" she asked through fits of laughter.

I smacked her arm hard enough that she stopped laughing and rubbed it.

"Have him over for a movie night," she said. "You love movies, and since you don't have to talk a lot during it, there's a smaller chance of you saying something incredibly stupid."

I blinked at her, slow and deliberate. If she hadn't hopped off the stool and created distance between us, I would have slapped her again.

Taylor went over to the fridge and pulled out two bottles of Cherry Coke, sliding one to me across the island.

I caught the cool bottle, my greedy hand tightening around it. "I don't want to be alone with him, though. I'll need you and Veronica there for support."

We twisted open our lids at the same time, the crisp sound of carbonation releasing, making my heart swell.

"Triple date!" Taylor said with a wide grin. "Zander has next Friday off, so let's do it then. That way, Veronica and I can prep you."

I tugged the hood of my onesie over my head. "I don't need any prep, thank you very much. I'm ready and raring to go."

"That's what I'm afraid of," Taylor mumbled. She snapped her fingers. "Text Bentley right now and ask him out for Friday. That way he'll be thinking about *you* during their 'study session.'" She used air quotes on the last two words.

I pulled my phone from my pocket. "Why did you use air quotes?"

"Huh?"

"You used air quotes around 'study session.'" I shot off a

text to Bentley, asking if he wanted to join all of us for a movie night next weekend.

She smiled mischievously, lifting her fingers. "Does anyone actually 'study' during 'study sessions'?"

I stuck my tongue out at her. "Stop using quotes!"

My phone pinged. Bentley had already responded. Taylor was at my side seconds later, reading over my shoulder.

That sounds awesome! What can I bring?

"Chapstick," Taylor purred next to me. "Some mints and his sexy smile."

I elbowed her, making her laugh. Her laughter faded when I responded with, *your favorite treat to share.*

"Boring," Taylor whispered. "You also made it sound like friends hanging out, not a date."

I turned so I was facing her. "Bentley doesn't strike me as the type who would want the aggressive approach."

She pursed her lips. "You're right. He wouldn't." She patted my shoulder. "Look, you being a dud is coming in handy for once!"

Baring my teeth, I slammed my body into hers, trying to push her to the floor, but her socked feet just slid across the tile as she roared with laughter.

"You're supposed to fall over!" I yelled into her stomach.

She patted my head. "There, there, my little cub. One day you'll be just as fierce as all the other lions."

Straightening myself, I glared at her. "We can't all be Wonder Woman, Tay-Tay."

She pressed her hands against my cheeks, smooshing my face together. "Not with that attitude." Leaning forward, she kissed my forehead like a coddling mom, and it was my turn to laugh.

CHAPTER THIRTEEN

$\mathcal{W}$e waited on the living room couch, peering out the window to watch for Bentley. Right on schedule, he pulled along the curb and got out of his car, throwing his backpack over his shoulder. It was too dark to see what kind of car he drove, but knowing how loaded his family was, it was probably something fancy.

"Flannels and Converse," I said, holding two slats of the blinds apart. "I do love his casual style."

He glanced sideways down the street, running his fingers through his thick hair like he was in a photoshoot.

"You should be grateful it was Bentley sitting between you and Sierra," Taylor said, looking through a crack in the blinds. "What if it was someone you couldn't stand, like the guy who talks about himself in the third person?"

"I don't think I would have made the bet."

"I was a little surprised when I heard about it. I'd been under the impression that Sierra and Bentley were dating."

I turned to her in shock. "What?"

She shrugged. "They hang out a lot, and I swear I've seen them flirting. But maybe I read the situation wrong."

Was that why Sierra made the bet with me? She knew Bentley already liked her, so it would be easy for her to win? I wouldn't put it past her.

My mind pictured me in the classroom, staring at Bentley sitting to my left. I glanced past him at Sierra, trying to remember if they ever did anything to indicate they liked each other. Like *like-liked* each other. There was a ruffle of papers to my right in the scene playing in my head. I snapped to that direction and saw Weston fumbling through his backpack, his reddish-brown eyebrows pinched together in serious concentration that made me smile. He was adorable when he focused.

I shook the scene from my head, scampering back to reality in front of me. Why had Weston intruded on my moment with Bentley?

Taylor pushed my arm. "Stop playing whatever song is blaring in your head and pay attention to me. I can't climb a tree in this skirt."

My gaze wandered to her cut-off jean skirt. It was very rare for Taylor to *not* wear skirts.

"You know where my room is," I said.

While she went to change, I stretched out in the front room. It had been years since I climbed a tree. I wasn't sure if I'd be able to.

Taylor came back in my pink Love-a-Lot Bear onesie with hearts. "Okay, I see why you're obsessed with these."

I grinned at her. "I thought you were just going to grab some sweats or something."

"I was." She motioned to the onesie. "Then, I saw this beauty and needed in on the action."

"They're amazing, right?"

Post Malone rang out from my phone. I picked up the call from Veronica, about to ask where she was.

"I'm on my way!" she yelled. "Just hold on. Don't do anything too crazy without me!"

The call ended.

I stared at the blank screen. "Okay, then."

Taylor and I crept outside, already in stealth mode. All the lights were out in the back yard, cloaking us in darkness. It had been so long since I'd been in my grandparents' back yard, I didn't really know the terrain.

Taylor turned on the flashlight on her phone, lighting up the cement path.

I slapped her arm. "Turn it off!"

She glared over her shoulder at me. "They aren't going to notice a small light in the next-door neighbor's back yard."

She'd better hope not.

We rounded the corner, heading to the side of the house, where Sierra's room was. I kept my steps light, not wanting to make too much sound.

Grams and Gramps planted a few rosewood trees on both sides of their house, wanting to create privacy from the neighbors. I went to the one closest to Sierra's bedroom and slapped the side of the trunk.

"When's the last time you climbed a tree?" I asked.

Taylor shined her phone light on her face so I could see her look that said, "really?"

"Do I look like someone who would climb trees?" Her flat tone matched the look on her face.

I thought back to elementary school, when she'd pretty much branded herself as the girl who always wears skirts back in kindergarten. It started out because her mom was so excited to finally have a daughter after six boys that she went crazy with the girly clothes. As Taylor got older, and noticed it made her brothers mad to have guys checking her out, her skirts got shorter.

With a great heave of effort, I worked my way up the tree, clinging on for dear life. Beads of sweat broke out on my forehead from all the effort. Each shimmy up took an amount of strength I didn't know I had.

"How much farther?" I asked Taylor.

"You've barely moved," she said.

"What?" I glanced down, seeing the grass right beneath me. I lowered my legs, my feet instantly connecting with the ground. "Well, this isn't going to work."

"Do you have a ladder?"

"Gramps probably does in the garage."

By the time Taylor and I got the ladder, carried it into the back yard, and set it against the side of the tree, we were both huffing and puffing.

Taylor aired out the top of her onesie. "Okay, maybe these aren't the best idea."

I fanned my face with my hand. "They make so much more sense in Utah where it would be twenty degrees out right now, not sixty-five."

Once I collected my breath, I tested the first step of the ladder before I climbed my way up. It didn't take long for the branches to surround me. The tree was a lot thicker than I expected. Pushing the leaves out of my face, I shimmied onto a branch, working my way toward Sierra's window.

As Taylor climbed, I inched closer to the window, using the light shining from it as my guide. The branches below me sunk with my weight. I held on tight to the branches around me as I pushed one to the side, trying to get the perfect angle.

Sierra was sitting on her bed, still dressed in her pastels

that so clashed with who she was. I'd done some "light" social media stalking to size up my competition, so I got a feel for her personality before I'd moved here. She used to be cool and nice. Something sure had changed, though. She'd turned all fake and stoic.

Sierra's binder was open in front of her as she leaned forward, laughing. I followed her gaze, but couldn't see anything.

With a quick prayer that I wouldn't fall, I scooted over, trying to get a better view of her room. Suddenly the branch I was on started bouncing, and I clung on for dear life.

Taylor was behind me, coming closer.

"I swear, if this snaps under our weight ..." Taylor trailed off.

"Then you'll be on the ground," I finished for her. "Stop shaking the tree so much!"

"This isn't easy!" she hissed back.

We finally got into a spot where we could peek through the trees and see both Sierra and Bentley. Taylor and I were squished close, our heads pressed together.

"He's sitting on a chair," I whispered. "Not the bed. That's a good sign, right?"

"Yes, but he's leaning toward her with very open body language."

"Open?"

Taylor sniffed, rubbing her nose with the tip of her index finger. "Yeah, like, inviting. Not closed off."

"Well, he should close himself off. This is their first study session, after all. Don't want to appear desperate or easy."

Taylor snorted next to me, then sniffed again.

"Oh, he's getting up!" I said.

Bentley moved toward the bed, sitting down on the edge

next to Sierra, looking at her notebook where she was pointing. He was focused on the notebook, talking with a lot of animation.

Sierra leaned closer to him, but Bentley didn't seem to notice. She laughed—way over the top—at something he said, so he turned to face her, their faces inches from each other. Her laughter faded as they stared at each other, and I suddenly felt like I was interrupting a very private moment.

"Well, this just got awkward," Taylor whispered. "Should I throw something at the window to distract them? Break it up?"

"Like what? A leaf?"

Taylor sniffed yet again. "I think I might be allergic to something." She pressed her hand to her nose. "I have to sneeze."

"Hold it in!"

"I can't," she squealed. "It's ..." She took deep breaths, her face switching to pre-sneeze mode, and, oh my, she was going to blow.

I slammed my arm into her nose right as she let loose, sneezing into the fabric of my onesie. So going to have to wash it.

She sucked in another breath like she was going to sneeze again.

I glanced over, seeing Bentley and Sierra both standing near the window, squinting at the tree.

"Do you think they can see us?" I whispered.

Taylor was able to hold in her sneeze. She tugged the hood of the onesie so it was covering her face. I did the same. So, if they could see us, it would be two Care Bears staring at them through the trees. Which wasn't creepy at all. It actually sounded like the start of a good horror movie.

My mind went deathly silent, no music playing, as if they'd be able to hear a track playing in my head.

"What do we do?" Taylor asked in a hiss. "Go down?"

"Maybe if we don't move, they'll think it's just their imagination playing tricks on them."

"I can't stay frozen up here all night."

"I'm afraid to move," I said. "I want to look to see if they're still watching, but that would require moving."

"Maybe we should count to thirty or something," Taylor said, "and then head back down. Like, really slowly."

"Daphne?" Veronica's voice booming from the bottom of the tree startled me so badly, I lost my grip.

I flailed my arms out, trying to grip one of the branches, but my fingers just slid off the leaves, my momentum already taking me down. I fell, back first, toward the ground, the hood of my onesie covering up my eyesight.

Someone's arms caught me, and I fell into their chest.

"Nope," Weston said through a grunt as he stumbled backward. "Can't do this."

We both fell to the ground, me landing on top and rolling off. I lay on my back, gasping for air. I yanked the hood off my head, trying to get everything back in focus. Everything above me spun, swirls of colors and lights, and if I hadn't been so horrified, I would have loved how pretty it was.

"Daphne?" Veronica's concerned voice came somewhere from my left. "Are you okay?"

I tried to speak, but nothing came out. Instead, my breathing became deep and ragged.

Weston rolled onto his side, grunting through the pain, so he could face me. His hand came forward, brushing some hair out of my face, and I don't know why, but I took hold of his hand and held on tight.

"Just breathe, Daphne," Veronica said in her soothing tone. "In and out. Shut out the noise."

Taylor kneeled next to her, placing her hands on my leg. "Slow it down. Picture all the happy things."

The fire in my lungs outweighed all the pain radiating from the fall. Closing my eyes, I concentrated on their voices, the warmth of Weston's hand, and everything that made me happy.

"In and out," Veronica sweetly said.

Taylor spouted things out. "Cherry Coke. Care Bears. Captain America. Your mom. Grams and Gramps. Veronica. The beach. Disneyland."

"Taylor," Veronica put in.

"Should I get her some water?" Weston asked, concern in his voice. His thumb stroked my hand, calming me.

"Give her a minute," Veronica said. "It will subside. Then, all the water."

"And Cherry Coke!" Taylor said.

Someone knocked on the side gate. "Hello?" Sierra. She did not sound happy.

My wide eyes went to Veronica, but she was staring at Taylor, the two of them mouthing words I couldn't make out.

"Daphne, I know you're back there," Sierra said.

"We just want to make sure you're okay," Bentley said from the other side of the fence. "That was a long way down."

Why was this happening? Oh, because I decided to spy on them. But, hey, I broke up a maybe almost kiss, so, win?

My breathing started to settle, finding a rhythm that didn't sound like I was running a marathon.

"She's fine," Weston said.

Both Taylor and Veronica's heads snapped toward him, but he just shrugged.

"We'll talk to you tomorrow," Bentley said. He and Sierra began whisper arguing, but it was too muffled to make out the words.

How in the world would I face them tomorrow?

I stared into Weston's calm eyes, the crooked smile landing on his face that made his nose inch up. "Speech-less" by Dan + Shay played in my mind, and suddenly, I didn't care.

CHAPTER FOURTEEN

The next morning, I hobbled down the hall and into the kitchen. Every muscle ached something fierce. Falling from a tree was so not recommended, even if there was someone at the bottom to kind of catch you.

I wondered how Weston was feeling. That was a lot of weight to catch and land on top of him.

I'd dressed in full Captain America gear—shirt, belt, socks, and earrings—to try to give myself courage for the day.

Mom was whistling in the kitchen, the smell of omelets in the air. I immediately went to the fridge, grabbed a small bottle of Cherry Coke, and downed the entire thing in seconds.

"Good morning, sunshine," Mom said with way too much pep at seven in the morning.

"How was your date?" I asked, though part of me didn't want to know. Her mouth split into this teenage girl grin, and now I really didn't want to know.

Mom flipped the omelet in the pan. "We had so much fun! We ate, danced, talked. I haven't had that much fun in the longest time." She glanced over at me. "Next month's theme is 'Regency Era.' I need to go through my mom's costumes in the attic. I bet I could find a dress there."

I tossed my empty bottle in the recycle bin. "A second date?"

"We're going out on Friday," Mom said through her smile. "He's taking me to a local art museum and ..." Her eyes landed on my arm, and she gasped. "What happened to your arm?"

"What?" I glanced down to see a bruise the size of a softball right below my elbow. "Huh." Must have happened during the fall. I bruised so easily, I wasn't all that shocked.

She turned off the stove and came over to me, examining my arm. "Does it hurt?" When her fingers pressed against my skin, I sucked in a breath.

I slapped her hand away. "When you touch it, yeah."

"What on earth did you do?" She got some plates from the cupboard and handed them to me. I held them while she scooped the omelets onto the plates.

"Just remember, you're the one who wanted me to take this bet."

We sat down at the table, saying a quick prayer before we dove into our breakfast. Mom kept her eyes on me, waiting for me to spill.

I sighed. "I may have fallen out of a tree at some point last night."

Mom's hand went to her mouth, covering up her smile as she chewed. "You fell out of a tree?"

"I had to get a better angle of Sierra's room!" Taking a bite of the omelet, I let the savory flavors explore my mouth. Mom sure knew how to make an omelet.

Mom pointed her fork at me. "Climbing back down would have been a lot easier."

"Veronica showed up and scared me. Thank goodness Weston was there to soften the blow."

"Who's Weston?"

My cheeks flared, and I quickly shoveled another bite into my mouth.

Mom grinned. "Oh, *Weston*. The guy Veronica showed me pictures of."

My eyes widened. So, it was Weston who had a thing for me. I didn't know how to feel about that.

"Daphne hot." She leaned toward me, her tone scandalous. "What was *he* doing here last night?"

Another round of blushes attacked my skin, sucking out my ability to speak evenly. "I'm actually not sure. He showed up with Veronica. With everything that happened, I didn't think to ask why he had come with her."

Mom tilted her head to the side. "To see you, of course. That's so sweet." She cut off another piece of omelet. "Do you like him?"

Another bite of the omelet went into my mouth, way bigger than was comfortable.

She winked at me. "So, that's a yes. You going to call off the bet with Sierra?"

I vigorously shook my head, trying to finish off the bite in my mouth.

"Just asking."

I swallowed the huge lump in my mouth. "I'm not calling off the bet. Prom is still months away, and anything can happen between now and then. I mean, they're called crushes for a reason, right? I'll probably find out he has a secret doll fetish or something."

Mom choked on her bite of food, pounding at her chest. Her phone buzzed on the table, and a goofy grin spread on her face when she looked at the screen. She held it up for me to see. It was a candid picture of her and Cody at the party, all cozied up and laughing.

"Someone apparently snapped this of us last night." She moved the phone, so she could stare at it better. "He has the greatest smile."

I quickly got up from the table, not wanting to say anything that would make her mad. It wouldn't last, her and Cody. I just needed to brave through the next couple of months, and all would be well again.

*S*ierra was waiting for me at the school entrance, her face a mix of anger and annoyance. A girl stood next to her, equally upset, her black, curly hair gelled to perfection. If she hadn't looked so pissed, the girl would have been pretty. A part of me wanted to walk up, put my fingers on the sides of her lips, and pull her mouth up into a smile, fixing the scowl. But, you know, that would be totally weird since I'd never met her before.

I'd seen her before, though. On Sierra's social media pages. But for the life of me, I couldn't remember her name.

Veronica stayed close to my side, linking our arms together so I couldn't run away.

"Choose your words wisely," Veronica whispered as we approached.

That wasn't something I knew how to do.

Sierra was back in her all-black outfit with red lipstick.

"Realized the pastels clash with your dark personality?" I asked.

The girl next to her moved as if she wanted to lunge, but Sierra put her arm out to stop her and went straight to the point. "I can't believe you spied on me!"

"I can't believe you tried to kiss him!" I said, my eyes darting to the scowling girl. What was her name?

Sierra had her hands balled into fists. "I was *not* trying to kiss him. We were just ..." She trailed off, her thick lips twisting to the side.

"About to kiss?" Veronica offered.

Sierra glared at her. "You're just upset that our study session went well. We're having another one tomorrow." She lifted her chin with a smug look on her face. "At *his* place, so you can't spy on us."

Was that a challenge?

Veronica, in all her freakiness, whispered in my ear, "That's not a challenge."

I smirked at Sierra. "Aww, talking about dead people and things they did years ago for a date." I fanned my face. "How romantic." I pointed a finger at the girl. "Who's this?"

The girl's jaw dropped, completely horrified that I didn't know who she was. Yeesh. I'd just moved back here.

"Rosalind," Sierra said, her tone oozing with, 'duh.'

"Right," I said dryly. "Rosalind. The girl I've never met before, and no one has introduced me to." I waved a finger gun and winked. "Got it."

Rosalind sneered. "You have P.E. with my brother." She said it like it was another thing I should have known. "Sebastian."

My eyes lit up. "Oh! Sebastian. He's a nice guy." I motioned to her magenta tunic. "Love your shirt, by the way. Best color ever. I think you might rock it better than I do."

Rosalind's glare faltered. "Uh, thanks."

"You're welcome." I turned back to Sierra. "Are we done here, or—"

With a huff, Sierra turned on her heel and stalked off, with Rosalind right behind her.

Veronica rubbed my arm, but then stopped when I sucked in a sharp breath from the pain. Did she have to rub right over my massive bruise? It wasn't like it was hiding or anything.

"Sorry," she said. "That went better than expected." She glanced sideways at me. "I'm more worried about how it's going to go with Bentley."

We'd only taken a couple of steps when someone called my name. I spun around to see Weston jogging toward me, also in a Captain America shirt. Oh, and belt.

"No matching earrings?" I asked when he got to us.

He chuckled. "Not yet. One day." He held out a bottle of Cherry Coke dripping with condensation. "Thought you could use it this morning."

I took it from him, our fingers brushing against one another, and boy, howdy, was it hot outside?

"Thank you," I said, holding the cold bottle against my neck. Oh, that really helped. Maybe I needed to invest in one of those misting fans.

"Holy bruise!" Weston shouted, looking at my arm.

"I would make up a really cool story of how I got it, but you already know the truth."

His reddish-brown eyebrows inched up in concern. "Does it hurt?"

"Nah. I get bruises all the time." I moved the bottle, so it was pressed against the other side of my neck. It was definitely cooling me down, which was good, because every time Weston and I made eye contact, the heat inside me flared.

Veronica cleared her throat, making us both look at her.

"We should probably get to class, seeing as the bell just rang."

"The bell rang?" Weston and I asked at the same time.

"Jinx!" I yelled. I counted to ten so fast, he couldn't stop me. "You owe me a Coke." I took the bottle away from my neck. "This one doesn't count."

Veronica tugged on my arm, taking me into the school and away from a smiling Weston.

CHAPTER FIFTEEN

*M*r. Buckley had opted for a pastel pink suit today. It clashed with the stern look on his face when class started.

I'd made sure to come in at the very last second, so Bentley couldn't talk to me. I knew he'd ask questions about last night, and I so didn't want to answer them.

"Listen up," Mr. Buckley said, his booming voice commanding everyone's attention. "I was reading your book reports last night and was completely horrified."

There were some murmurs from the class, a few people shifting uncomfortably where they sat. His tone was unsettling, to say the least. I mean, I thought mine had been pretty good, but maybe he didn't appreciate my comment that everyone in the Scarlett Letter could have learned a thing or two from the Care Bears.

"Your grammar and spelling are horrendous," Mr. Buckley continued.

Okay, now he better not be talking about me. I took great pride in my grammar awesomeness.

"I blame it on texting and social media." He folded his

arms, making his muscles bulge through his pink blazer. "You have to know how to spell out there in the real world."

"Why?" Sierra asked. "Isn't that what autocorrect is for?"

Mr. Buckley clenched his jaw, clearly annoyed. He pointed a thick finger at her. "It's comments like that that make me worry for our future. I swear, the English language is going to be non-existent within a few years. The whole dictionary is going to be full of acronyms and emojis." He swept out his arms. "This is our language. You should be proud of it. Explore it. Not shorten it and snuff it out altogether."

"There really are so many fun words," I said. "Fickle, lollygag, catawampus, boondoggle."

"You're just making up words," Bentley said, smiling over at me.

I shook my head. "Oh, they're real, mister. Very real." I held up a finger. "My use of they're being t-h-e-y-apostrophe-r-e. They are. Just to clarify."

Mr. Buckley cracked a small smile. "Nice to know someone gets it. That's probably why she's only one of two in this class who got an A."

Relief washed through me. He hadn't been talking about me. Then I did a fist pump under the table, because I freaking got an A.

He went over to his desk and lifted a stack of papers. "Which is why we're going to have a pop quiz!"

Groans rippled throughout the room, tearing through the silence.

I clapped my hands together. "I'm just aflutter with delight!"

Weston snickered next to me, while Zander turned around to shake his head at me, smiling the whole time.

Mr. Buckley pointed the stack of papers at me. "Ms. Richards, you don't have to take the quiz if you don't want to." His gaze slid to Weston. "Same with you, Mr. Ashworth. You both proved in your report that you know what you're doing."

Weston sat back in his chair, clasping his hands behind his head. "Sweet."

"But I *can* take it, right?" I asked.

"I'm certainly not going to stop you," Mr. Buckley said.

As Mr. Buckley passed the papers down the aisle, "Let's Get it Started" by the Black Eyed Peas provided the soundtrack in my brain, making me dance in my seat.

"How could you possibly be excited about this?" Sierra hissed from her desk.

"Words are fun," I said.

Bentley leaned toward me. "What song are you dancing to?" When I told him, he held out his fist for me to bump. "Classic." He glanced at the bruise on my arm. "You okay, by the way? I've been worried about you."

He was worried? That was a good sign, right?

"Totally fine," I said.

"Why were you in the tree, anyway?" Bentley asked.

I really had no sane reason for that. There was no way he'd believe that Taylor and I just liked to climb trees in Care Bear onesies.

"Veronica dared me," I said, finally taking the quiz from the girl in front of me. She'd been waving it in front of my face, trying to get my attention, but I was enjoying the nice breeze. "Thought we couldn't climb a tree in a onesie, but we proved her wrong." I glared at my bruise. "Well, until I fell."

Bentley stared at me for the longest time, and I wasn't sure if he bought my story. Sierra probably told him we were spying on them, and I mean, come on. Out of all the trees in my grandparents' backyard, we choose the one that just happens to be next to Sierra's bedroom window? I wouldn't believe me, either.

"Do you like to read?" I suddenly asked Bentley.

He shook his head. "Not really my thing."

"That just means you haven't found the right book," I said. "We should go to a bookstore this weekend. Find you a book with all the fun words."

Weston leaned toward us, a shy smile on his face. "There's this indie bookstore near the beach you could check out. Big selection. Cozy, beach vibe. Tons of places to chill. It's one of my favorite places to go."

I reached out, placing my hand on his arm. "That sounds amazing. We should all go!"

When I noticed he was staring at my hand on his arm, I quickly yanked my hand away, blushing. Why had I even put it there to begin with?

"Yes, we should," Sierra said from the other side of Bentley. She smiled at him. "You want to drive?"

Bentley nodded. "Sure. I can pick you all up Saturday afternoon, and we could head down there. Maybe grab something to eat, too."

"I'm in," Weston said.

Even though I was mad at Sierra for inviting herself, it was still time with Bentley at a place where I would feel comfortable. I stole a glance at Weston. He would be there as well.

"And, go!" Mr. Buckley said.

I quickly turned my eyes to the paper, hoping Weston didn't notice me checking him out. Which wasn't. Checking him out. I was just looking in an observatory way. Huge difference.

CHAPTER SIXTEEN

*a*fter chucking a box of Lucky Charms into the cart, I placed one foot on the bottom of the cart, then used my other foot to get some momentum going before I soared down the aisle. My foot kicked up behind me like I was an Olympic ice skater. Honestly, cart riding should have been an Olympic sport. I'd totally take home the gold.

When I got near Mom, I set my foot down, skidding across the linoleum until the cart came to a stop next to her.

She held up a box of healthy-looking cereal that had the look of, "you could eat the box, and it would taste the same." She tossed it in the cart with a frown. "Never get old, Daphne. It sucks."

I held out my open bag of Watermelon Sour Patch Kids, offering her some, but she declined. "I'm not planning on it. Is there an option on those end-of-life forms that's like, 'once my metabolism stops working like it used to, just pull the plug?'"

Mom chuckled. "Or, you could choose not to care and get fat and have a heart attack."

I grimaced. "Well, that sounds lame."

We rounded the corner, going down another aisle, only to come to a stop a few feet in.

Kimber Winters—with her cart full to the brim like she was stocking up for the apocalypse—stood chatting on the other end of the aisle with another lady, both of them smiling and laughing. Huh. Kimber looked like a nice, approachable person when she wasn't scowling like she wanted to rip you to shreds.

Also, for the record, I'd be the first to die in the zombie apocalypse, and I was okay with that.

I moved backward, taking the cart with me, whispering to Mom. "Maybe if we move quietly, they won't notice us."

Mom back-pedaled with me. "I was thinking the same thing."

We'd made it back to the start of the aisle, ready to turn the corner, when Mom accidentally kicked the cart, the clatter like a freaking siren, announcing our presence.

Both Kimber and the lady turned to us, Kimber's smile fading, and the other lady lighting up like I did when I opened a fresh bottle of Cherry Coke.

Mom sighed next to me. "Let's just get this over with."

"Want me to fake an illness?" I asked, leaning toward her. "A burst appendix, maybe?"

"Laura!" the lady exclaimed, jogging down the aisle with her cart like she was on a game show, heading for the finish line. When she got to us, she pushed her cart aside with flair before throwing her arms around Mom. "It's so good to see you!"

Mom hugged her back in a way that said she was at least happy to see this woman. "Hi, Heidi."

The song came into my head, then burst out of my mouth, luckily under my breath. "Hi-dee hi-dee hi-dee hi."

Man, I missed Gramps. Blues Brothers was his favorite

movie. Mom would probably kill him if she knew he let me watch it when I was ten.

"Kimber told me you were back," Heidi said, finally having released Mom from her hug-o-death.

"Ho-dee ho-dee ho-dee ho," I quietly sang, dancing a little where I stood.

Mom shot me a look, telling me I hadn't been as quiet as I thought.

Heidi just laughed. "I get that all the time." She smiled at me. "You must be Daphne. I'm Heidi. Went to school with your mom."

"Two sons and a golden retriever, right?" I asked.

Heidi beamed. "That's me!"

I grinned back at her. "I've seen your pictures on Instagram. Your youngest son is hilarious."

She rolled her eyes. "He likes to think so. I'll be glad when the potty-training days are behind us." She glanced over at Mom. "Thankfully, the hubby took the boys to the park so I could grocery shop alone. It's like trying to wrangle two monkeys at the zoo when I bring them."

Kimber cautiously approached us, walking with an air of sophistication. At least, I thought that was what she was trying to accomplish. She almost looked a little uncomfortable, like her Spanx were cutting off her circulation.

Heidi motioned to Kimber. "We were just talking about our twenty-year reunion! Can you believe it's been twenty years since we graduated? I swear, I still feel like I'm sixteen sometimes."

I pointed my bag of candy at her. "And you look it." She really did. She was one of those ladies that looked like she never aged.

She blushed, waving her hand. "Oh, I like you."

Kimber narrowed her eyes at me, clearly not liking my comment.

"Can't win them all, am I right?" I said to Kimber. "Thank goodness for those age-defying creams."

Mom whacked me in the stomach, trying to scold me, but she was trying so hard not to laugh.

Heidi's smile faltered, clearly confused by our interaction.

I twisted off the lid of my Cherry Coke, taking a sip, keeping my eyes on Kimber, my head bopping as "Eye of the Tiger" played in my head. I wanted her to know she didn't intimidate me.

Heidi cleared her throat. "Laura, you should join the planning committee! You always have the best ideas."

"The committee is pretty full," Kimber said, her "sophisticated" smile cranked high.

Heidi waved her hand. "One more person won't make a difference. Besides, Joanna is about to go into labor any day now. She'll need to focus on her newborn for the next couple of months." She grabbed Mom's hands in a plea. "Please say yes. We *need* you, Laura."

I tried to pull the cart back, wanting to leave the conversation, but Mom held onto it like it was the only thing stopping her from pouncing on Kimber.

Grabbing my soda and candy, I grinned at them. "I'll let you ladies talk about your reunion. I'm going to go gander around. Maybe check out the lip gloss aisle." I winked at Kimber. "Gotta be prepared for prom."

I scurried away before she could say anything.

Poor Mom. I felt bad for leaving her, but stupid things wouldn't stop coming out of my mouth. It was safer for everyone that I left.

I ended up on the makeup aisle, my brain probably still

thinking about lip gloss. After a search of the area, I found one named *kissalicious,* and another named *seduceology,* so I held onto them. Maybe I could make a show of asking which one I should get when I got back, though I already knew I was going with *seduceology.*

"Why are there so many choices?" A panicked voice rang out from the next aisle. A voice I knew.

I hurried around the corner to find Weston standing in the middle of the feminine products aisle, staring at the shelves of tampons. He held his phone in his hand, talking to the screen.

"Ivy, just tell me what to get," he pleaded.

"Tampons!" she yelled.

He threw out an arm. "There's like a million of them! Different sizes and scents." He picked up a box, grimacing at it. "Why would you want a scented tampon?"

There was a loud sniff on the other end of the call. She was crying.

I rushed over, snatching the box from his hands. "Never go scented. Ever." I set them back on the shelf.

Weston stared at me, beet red, his mouth slightly hanging open.

"Weston!" Ivy yelled from the phone. "Who *is* that?"

I handed Weston my soda, candy, and lip glosses so I could take the phone from him. I smiled at the girl on the other end. "Hey, I'm Daphne. Are you Weston's sister?"

Ivy wiped at her eyes, nodding. Man, she was adorable. Strawberry blonde hair, light freckles, and green eyes. She looked maybe twelve?

Oh. No.

"First time?" I asked.

She scrunched her face like a fresh round of tears was about to attack. "Mom's gone! They went out of town, and she's not answering her phone! I don't know what to do! Why did they pick this weekend to go to her cousin's wedding?"

"First," I said, trying to sound calm, "take some deep breaths. It's going to be okay. This is totally normal and natural." I scanned the shelves, taking in all the options. "Are you sure you want to start with tampons? Pads might be easiest until your mom gets home."

She shook her head, her eyes wide in horror like I'd just suggested she put scorpions down her pants. "No one in middle school wears pads!"

"I'm sure that's not true—"

"None of my friends do!" She bit her lip. "I'm the last one to ... you know."

I smiled at her. "Don't worry. I'll help Weston pick out the correct tampons."

She wiped at her nose. "Are there instructions on the back of the box or something?"

Weston whimpered next to me. When I glanced at him, he mouthed, *"Help me."*

I turned my attention back to Ivy. "I'll tell you what. I'll come over and walk you through the whole thing. Okay?"

Using her palm, she wiped the tears from her cheek. "Okay."

"Oh," I said. "What's your favorite treat?"

"Um. Kit Kats."

"Got it." I waved at the screen. "See you soon, Ivy."

I turned to hand the phone back to Weston, only to see him scarfing down my Watermelon Sour Patch Kids.

"I so didn't sign up for this," he said, mouth full.

I patted his shoulder. "None of us did." I grabbed a variety box of tampons and threw them in the basket he was holding. Then I found a bag of panty liners and threw them in there as well.

Taking Weston by the arm, I steered him toward the candy aisle where I got a jumbo size Kit Kat and threw it in the basket with everything else.

I snapped my fingers. "Wet wipes might be good."

After we grabbed some, I had Weston wait for me up front—he didn't want to go through the checkout alone—and turned to go find my mom, only to see her coming out from an aisle, a scowl on her face.

Uh-oh.

I tiptoed toward her, like a gazelle approaching a hungry lion, knowing it could end in my death. "Hey, Mom."

She snarled. "I'm on the stupid committee."

"At least then you can make sure the reunion doesn't suck."

She braced her arms on the handle of the cart, the snarl fading. "I don't even want to go, Daphne. Not without your dad."

I wrapped an arm around her. "I know. But just because you're on the committee doesn't mean you have to go."

"I said I would," she grumbled.

"Okay, well." I tapped my lips. "A lot can happen between now and then. We can find you a hot date."

She softly smiled. "Maybe I could rope Cody into going with me."

Well, not where I wanted that to go. That would mean she and Cody would still be dating months down the road. Ugh.

She looked past me, taking in the pale version of Weston. "Is he okay?"

"His sister just started her period, and their parents are out of town," I said.

Mom made an "O" with her mouth. "Poor girl." She pursed her lips, checking her watch. "Should we help?"

She had a date with Cody, and while I loved the thought of her canceling the date, I couldn't force myself to do it. Not when she looked so stricken at the thought of missing it.

"I picked everything out and said I'd go over and help."

Mom rubbed my arm. "That was sweet of you."

Weston came up, holding out the empty candy bag, and now empty soda bottle. "Sorry."

I took them from him, then set them in our cart so we could pay for them. "No worries."

He glanced at them in the cart. "Maybe I should pay for them."

I waved a hand. "You've been traumatized enough for one day. We got it."

He handed me the lip glosses, his eyebrows twerking up in amusement.

I took them with a frown and showed them to my mom. "I wanted to make a big show of getting these in front of Kimber."

"She already left," Mom said, smiling at the names of the lip glosses. She tossed them both in the cart. "We'll find a way."

Weston ended up giving me the cash and making me get the stuff alone while he waited out in the minivan. He kept quiet the whole ride to their house, where we found Ivy locked in the master bathroom.

I knocked on the door. "Ivy? It's Daphne. How are you feeling?"

"Really weird," she said. "I can't really explain it."

I glanced over my shoulder at Weston, who stood in the doorway to the master bedroom, shuffling uneasily. "Why don't you go order some pizza for all of us? I can take it from here."

Weston sighed in relief. "Now, that I can do."

"Ivy," I said, leaning into the door, "you're going to need to unlock the door for just a second so you can grab the bag of supplies, okay?"

There was a shuffle of steps before the lock clicked, the door opened, and her arm stuck out, snatching the bag from my hand before the door was back to being closed and locked.

I walked her through the steps, calming her every time she freaked out. Fifteen minutes later, she finally came out, immediately throwing her arms around me.

"Thank you," she said.

"Happy to help," I said, hugging her back. "Weston has my number, so if you ever have any questions, you can reach out to me. Us girls gotta stick together."

After stuffing our faces with pizza, we lounged on the couches, watching High School Musical—Ivy's favorite movie. She took up the whole couch, laying down, covered in a blanket, and munching on the huge Kit Kat.

Weston and I sat on the loveseat, snacking on Watermelon Sour Patch Kids. He'd gone back to the store and bought some more, along with other treats for the night.

"I'm so glad you were at the store," Weston whispered, leaning toward me. "That was my worst nightmare coming to life."

I snickered. "If that was your worst nightmare, then you must be living a cushy life."

He scoffed. "It was awful. All the crying. People staring at me at the store. So. Many. Tampons."

I looked at him, smiling. "You're a good brother to do that for her."

"She didn't give me much choice." He rubbed his neck. "She threatened to strangle me."

I glanced over at Ivy, lying peacefully, looking so young and innocent.

"Yeah, she seems vicious."

He bumped my arm. "You weren't there, man. She went all sorts of crazy."

I pointed a finger at him. "Never call her that. Especially during her time of the month. Unless you really do want to be strangled."

He rubbed his neck again. "Noted."

His hand came down, resting on the couch, his pinky brushing against mine. It sat there for a moment before it advanced, locking over mine, just a simple, sweet move.

Huh. I'd never held pinkies with a guy.

I had no idea what it meant, but I kind of liked it.

CHAPTER SEVENTEEN

Saturday morning, I met Mom in the kitchen, ready to go to Zumba. I had on my favorite lilac Care Bear workout leggings and a lilac shirt.

Mom wore her typical black leggings and tank, her blonde hair pulled into a high ponytail. She patted to a seat at the table. "Let's do something with that mane of yours."

I took a seat, getting comfy. "Just french braid it. Easy, and it will be out of my face." As she went to work brushing my hair, I brought up exactly what I didn't want to talk about. "How was your date last night?"

I didn't have to see Mom to hear the smile in the voice. "We had a really nice time. The art museum was amazing." She tugged at the top of my hair, starting the braid. "We also went to this cute little Italian restaurant. It was delicious."

"You came home really late."

She yanked at my hair, causing me to flinch. "We sat in the car forever, just talking."

"Talking? Or '*talking*'?" I held up the air quotes high enough so she could see them.

Mom snorted. "We weren't making out, Daphne. Just talking."

That was somewhat of a relief. It was weird to think about my mom making out with some twenty-four-year-old guy in his car, parked in the driveway, steam fogging up the windows, his elbow accidentally blaring the horn, everyone from the neighborhood running out of their homes in their pajamas to see what was going on.

I shook the image from my head.

The doorbell rang, followed by Alexa's voice from the Echo sitting in the family room. *"Cody Brooks is at the door."*

"What is Cody doing here?" I asked. "And you programmed him into the system?"

Mom finished up with my braid, jerking my head around with a little too much force. "Be nice, Daphne."

She hurried over to the door, smoothing out her tank top before she opened it. I leaned over in my seat, trying to get a better view. Cody's toothy grin greeted her, and he moved in as if to kiss her on the lips, but then his eyes traveled over to me, and he switched to a hug. Good boy.

Mom ushered him inside, where he waved at me, holding a plastic bag at his side.

His yellow shirt said, *I ♥ Zumba.* "Hey, Daphne! Ready to Zumba?" He did a little dance step, shaking his hips.

"You're going to Zumba with us?" I hadn't meant for my tone to sound so incredulous. It just came out like that.

Cody's smile faltered, and he turned to my mom. "You didn't tell her?"

"I hadn't had time," Mom quickly said.

Cody held up the bag. "Then, is this an awkward time to mention I got you matching shirts?"

Mom beamed. "You got us shirts?"

Cody pulled them out of the bag, tossing one to Mom. "They're the same as mine."

Mom tugged hers over her head, covering up her tank. "I love it!"

Cody swung his arms a few times toward me, waiting for me to give the go-ahead. I reluctantly held out my hands, and he tossed me the other shirt.

I held it up against my chest, taking in all the yellow. "This is really bright. And clashes with my lilac pants."

"You'll just look like a Lakers fan," Cody said.

"I'm not a Lakers fan."

His smile faltered again, his eyes darting to Mom like he was in search of rescue. She was too busy glaring at me. If looks could kill, I'd be a pile of ash on the floor, ruining the HGTV vibe my grandparents had going on.

I went out of Cody's line of sight and quickly traded my top for his yellow atrocity. Forcing a smile onto my face, I joined them in the entryway. "Let's get this over with." I pushed past them and out the door.

Tires squealed as the Winters' SUV pulled into their driveway. "Don't Start Now" by Dua Lipa blared from the vehicle. I immediately started dancing toward Cody's car, feeling the music. I loved that song.

Mom joined me, an impromptu dance party starting in our driveway, Cody impressing me with his own moves.

The music suddenly cut off, and the door to the SUV slammed shut. I glanced over to see Kimber standing there in workout clothes, her hand on her hip, glaring at us.

I gave her a thumbs-up. "You have great taste in music."

For a second, she looked taken aback by my comment. She quickly covered it up, her eyebrows quirking up as she took in our matching shirts.

"Did you accidentally sleep in?" she asked, all proud, like the fact that she'd already completed her workout made her ten times better than us.

"Don't want to wake up too early," I said. "Gotta get that beauty rest."

Kimber looked at Cody, then switched her attention to Mom. "I wasn't aware you had another kid. I have a boy as well. Looks just like his father." Her eyes narrowed at Cody. "Not seeing the resemblance to Ian, though. Different father?"

Wow. Cody looked young, yeah, but obviously he was older than me. I mean, the guy had a full-grown beard. Which meant Mom would have had him in high school, something Kimber would have known about.

A part of me wanted to jump over the bushes and maul Kimber for being so disrespectful to my mom. Only *I* could give her a hard time about her young boyfriend.

Ugh. Boyfriend. So didn't want to refer to Cody that way.

Cody, not missing a beat, put an arm around Mom's shoulder, pulling her close to his side and giving her a soft kiss on the temple. All the tension in Mom fell away, saving Kimber from a beat down. I hated that I was liking this guy, but I was.

"You must be the eccentric neighbor I've heard so much about," Cody said through his genuine smile. "Heard your husband's a cop. My dad is a detective, so they might know each other. Is your husband here? I'd love to meet him."

Kimber's eyes went wide for the briefest of moments. She scratched at her forehead, letting me see that her ring finger was bare, which didn't mean too much since she'd just been working out. A lot of people took off their rings to exercise.

"Already at work," she said. When she saw me checking out her hand, she rubbed her thumb over her ring finger. "It's being resized right now. My wedding ring. I've lost some weight recently, so it didn't fit anymore."

"Good for you!" Cody said. "It's never easy to lose weight. Especially as you get older." He smiled at me, then at my mom. "Well, ladies, we should probably get going. Don't want to be late." He waved at Kimber, his hand rubbing Mom's arm as he did. "Nice to meet you. Kimmy, right?"

Her jaw clenched as she forced a smile on her face. "Kimber."

"Well, have a nice day, Kimber." Cody turned around and opened up both passenger side doors, holding them for Mom and me. As we drew near, he spoke quietly, not hiding his disdain. "Man, she really is a piece of work, isn't she?" He winked at Mom. "Safe to say Ian made the right choice all those years ago."

So, Mom had told him *everything* about her past. And he was still here, happy to get to know her and her teenage daughter. I loved that he'd said my dad's name with such ease, like he didn't mind talking about him and knew he was a big part of our life.

And I hated that I loved it. I was supposed to loathe Cody.

I'd find another reason.

CHAPTER EIGHTEEN

Cody tried all the small talk he could on the way to the class, but I was too busy taking in his car to pay attention. Nice blue Honda Civic Hatchback. Four doors. Backbench kept exceptionally clean. Had the new car smell I absolutely loved. Tinted windows, which would help on sunny days. I ran my hand along the smooth leather seat.

"Those heat up," Cody said, really loud so I'd actually hear.

"Really?" I asked.

He nodded. "I can turn them on if you want."

"I'm good, but thanks." I finally turned my focus to him. "What's the gas mileage?"

"Forty on the highway," Cody said, all business. "About thirty in the city."

Not bad.

We pulled into the parking lot, and I got out of the car as quickly as I could. I enjoyed it way too much. I couldn't like anything Cody. Those were the rules.

Cody held the door open for us as we went inside the building.

"Your mom says you're saving up for a car," Cody said to me.

"Truth," I said.

He rubbed the back of his neck. "How much have you saved up?"

"Close to four thousand."

His eyes widened, impressed. "That's great. I'm looking to sell my old 2008 Civic if you're interested."

My eyebrow inched up on its own accord, betraying me and giving away my interest. "Oh, really?"

"It's in great condition," he quickly went on. "I can bring it by the house sometime so you could check it out. If you want."

Out of the corner of my eye, I could see Mom eagerly nodding, wanting me to agree.

I paused for a few beats, just to make them both uncomfortable. "I think that could be arranged."

Cody let out a breath of relief. "Great. I'll bring it by tomorrow."

I opened my mouth to tell him he really didn't need to bring it by so soon, but Mom tugged us into the classroom.

We got into position in the middle, and I focused on the fact that I loved Zumba, and it was the perfect stress release for me. Who cared if Cody joined us? Who cared that they kept stealing lovesick glances at each other and that Mom checked out his butt multiple times? This was one of my happy places, and I wouldn't let Cody take that from me.

After about ten minutes, I was fully submersed in the movements, dancing along with all the energy I had in me. I loved Zumba. It was a much-needed escape and such a good workout.

A couple people came in late, finding a spot next to me and quickly falling into the groove. I about lost my footing, though, when I looked over to see none other than Bentley Anderson.

He winked at me, moving along with the beat like a pro. He'd definitely done Zumba before.

He leaned toward me. "I didn't know you did Zumba."

"Me? What about you, Mr. Two-Left-Feet?" I forced out of my dry mouth.

He chuckled, pointing his thumb at the lady next to him. "Mom got me into it a couple of years ago. It's my secret hobby. Also helps keep me in shape when it's not swim season."

The image of Bentley in a speedo flashed through my mind, causing a heatwave to crash through me. I stared straight ahead, doing my best to concentrate on the steps and Bentley being fully clothed.

All through the workout, I kept stealing glances at Mom and Cody in the mirror. Watching them smile and laugh with each other caused my heart to soften. Just a little. He was still way too young for her. But, maybe a short relationship with him would help her feel young again. See the world in a new light. Then, they could break up, and she could date someone who was old enough to be my father.

Wait, did this mean I was okay with her marrying someone else?

When the session ended, Cody tossed both Mom and me a towel so we could wipe down, which I happily did. Sweat practically rained from my body. Very sexy.

Bentley used a towel to wipe his forehead. "Nice work out there, Daphne. You really know how to dance."

I wrapped my towel around my neck, so it was draped over my shoulders. "It's one thing in life I'm actually okay at."

He grinned. "Definitely better than okay."

Cody stepped up to us, reaching his hand out to Bentley. "Cody."

Bentley shook his hand, his gaze glancing over all our matching shirts, then landing back on Cody with a curious expression. The shirts said, 'Hey, look at us, we're all together!' but didn't explain our relationship. Maybe I could tell Bentley that Cody was my uncle or something.

I introduced Mom to Bentley to steer the focus somewhere else.

"Daphne said you're planning a bonfire," Mom said, smiling up at Bentley.

Cody put his arm around Mom's shoulder, and all I could think about was all the sweat they were sharing, and, gross. Also, shut down the option of claiming Cody was my uncle. Unless I could pass it off that we were a very affectionate family.

"In January?" Cody shivered. "Don't think I could handle that."

Mom laughed. "Daphne is good at roping people into doing random things."

I brushed off my shoulder. "Yet another thing I'm good at. You guys mustn't flatter a lady so."

Cody motioned between Bentley and me. "How do you two know each other?"

"School," I said. "Poor guy is stuck sitting next to me in English."

Bentley pushed on my arm, grinning. "I think she means that she's stuck next to me."

Cody snapped his fingers like the most brilliant idea just crossed his mind. "You two should come to my friend's costume party next month! It's Regency themed, so you can dress like you're in a Jane Austen movie. And you'll be able to show off your dance moves."

Bentley stroked his chin. "Do I have to pick a character? I know everyone loves Mr. Darcy, but honestly, I'd pick Henry Tilney from Northanger Abbey."

I stared at him with my jaw dropped. He knew the men from Jane Austen novels? I yanked the towel from around my neck so I could dab at my face. Why had I started sweating again?

"No particular character," Cody said. "It's all just for fun. A chance to dress up and be someone else for a night."

Bentley looked down at me. "I'm in if you are."

I kept dabbing at my face, my breaths getting more shallow. Okay, they'd definitely turned on the heat or something.

Mom elbowed me, snapping me from my trance.

"Yeah." I cringed at the crack in my voice. "That would be great." Wait. What? Was I agreeing to go to a party with Cody?

But Bentley would be there. As my ...

"Is this a date?" I blurted.

Mom closed her eyes, her sigh barely audible, but it was magnified to me.

Bentley just shrugged. "Sure. Why not?" He offered a bow, sweeping his arm in front of him. "If you would do me the honor, my lady."

I couldn't help but snort. With a deep flourish, I curtseyed. "It would be my pleasure."

"Oh," Cody said, patting his stomach. "Chick-fil-A does sound good right now."

"I was thinking the same thing!" Mom said.

I loved and hated that his mind went there from me saying, *my pleasure.*

Bentley tapped my arm. "I'll see you in a couple of hours. I'll pick you and Sierra up at two."

I curtseyed again, trying to hide my annoyance at the mention of her name.

When he walked away, Mom let out the smallest of squeals. "A date! And he knows Jane Austen?"

"And does Zumba," Cody put in. "He seems like quite the catch."

I watched Bentley leave with his mom, the two of them chatting and smiling. "He is."

Thanks to Cody using the word 'catch,' "Grenade" by Bruno Mars entered my mind. Seriously, that song was intense. If I were the girl, I wouldn't want to be with a guy like that, either. I mean, he'd catch a grenade for her? If I saw a grenade coming for me and the one I loved, I'd be hightailing it out of there, dragging the guy along with me.

That was true love.

CHAPTER NINETEEN

*W*e ended up sitting at Chick-fil-A, chatting for a couple of hours. I was starting to understand why Mom liked Cody so much. He was a charming guy, easy to talk to and get along with. He had a lot of the same interests as us and worked hard to make sure I was included in the conversation, all the while sprinkling my mom with compliments.

I was warming up to the idea of having him in our life. He'd be a good friend for Mom, even after their relationship fizzled.

I'd just gotten another refill of Cherry Coke—they were one of the few places that actually carried it, so I didn't need to add my own syrup—when I looked at my phone and saw the time. I rushed back to the table, clearly interrupting a sweet moment between Mom and Cody.

"We have to go!" I yelled.

They both jumped, breaking eye contact to look up at me.

"Bentley is going to be picking me up soon." I motioned

to my body, still wearing my Zumba outfit. "I'm not going to have time to shower!"

Mom and Cody went into code red mode, quickly cleaning off the table and rushing outside to the car. We all piled in, and Cody was off.

"You have time to rinse off," Mom said, looking back at me. "Just not to wash your hair."

Cody chanced a glance at me as he drove. "Maybe if you washed it really quick, your mom could re-braid it for you."

"What about makeup? Outfit?" I screeched.

"You don't need makeup," Mom said. "You look beautiful without it."

"I'm in a competition here, Mom!" I yanked out the tie holding my hair back and went to undoing my braid. My leg bounced, like doing so could get us home faster.

I swear we hit every red light until Cody turned sharply into our subdivision. "Daphne, you head straight for the shower. We'll pick out your outfit."

"But—"

"We don't have time to disagree," Cody said, pulling into the driveway. "Just go!"

I scrambled out of the car and into the house. If I knew Cody wouldn't be following us into the house, I would have been stripping in the hallway on the way to the bathroom.

I probably set the record for the fastest shower in history. I'd never moved so fast.

When I got in my bedroom, my outfit was laid out on the bed, sans underwear. I grabbed a bra from my drawer, then noticed the underwear side was practically empty. I'd forgotten to do the laundry, and some things were still on their way from Utah.

Which meant I had a limited supply of underwear. I

picked up the only pair I had, twisting my lips to the side in thought. My lucky Care Bear underwear I'd had since I was in elementary school. I'd always kept them in my drawer to remind me of the good ol' days, but I never actually wore them. They were about three sizes too small.

So, did I go commando, or wear my Care Bear underwear?

Yeah, so not going commando.

It was a struggle, but I got the underwear on, a wedgie already taking form. I hurried into my outfit, softly smiling at Mom and Cody's choices. A Cherry Coke shirt, plus the newly cut-off Cherry Coke sweatshirt, and tennis shoes. So comfortably me.

The black pleather pants, though, I'd never seen before.

"Daphne," Mom yelled from outside. "Hurry up!"

With a shrug, I slipped into the pants, trying not to think about the fact that they were a hair too snug. Hey, I was able to get them zipped, and that was all that mattered.

Mom and Cody were in the kitchen when I ran out. Mom practically shoved me into the chair and went to braiding my hair.

"Whose pants are these?" I asked.

"Mine," Mom said. "They were my lucky pants in high school."

Apparently, my family had a thing for lucky bottoms.

"Your dad always went nuts when I wore them," Mom said, brushing the tangles from my hair.

I glanced at Cody, wanting to see his reaction to the mention of my dad, but he was just smiling at my mom, so sincere and sweet. Ugh. Would it kill him to be a jerk for once?

"Well, FYI, you were slightly smaller than me back then," I said. "I'm surprised I got these babies on."

Cody kneeled before me with my makeup bag. "Have I told you I have three younger sisters?"

I tried to shake my head, but Mom was holding it too tight.

Cody glanced up at her. "Two Dutch braids." His gaze went to me. "Well, they're the reason I know a lot about hair, makeup, fashion, anything girly." He zipped open the kit and searched around in it. "Our mom died when the girls were young, and Dad worked like crazy, so I kind of became the stay-at-home parent." He pulled out the foundation in the bag and held it up to my face. "Isn't this *your* makeup?"

I glanced down at the Care Bear bag. "Yes."

He shook his head, tossing the foundation back in the bag. "That's the wrong color for you. It'll wash you out." The next thing I knew, he was applying eyeliner, eye shadow, blush, mascara, and lip gloss.

"How old are your sisters?" I managed to ask while he was putting on the mascara.

"The twins, Elizabeth and Elinor, are twenty," he said, steely determination in his green eyes. Huh. His eyes were green. Like mine.

"Emma is seventeen," he said. "I think the two of you would get along."

Nope. That was weird. Being friends with his *sister*? If they got married, she'd be my *aunt*. Was that better than Taylor being my aunt? Probably.

"I'm sensing a theme with the names," I said.

He chuckled. "Mom loved Jane Austen."

"Then why are you Cody?" I asked.

"Dad intervened when she tried to name me Edmund." Cody grinned widely when he finished, standing up and stepping back to survey his work.

Mom had finished with my double braids and stood next to him, smiling at me in a total proud mom fashion.

"You look gorgeous," Mom said.

Cody held out a mirror for me to look in. I was worried with all the product he was putting on me, I'd look like a clown. But it was done so well, subtle, the colors matching my outfit.

"This is better than I do!" I said, turning my head side to side.

"I'm more than happy to give you some techniques," Cody said with a laugh.

"You know, I kind of like the name Edmund," I said.

Cody ran a hand over his beard. "It's my middle name. Mom stuck it on the birth certificate when Dad wasn't looking."

Man, I really liked his mom. Wish I could have met her.

Wait, what? I didn't want to meet *anyone* in his family. This was all moving way too fast for me.

The doorbell rang, so Cody went to answer it.

Mom clapped her hands. "Perfect timing." She leaned in and kissed me on the cheek. "Just be yourself, Daphne. Don't let Sierra get to you. Stay focused. Stay strong."

I stretched out my neck like I was headed into battle.

"Hey," Cody said from the doorway, talking to whoever was on the other side. "I'm Cody."

"Weston." Weston's shaky voice made my heart do this weird flip.

Mom's eyebrows scrunched together. "Weston's going?"

I ran my fingers over the Dutch braids. "Didn't I mention that?"

She shook her head. "You just said, 'some people from my class.'" She'd switched to a weird, nasally voice.

"Okay, I do *not* sound like that."

"Daphne?" Cody called out.

Both Mom and I turned to see Cody and Weston standing in the entryway. Weston's nose inched up as he smiled.

"Love Story" by Taylor Swift started up in my mind, and whoa! Where did that come from? This wasn't a freaking fairytale. I turned it off as quickly as I could, replaced by "You've Got a Friend in Me," and, man, that was much better.

CHAPTER TWENTY

*W*hen Weston and I walked down the walkway, I noticed Bentley had been the one to knock on Sierra's door, and I tried not to read too much into that. Maybe he drew the short straw or something.

Sierra and I stopped on the sidewalk, locking eyes. It was a moment of just the two of us, sizing up the enemy. Then our eyes flicked toward the passenger seat, and we both took off.

The William Tell Overture blared in my head like we were off to the races, giving me the energy I needed.

"Shotgun!" I screamed as I sprinted toward Bentley's car.

Sierra and I arrived at the same time, slamming into the door as our hands scrambled to latch onto the handle. Sierra tried to shove me to the side, but I held firm.

"I'm sitting up front," Sierra hissed at me.

"I called shotgun!" Using my hip, I pressed her to the side, slowly inching her back.

"Uh, ladies?" Bentley said from somewhere nearby.

It distracted me just long enough for Sierra to shove me

with all her might, swing the door open, hop in, and slam the door shut. She smirked at me through the window.

Standing straight, I adjusted my bag that had gotten all wonky from the race, making sure it laid right against me. I looked up to see both Weston and Bentley staring at me, both in a mixed state of shock and confusion.

I cleared my throat. "Passenger gets to pick the song selections, and we all know what horrible taste Sierra has in music."

"What does she like?" Weston asked.

I had no idea. We'd never talked about that. Or anything about ourselves, for that matter.

"Crappy music." I wrapped my hand around the door handle, ready to pull it open, when I finally realized what kind of car Bentley had.

"You have a Bentley?" I asked, watching him walk around to the driver's side of the car. On top of that, it was gold, and it doesn't get much more pompous than that.

He shrugged, a small smile on his face. "Parents thought it fitting with my name and all."

Yeah, because getting your teenage son a two-hundred-thousand-dollar car just because it shares his name was totally reasonable.

"Thank goodness they didn't name you Pinto or Chevy," I said, opening the door.

"Or bicycle," Weston said, smiling over the car at me.

I couldn't help but laugh.

"Very funny," Bentley said with obvious sarcasm.

As soon as I sat down, I took in the back seat. Much different from Cody's back seat. Papers, hamburger wrappers, and dirty gym clothes were on the floor and the seat, which answered why it smelled so bad. Did his parents know how Bentley treated his two-hundred-thousand-dollar car?

Weston got in the back, wincing like he'd forgotten about the smell and was just remembering.

Something lumpy was underneath me, so I shifted and pulled it out, holding the dirty sock between my fingers before dropping it to the ground. I had to ignore the fact that I was now in full wedgie mode, thanks to my way-too-small underwear.

Weston leaned close to me, his breath minty fresh, and I practically inhaled the scent, welcoming it over what Bentley had going in his car. "Sorry, I should have warned you."

"That I should have worn a hazmat suit? Yes, you should have."

Bentley hopped in the front, smiling wide at everyone, completely oblivious that we were all grossed out by his car, including Sierra, who had her fingers pressed against the bottom of her nose like she was trying to hold in a sneeze, but was really probably trying to block the smell.

"Who's ready for some fun?" Bentley asked, starting up the car.

Weston and I shared a smile, and I realized we were still leaning toward each other. I casually righted myself, looking out the window as Bentley pulled away from the curb. Mom and Cody were both standing in the doorway, arms around each other, both waving.

"Okay, who *is* that?" Sierra asked, turning around to face me. "I've seen him over at your place a lot."

"Sounds like you've been spying on me," I said.

Her cheeks flared. "You live next door to me, Daphne. There are some things I can't avoid, even if I want to."

Bentley quickly glanced back at me before turning his eyes back to the road. "I'm dying to know, too."

"He's really hot," Sierra said.

Bentley pretended like he was rubbing a long beard. "Love the beard on the guy. Do you think I can pull that off?"

"No," Sierra and I said at the same time.

He'd look so weird in a beard. I glanced over at Weston, taking in his reddish-brown hair. I reached up and rubbed his cheek. "Is your facial hair red?"

His cheeks flared, and I realized I was touching his face. Who does that? I snatched my hand away, tucking it under my leg so I wouldn't do anything else weird with it.

"I think Weston would look awesome with a beard," Bentley said.

Sierra put up a hand. "We're getting off-topic here. Who was that guy, Daphne?"

Ugh. I was hoping she'd forget about that.

I could say Cody was my uncle, but Bentley had already seen him and my mom flirt. Also, there was a chance Sierra could come home one night and see my mom and Cody making out in his car. She'd think she was either making out with her brother, or her dead husband's brother, neither of which were ideal.

But if I told them the truth, Sierra might mock me. She might mock my mom. Or get her mom to try and sabotage Mom and Cody's relationship like she did with Mom and Dad.

Wait. Maybe that would be a good thing. Make Mom realize how ridiculous it was for her to date a twenty-four-year-old.

"He and my mom are dating," I finally said, hoping I wouldn't regret it.

"What!" Sierra's eyes practically bulged from her sockets. "How *old* is he?"

Even though I wasn't happy with the situation, I had a sudden urge to defend my mom. I mean, really, they were both adults.

"Old enough to date my mom," I said with a snappy tone. "I mean, Nick Jonas married a woman ten years older than him."

"So, they're ten years apart?" Bentley asked.

"More or less." With an emphasis on the *more*.

"She looks happy," Weston said, smiling at me.

I returned the smile. "She is." As much as it pained me to admit, she was happy. But I'd be keeping a very close eye on the guy.

Sierra scoffed. "So weird."

With pinched eyebrows and the saltiest glare I could muster, I opened my mouth, ready to tell her off, but Weston's warm hand landed on mine. As soon as my gaze—which had immediately softened at his touch—landed on our hands, he quickly yanked his hand away and held it close to his chest, his worried eyes telling me he wished he could take the moment back. He offered an apologetic shrug and unsure smile.

When I smiled warmly back, he blew out a relieved breath. He'd only been trying to stop me from lashing out at Sierra, and it was probably a good thing he had.

Maybe it was a good thing he was with us. He read me as well as Veronica or Taylor did and knew when to stop me from doing something stupid.

CHAPTER TWENTY-ONE

The bookstore we went to was everything I dreamed of and more. The moment we stepped inside the quaint store, that lovely, intoxicating smell of books welcomed me, and I wanted to bathe in it. Honestly, it should be bottled up as a fragrance because I would douse myself in all that enticing glory and prance around for everyone to enjoy it.

"Do you think they'd let me move in?" I asked, staring at all the rows of books.

Weston chuckled next to me. "I've always wondered that same thing. The smell alone is amazing." He looked at me, his nose slightly inched up with his crooked smile. "You know how people say they enter Disneyland, and they suddenly breathe in the smell of Main Street, and they feel like they're home?"

"It is a great smell." I twisted my lips in thought. "Well, that I can remember. It's been a long time since I've gone to Disneyland."

Weston glanced around the bookstore, a sense of wonder in his eyes. "That's how I feel about this place."

Bentley came up on the other side of me, one hand in his pocket, the other scratching the back of his head. "So, what are we supposed to do in here?"

I threw my arms wide. "Soak it in. Bask in the moment."

Sierra had wandered down an aisle, perusing the books. It seemed like she knew exactly where she was going, like she'd been here before. Did she like to read?

I motioned to her. "Take a look around, Bentley. Check out the different genres and titles. Read the first few paragraphs of a book that catches your eye."

He scrunched his face. "That sounds like a lot of work."

"It'll be worth it, I promise," Weston said.

Bentley linked his fingers together and pushed them out in front of him, his knuckles cracking. "Let's do this." He headed for the aisle right in front of him and picked up the first book he saw. He turned it so we could see. A lady in a skimpy outfit clung to the bare chest of a muscular guy, both staring at each other like they wanted to devour the other. "Now, this looks promising."

I covered my mouth, holding back my laugh.

"Classic," Weston said. "One of my favorites."

Bentley cocked his head to the side. "Really?" He skimmed the pages of the book, settling on a page toward the middle.

"I'm kidding." Weston pointed to the right of the store. "Try the crime thrillers over there. They're my real favorites."

Bentley's eyes were wide as he read, his face scrunching up in disgust. "Okay, my mom reads books like this, and now that I know what's inside, I'm totally grossed out."

A middle-aged lady waddled down the aisle, stopping next to him. "The best scene is on page two-thirty-five." She waved her hand in front of her face. "Always gets me going."

With a wink at him, she sauntered toward the cashier, a stack of romance books in her arms.

Bentley gently tucked the book back into its spot, barely touching it, the look of disgust on his face not gone. "So, where are these crime thrillers?"

With a laugh, Weston took off toward the right. "Follow me."

Bentley was quick at his heels.

It gave me a moment alone in the bookstore. Aside from the rows of books, there were couches and chairs lined up around the perimeter, all cushy and inviting. Origami of all different sizes was randomly scattered through the store, all folded from pages from a book. 3D artwork lined the walls, all from book pages that had been shaped and painted. One was a bouquet of flowers, the stems made from old spines.

I stopped in front of one, staring at it with a smile. The artist had created a masterpiece, using the pages to create waves in the ocean, a sandy shore, birds flying in the air, and seashells on the sand.

"Don't worry," an older gentleman said next to me. "I only use books that have been so loved, they're no longer staying together." He stared at the picture. "Why throw a book away when you can turn it into something else to love?"

"You made these?" I asked, not able to hide the awe in my tone.

He turned to me, grinning, showing off what had to be dentures. "Keeps me busy when the store is slow."

"Do you own this place, too?"

He nodded. "Opened it all the way back in nineteen-seventy-four with my sweetheart."

I glanced around. "Is she here? I'd love to meet her. This store is *amazing*."

Smoothing the top of his white hair, he shook his head. "She passed away last year."

"I'm so sorry," I said.

Using his finger, he brushed some dust off a 3D bird. "She lived a good life. I buried her with all her favorite books, so she'll have something to keep her occupied until I join her."

This was hands down the most adorable story I'd ever heard.

"What did she like to read?"

He chuckled, all raspy and wet. "Horrors. That woman loved to be scared."

"Sounds like we'd get along." My perma-wedgie was starting to get to me, ruining this whole moment. I wanted to pick it so badly, but there was no way I was doing it in front of someone. Especially not an old man talking about his late wife.

His white, bushy eyebrows shot up. "You read horrors?"

"I know it doesn't match with me," I said, motioning to the pink Cherry Coke sweatshirt and Dutch braids. "But I'm a sucker for them."

I'd always had a great relationship with books, and now "Sucker" was officially our love song.

He pointed a wrinkly finger at a spiraled set of stairs near the back. "Margot's favorites are up in the loft. There's a whole shelf of them. Why don't you go pick one out? On the house."

I quickly shook my head. "I can pay for it. I *want* to pay for it."

There was a twinkle in his eyes. "Buy one get one free. Special offer that you can't pass up."

"I think I can handle that," I said with a smile.

Getting up the old spiral staircase was more difficult

than I thought it would be. Mostly because of my too-tight pleather pants and too-small underwear. The pants made a weird squeak with every step.

I was practically winded when I got to the top of the stairs. The moment I looked around, though, a new high entered my system, and the *Stranger Things* theme song gave my mind the ambiance it needed.

A black couch and end tables sat in the middle of the loft. The black coffee table was decorated with skulls, spiders, and everything scary.

The black shelf on the left had a sign that said, *Customers' Favorite Horror Picks*. Fake spiderwebs clung to the sides of the shelves, adding the perfect creepy feel.

On the wall straight ahead was a black shelf with a sign that said, *Margot's Little Shop of Horrors*.

With a smile, I headed straight for that shelf. I perused the titles, my fingers hovering next to them, but not quite touching the books. When I passed over one, my spidey-senses tingled. Sorry, Captain America, but Spiderman would always be a part of my life. The Tom Holland version.

I picked up the book, and something inside me warmed, like I needed to read this book. Flipping it over, I read the summary on the back.

My wedgie was so far up that I really needed to do something about it. After a quick glance around, I noticed I was the only one on the loft, so I set about the task of fixing my stupid underwear.

Problem was, it was such a small pair to begin with, there wasn't much material to pick out. But even what I did get out gave me the slightest relief.

"This place is awesome!" Bentley's sudden voice behind

me made me jump, sending the book I was holding into the air.

It thudded on the ground, and I cringed at the sound, like I'd just dropped a masterpiece, totally disrespecting it. I quickly bent down and scooped it up, wiping off the sides and front.

Sierra let out a mixture of shock and laughter. "Oh. My. Gosh."

I looked over my shoulder at her. "What?"

She was staring wide-eyed at my backside. In fact, so was Bentley.

I pressed my hand to my butt, and my own horror story started right up. My pants had torn. Right down the middle of my butt, exposing not only my Care Bear underwear, but *way* too much skin for my liking. Well, no skin would be my ideal liking. And no underwear showing. And pants without rips.

I didn't know where to turn. I didn't want to face them with my bright red face and their shocked expressions, but I didn't want my backside facing them either.

I twisted side to side, not knowing what to do. Heat flared inside me, and my lungs started to burn. Breathe. I needed to breathe.

Weston trotted up the stairs, pausing when he saw Bentley and Sierra still staring at me.

"What's going on?" he asked.

Oh no. Another person to add to the humiliating situation.

Bentley just pointed at me, like he had no idea what to do. That made two of us.

I needed to cover up. I tried to take off my sweatshirt, but my arms were practically locked into place, not bending how I wanted them to.

Sierra lifted her phone like she was going to take a picture.

Weston gasped. "Oh."

Now my sweatshirt was stuck over my head as I tried to tug it off. Footsteps pounded toward me, and suddenly two warm arms wrapped around my waist, tying something around me.

"Your sweatshirt is too short," Weston said. He tugged it back down so I could see. He'd taken off his zippered hoodie and tied it around my waist.

I couldn't breathe. Why was this happening to me?

Bentley and Sierra argued in the background, but I couldn't make out their words. Everything closed in on me. Each breath was ragged and quick, drying out my lips. I slid down to the ground, pulling my legs into my chest and rocking.

What was I supposed to do during a panic attack? My mind reeled but came up empty. All I could do was breathe in a deep wheeze, my chest heaving in and out.

Weston knelt in front of me, softly putting his hands on my shoulders. "Breathe, Daphne. Slow it down."

Slow, yes, that was what I needed to do. Slow my breaths. But how?

"What did Veronica have you do?" he asked, his eyebrows pinched in concentration. "Oh, yeah, happy thoughts, right?"

I nodded, my head bouncing as rapidly as my breathing.

Weston glanced at my sweatshirt. "Cherry Coke. Um, Captain America. Care Be ..." He trailed off, his eyes going wide. "Probably not them right now."

I shook my head. Definitely not Care Bears right now. I mean, sharing was caring, but not like this!

"What else?" Weston kept his tone low and even,

calming me. "Your mom. Veronica. Taylor. Uh. Grandparents? Oh. Pets?"

My head shook so fast, I worried it would fall off.

"No pets," Weston said with a nod. "Just breathe, okay? Slow your breathing. Everything is okay, I promise."

"Is there something I can do?" Bentley asked, kneeling next to Weston.

"Get her some water," Weston said.

With a nod and a soft smile thrown my way, Bentley stood and trotted down the stairs. Sierra had sat down on the couch, her arms folded in a pout. What could she possibly be upset about? She wasn't the one who got humiliated.

I hadn't noticed my breathing had sped back up until Weston placed a finger under my chin and turned my head away from Sierra and toward him.

"Slow down," he said, concern in his eyes. "Don't worry about her. She doesn't matter."

She shouldn't, but she did. Everyone's opinion of me mattered. I hated that about myself. I shouldn't care what they thought.

I needed to shut out the noise, like stupid Sierra and my pessimistic thoughts.

"In and out," Weston said, soft like Veronica always did.

Happy thoughts.

"In and out," he said.

Dancing in the kitchen with my family as we cooked dinner. Trips to Disneyland.

"In and out."

My dad's laugh. Our family hikes in the Wasatch Mountains in Utah.

"In and out."

Making snow angels with Mom and Dad in the front yard.

The burn in my lungs subsided, my breaths slowing down.

Bentley came back up the stairs with a bottle of water and handed it to me. The cool water felt nice against my dry throat.

"Are you done freaking out?" Sierra asked.

"Sierra!" Both Weston and Bentley shouted. She shrunk back on the couch, her face turning red.

I smacked my dry lips together. I needed Chapstick. Pronto. My shaking hands tried to open my bag.

"What do you need?" Bentley asked.

"Chapstick," I managed to squeak out.

Bentley unzipped my bag and rummaged inside until he came back out with my cherry Chapstick. He grinned as he handed it to me. "Why am I not surprised it's cherry?"

My lips absorbed the moisture, immediately reducing the sting. "Much better."

"You okay to get up?" Weston asked.

"I think I'd rather curl up in the corner and die if that's okay with you guys."

Weston glanced at Bentley, then back at me. "No one will ever know this happened, we promise."

Bentley held up his hand. "I solemnly swear I won't tell a soul."

They both turned to Sierra, their eyes narrowing in on her.

With a huff, she rolled her eyes. "You already made me delete the photos." When they continued staring, she grunted. "Fine. I won't tell anyone, okay? What happens in the bookstore, stays in the bookstore."

Bentley relaxed, satisfied by her words, but both

Weston and I stayed a little stiff. No way Sierra could keep something this juicy to herself. Thank goodness Bentley made her delete the photos.

It would be her word against ours.

Weston held out his hand and helped me to my feet. His warm arm wrapped around my waist, holding me steady. "Think you can walk down the stairs?"

I slowly nodded. "I think so." I pointed to the book on the ground. "I want that book, though. It talked to my soul."

Bending down, Bentley snatched it up, his eyes roaming the cover. "A creepy mansion with the title dripping blood speaks to your soul?"

"Always," I said.

Both he and Weston chuckled.

Sierra stood and joined us. "Can we go eat now? I'm starving."

All my appetite had left. All I wanted to do was go home, put on my Grumpy Care Bear onesie, and listen to all of Kelly Clarkson and Taylor Swift's depressing songs. I already had the playlist created: Grumpy Grooves.

Weston rubbed my arm. "What do you want to do, Daphne?"

"I want to go home," I muttered.

Bentley nodded. "Then, we'll get you home."

With another grunt, Sierra stormed down the stairs.

Bentley smiled after her. "Guess someone gets hangry."

The owner of the store insisted I take the book for free, especially after he heard about my panic attack. I promised I'd be back to make tons of purchases.

When we got into the backseat of Bentley's car, Weston hesitated a second before moving to the middle seat to be next to me. I leaned into him, so grateful for the support.

CHAPTER TWENTY-TWO

*W*eston called Taylor and Veronica, so they were both waiting on the porch when I got home. Weston quickly got out of the car, jogged around, opened my door, and helped me out.

"I'll text you later, Daphne," Bentley said from inside the car. "To make sure you're doing okay."

"Thanks, Bentley," I said.

Sierra just huffed a goodbye, her nose buried in a book she'd bought at the store. She didn't get out of the car, which meant she was staying with Bentley. Time alone with him. It would have bothered me more if I didn't already feel like crap.

Veronica and Taylor rushed to my side, hugging me from both sides, making Weston release his grip on me.

I strained my neck to look at him. "Thank you, Weston. For everything. I'll bring your jacket to school on Monday." No way I was taking it off now so more people could get a good look at my butt.

"Yeah, of course," he said. His eyes traveled to the car, and then back to me. Clearly, he didn't want to get back into

Bentley's awful smelling car with just Bentley and Sierra in there.

I debated whether I wanted him to stay or not. He was a nice guy, and had calmed me down, but I could be more open with Veronica and Taylor.

But then "I Like Me Better" by Lauv entered my thoughts, reflecting how I truly felt about Weston. I did like myself better when he was around. He brought out the lighthearted and easy-going Daphne, free to be me.

Veronica looked at Weston and spoke, interrupting my song. "You *have* to go with them."

Weston furrowed his eyebrows. "Why?"

"You have to make sure nothing happens between Bentley and Sierra," Taylor said with a tone that said she couldn't believe he was even questioning them.

"You're our eyes and ears," Veronica said to him. "Keep them apart. Then report back to us with *everything* that happens."

Weston's nose inched up, not in his cute, smile way, but in a cute, you girls are crazy way. "That sounds awful. Can't I stay here?"

I opened my mouth to say *yes*, but Taylor cut me off. "Weston. In the car, now. Then report."

He saluted her. "Okay, captain." His eyes flickered over to me. "Hope you're feeling better, Daphne. I'll text you later as well."

"Sounds good." I pushed away from Veronica and Taylor so I could hug him. "Seriously, Weston, thank you. I don't think I would have survived without you." I must have still been in a weird/shocked state, because I kissed him on the cheek before I went inside my house.

The first thing I did when I got inside was change out of the stupid pleather pants and toss them in the trash. Then I started the laundry, eager to get on a different pair of underwear.

Shuffling back into the front room, I tugged the hood of my blue Grumpy Care Bear onesie over my head, wanting to disappear.

Veronica was sitting on the couch, scrolling through Netflix. She had Alexa playing Kelly Clarkson's *My December* album, setting the dismal mood.

I sank into the couch next to her. "Where's Taylor?"

"She went to get you a Double Western Bacon Cheese-burger from CJ," Veronica said. I loved that she knew I referred to Carl's Jr. as CJ. "Do you want a sappy movie, or a scary movie?"

"Scary," I mumbled. "Might scare the embarrassment out of me." I lay my head back on the couch, staring up at the ceiling. "Is she getting regular or criscut fries?"

"Criscut, obviously," she said. "You won't eat regular fries without Utah's stupid fry sauce."

"Fry sauce is not stupid. It's delicious." It had taken me a while to get used to it after moving to Utah. Now, I couldn't get enough. Aunt Shannon was going to send us some bottles from a favorite local restaurant of ours.

"And, she's replacing the drink with an Oreo shake."

"You two are my heroes."

Veronica patted my leg. "We got you, girl."

I lowered my head so I could look at the screen. "Why didn't she just order it through an app?"

"And pay those delivery fees?" Veronica snorted. "No, thank you." She turned to me. "Any of these titles stick out?"

"Let's just binge-watch *The Haunting of Hill House*."

She grinned. "Good thing we've already got the okay from our parents to spend the night. We're all yours, baby."

I curled up on the couch, facing her. "They saw my underwear, Veronica. And practically my butt."

She turned toward me, taking my hands in hers. "I'm so sorry that happened. If I would have been here before you left, I would have talked you out of those stupid pleather pants."

A thought crossed my mind. "Don't you have a date with DeShawn tonight?"

She squeezed my hands. "I'm right where I'm supposed to be. Besides, he and Zander are playing some online game instead. Siege the Rainbow, or something?"

"*Rainbow Six Siege?*"

"Whatever. It's a dumb computer game."

"That you've never played or seen, so you can't comment on it."

Her eyes narrowed. "Don't make me regret my decision of staying here with you."

"Single Ladies" by Beyoncé rang out from my phone. Mom was video calling. I answered the phone, my heart melting a little at the worry etched on her face.

"Hey, Mom," I said, grabbing a piece of hair and twirling it around my fingers.

Her eyes teared up. "Are you okay? Taylor called me and told me what happened."

I played with my hair, taking my anxiety out on it. "I think I'll survive. I'm just forever traumatized."

"This is all my fault," she said.

"How?"

She wiped a tear from her eye. "I made you wear those stupid pants!"

"You didn't know they would rip down the middle." I arched an eyebrow. "Did you?"

"Of course not!" She looked mortified that I would even ask the question.

"I was kidding," I said, a smile finally breaking through.

She let out a breath of relief. "Should I come home?"

I looked past her to see where she was. Two doors were open behind her, revealing a gym. "Where are you?"

"Emma has a volleyball game," Mom said. "Cody and I came to watch. But I can have him take me home. I should be there."

I shook my head. "Stay. I have Veronica and Taylor to keep me company."

"Are you sure?" The worry on her face hadn't eased.

"We're watching *The Haunting of House Hill*."

She blanched. "I hate that show."

"I know. So, stay with Cody. Cheer for Emma. And bring me home a slice of cheesecake."

She grinned. "There's a Cheesecake Factory down the street. Oreo?"

"Yes, please."

She blew me a kiss. "Love you, Daphne. I'll squeeze you tight when I get home."

"Looking forward to it. Love you, too."

*L*ater that night, during a break between episodes, I saw a text from Weston. *You okay?*

Me: *Much better, thanks. How was the rest of your night?*

Weston: *Awful. I was the freaking third wheel! I still don't know why your friends forced me to stay with them.*

Me: *Just looking out for Bentley's best interest, I guess.*

Weston: *Well, his interest seems to be Sierra right now.*

My heart lodged in my throat. *What do you mean?*

Weston: *It was like extreme flirting. I finally made them take me home because I couldn't handle it anymore.*

Well, that wasn't what I wanted to hear. My stupid panic attack had ruined everything. What if they kissed after they released Weston from third-wheel prison? Could I even stand a chance now? But Dad had kissed both Mom *and* Kimber, and, wow, did that thought make me sick to my stomach.

I mean, I figured they'd kissed other people, but that didn't mean I wanted to like visualize it or anything. And with Kimber. So gross.

Weston: *DeShawn and Zander invited me to play R6S with them, so my night is looking optimistic now.*

Rainbow Six Siege. At least I knew that acronym.

Me: *Have fun!*

Weston: *I'm glad you're doing better. See you Monday.*

Me: *Thanks for being awesome today. I'm lucky to have you*

My thumb hit *send* before I could finish the sentence. It should have read, *I'm lucky to have you in my life.* But no, of course, it had to sound like a declaration. Did I finish the sentence? Send the other half?

Weston replied before I could get my crap together. *Pretty sure the luck is all mine.*

Oh, no. A huge smile was coming to my face. Like, ginormous. I needed to shut it down. My focus was Bentley right now. Bentley Anderson. Diver and swimmer extraordinaire. Handsome and fun. Knew his Jane Austen and how to Zumba.

But ...

I couldn't shake the feeling that Weston Ashworth and all his perfectness could make me lose the bet.

CHAPTER TWENTY-THREE

Thank goodness Grams loved Halloween and did community theater. She had so many costumes, they were practically overtaking the attic.

"Attics always creep me out," I said, my fingers pinching the very edge of a tote to pull open the lid.

"They creep everyone out," Mom said, rummaging through some boxes.

I peered inside the tote, still barely hanging onto the lid. A big red nose, creepy eyes, a mop of curly red hair, and a disturbing smile that made the Joker seem like a nice guy gazed up at me.

Screaming, I let go of the lid and jumped back, my hands flying to my chest.

"What?" Mom asked, rushing to my side. "Are you okay, Daphne?"

I pointed a shaky finger at the tote. "Burn that and everything in it."

Frowning, Mom glanced inside the tote before she rolled her eyes. "What's your problem with clowns?"

"Oh, I don't know. The fact that they're always laughing, always smiling, love to be around children, want you to squeeze their nose, don't know the meaning of personal space, and like to dress up in a stupid suit and paint stuff on their face?"

Mom chuckled. "You practically described Santa, too."

I pointed a finger at her. "His laugh is jolly, full of warmth and love. Clowns, though, their laugh is menacing, full of malice and hate. They're pretty much the equivalent of a serial killer."

Mom patted my arm. "You might be overreacting just a tad."

"Santa brings cheer. Clowns bring fear." I needed that embroidered on a pillow.

"You really need to stop." Mom opened another tote near us, sighing in relief. "Found the dresses."

I hightailed it toward the ladder that would bring me back to a safe place. "Bring the tote with you! I'll be downstairs taking a shower!"

Mom's grunt echoed behind me as I descended the ladder. As soon as my feet hit the ground, I let out a shudder. "I hate attics." I sniffed. "And clowns."

After my long, hot shower—the water practically scalding my skin—I tried on a coral Regency dress my mom found in the tote.

I waddled out of my bedroom and into the living room, where Mom was sitting on the couch in a navy-blue Regency dress.

"I'm drowning," I said, holding out my arms.

Mom bit back a laugh as she came to my side, taking in my dress. Hers fit like a glove. "I can fix this. Don't worry."

"How come yours fits you like it was made for you?" I asked, putting my hands on my hips.

Mom went to the sewing basket and pulled out some

pins. "Because it was. Grams made it for my Halloween costume when I was ..." She twisted her lips in thought, coming toward me. "Sixteen, I think."

"And you still fit in it?" I shook my head. "That's not right, man."

She came up behind me, cinching the back of my dress. "It was a little too big on me then. Grams hated anything tight on me."

"If she could only see you now. How disappointed she would be." A pin pricked my back. "Hey!"

"Oops." Mom didn't hold back her sarcasm. "Accident."

I huffed. "It actually looks stunning on you."

"Well, just some minor alterations, and this one will look stunning on you."

I shook my hips, causing her to laugh.

"Stop moving!"

"Alexa, play 'Bootylicious' by Destiny's Child," I said.

The song started up, booming around the living room.

"This brings back memories," Mom said. "I used to sing this song to your Dad all the time."

I scrunched my face. "Ugh. Alexa, stop."

Mom came in front of me, putting more pins at my waist. "You know they'll be playing Regency music at the ball, right?"

I smiled. "How funny would it be to see everyone doing the La Galante dance to 'Bad Guy' by Billie Eilish?"

Mom looked up at me, a huge smile on her face. "Now, *that's* a great idea for a party. Regency dances to modern songs."

I tried to twerk, but the dress wouldn't let me squat.

Mom tapped my chin. "I never want to see you do that again."

"Well, yeah, it was all wrong. Can't get a good range of movement in this dress."

The doorbell rang, so I jogged over to the door, leaving a laughing Mom in the living room.

When I opened the door, the smile on my face grew bigger. "Weston!"

He took in my dress, his nose inching up as he smiled. "Hey, Daphne." He held out a twelve-pack of Cherry Coke.

I took it into my arms, holding it close. "What's this for?"

He stuffed his hands in his pockets. "I know I said I'd see you Monday, but I had to see in person that you were okay."

Yeah, probably thanks to my declaration, telling him I was lucky to have him. Like he was mine or something.

"Plus, I still owed you a Coke," he said.

I gestured to myself. "I'm alive. And the pants are burned, so all is well.".

Mom came up behind me. "You burned my pants?" She waved at Weston. "Hi, Weston."

"Hey, Mrs. Richards."

I turned to her. "Okay, I just tossed them out. But in my mind, it was a huge inferno, burning all my embarrassment to ash."

Weston looked at Mom's dress, then at mine. "Uh, what's with the dresses?"

"They're for a party we're going to in a couple of weeks," Mom said. "How's Ivy doing?"

He grinned. "So much better. Daphne seriously saved both our lives." His gaze slid to mine. "She can't stop talking about you."

I waved a hand, hoping to wave off the butterflies

invading my stomach. "No big deal. Anyone else would have done the same."

"Not so sure about that," Weston said.

Around the corner, just out of sight, it sounded like a car had pulled into the driveway. The next thing I knew, Cody was coming up the walkway, saying hi to everyone—including giving Mom a kiss on the lips. His blue and white checkered Vans were awesome, but I kept that bit of information to myself.

"You ladies look beautiful," Cody said. "Are these the dresses you're wearing for the party?"

I pointed to the pins at my waist. "Hopefully sans pins."

"I'll fix it, don't worry," Mom said, squeezing my arm.

Cody motioned for me to come outside. "I brought my old Civic for you to test out."

Excitement bubbled to the surface of my chest, coming out before I could stop it. I couldn't have Cody thinking I actually *liked* him. "Really?" I quickly set the soda in the entryway and almost stepped outside, but then remembered I was wearing a Regency dress full of pins. Then I decided I didn't care.

I followed him to the driveway, pulling back in surprise when I saw his old, blue Civic sitting there in near perfect condition. The only thing that really said it was older was the outdated frame.

"I've had her since I was sixteen," Cody said, beaming with pride. "Great mileage, no accidents, everything inside is holding up well." He tossed me the keys, which I caught against my chest. "Take it for a spin. See what you think."

"Uh, you sure about that?" I asked, my gaze sliding to my mom. This guy was being way too trusting of a teenager he hardly knew.

Mom was too busy ogling Cody to see me trying to catch her attention. Guess it *was* smart on his part to do this.

Cody's smile faltered. "Why wouldn't I? You have a license, right?"

Ignoring him, I turned to Weston, shaking the keys in my hand. "Want to go for a ride?"

Weston's eyes lit up. "Heck yeah."

We quickly hopped in the car, well, as quickly as I could for wearing a pinned Regency dress.

"You have a license, right?!" Cody yelled from outside the car.

I glanced around, noting how everything was immaculate. "I'm really impressed." I ran my hand across the center console. "The guy really takes care of his vehicles."

Weston arched an eyebrow at me. "You *do* have a license, right?"

I couldn't hold back my grin. "Yeah. Just enjoying freaking him out. I mean, if he's going to date a girl with a teenage daughter, I feel it's my duty to give him the full teenage experience. Gotta crank up the drama." My eyes went to the dashboard. "Speaking of cranking, let's test out the speakers in this baby."

Popping the key in the ignition, I started the car, my wide eyes turning to Weston when I heard the music. Jason Aldean played from the radio station.

"A country music fan." I glanced out at Cody, who was currently being consoled by Mom. After adjusting the mirrors, I started to back out of the driveway, but Mom suddenly appeared at the driver's side window, holding my bag.

I guess bringing my driver's license with me would make sense.

Rolling down the window, I smiled at her before I took

the bag and went to toss it in the back, then thought better of it and gently placed it on the floor behind the driver's seat. "Thanks, Mom."

She patted the top of the car. "Be safe." She leaned in the window, kissing me on the cheek. "And quick."

Right. It was Sunday, the day of the week we usually saved for church and family.

I gave her a thumbs-up. "Ten minutes, tops."

As I drove away, I checked in the rearview mirror, seeing Mom and Cody waving at us.

"I can't peg that guy," I said.

"What do you mean?" Weston opened the glove compartment, peering inside. He pulled out the owner's manual. "Only thing in here."

I flipped on the blinker, getting ready to turn out of my neighborhood. "He likes country music. Loves to Zumba. Obsessed with costume parties. Dates women fourteen years older than him."

Weston held up a hand. "Do you know if he's dated other older women?"

"Okay, no, I haven't done a thorough background check on the guy, but maybe I should." I mean, Sierra's dad *was* a cop. I had an in. Well, except for the fact she hated me.

He motioned to the car. "Well, he takes great care of his property, likes to have fun, generous, friendly." He shrugged. "It seems like your mom could do a lot worse than this guy."

I groaned. "I know. And I hate it."

"What happened to your dad?"

My heart softened. "He died a few years ago. Pancreatic cancer." I sighed. "I knew Mom would start dating again, it's just weird. Especially when he's closer to my age than hers."

He snapped his fingers. "Aha! You're jealous."

I tried to hold back my snort, but it came out when I laughed. "*So* jealous."

"I mean, did you see those gorgeous locks on the guy?" He fanned his face. "And that beard? I'm swooning over here."

Reaching across the center console, I shoved his arm. "Yeah, okay, maybe I'm being ridiculous."

"You're not," he said. "I'm not sure how I would feel if my mom started dating someone else." He fiddled with some of the nobs on the dashboard. "Especially since my parents are still married."

"10,000 Hours" by Dan + Shay came on the radio, and I reached for the dial at the same time Weston did, his hand landing on top of mine, both of us cranking up the volume. We smiled at each other before we started singing along, our off-key harmonies music to my ears.

CHAPTER TWENTY-FOUR

*M*om and Cody had gone inside while I went for my test drive with Weston. When we came inside, we caught them kissing on the couch, and the song in my head—"Believer" by Imagine Dragons—came to a screeching halt. Every single awkward moment before this paled in comparison. I mean, *I* should have been the one making out, not Mom.

They jumped off the couch, straightening out their clothes, Cody wiping pink lip gloss off his lips, Mom running her fingers through her tangled hair, trying to smooth it out. She still wore her Regency dress, which added to the weirdness of it all.

Cody cleared his throat. "How did you like the car?"

Seeing my mom tangled up with such a young guy that definitely was *not* my dad put my mind in such a strange place.

Words just flew out of my mouth. "Great. Smooth. Smelled nice." I motioned to Weston. "We really enjoyed the back seat."

"What?" Mom asked with her eyes wide.

"What?" Cody and Weston said at the same time.

"Nothing." I picked up the twelve-pack of Cherry Coke off the floor in the entryway. "I need a drink." I hurried into the kitchen, tossing the soda on the counter before I snatched a bottle of Cherry Coke from the fridge. I had it open and chugging it down my throat in about two seconds.

Weston cautiously approached me, his hands out like I might spring on him at any moment. "Do you prefer bottles?"

I nodded, still chugging away.

"I'll remember that for next time," he said.

I gave him a thumbs-up.

Mom crept into the kitchen, more cautious than Weston. She smiled sheepishly at me, and all I could hear were little *baas* frolicking through my mind.

"Daphne, sweetie," Mom said, taking slow steps toward me. "Are you doing okay?"

Shaking my head, I put my hand out, telling her to stop in her tracks. I finally lowered the bottle, taking a huge gulp of air. I opened my mouth to speak, but no words came.

"How'd you like the car?" Mom asked.

Changing the subject. Typical Mom move. Although, I really didn't want to talk about her kissing escapades.

"It's really nice," Weston said since I still couldn't word at the moment. "If Daphne doesn't want it, maybe I'll buy it."

"Dibs!" I finally found my voice. Then my cheeks flushed, thinking about the song "Dibs" by Kelsea Ballerini that came into my mind the first time I met Weston.

Cody came around the corner, grinning widely. "You want it?"

I nodded. "Definitely. Although, I don't think four thousand is enough for that car."

"Maybe I could help some," Mom said. "Early graduation present."

Cody waved a hand. "Four thousand is perfect. I know you'll take great care of it."

All the awkwardness left, replaced by a giddiness that I couldn't contain. I ran at Cody, throwing my arms around him. My own car. Something I saved up for and bought myself. A freaking car!

When I finally released him, Cody was still all smiles.

"Thanks, Cody," I said. "This means so much to me."

"Glad to help," he said.

If the guy thought this meant more make-out sessions with my mom, he was sorely mistaken. I needed to install cameras inside. Make sure no hanky-panky was going on when I wasn't home.

How did *I* become the responsible one in this relationship?

Mom clapped her hands together, her eyes lighting up. "Weston, can you stay for a bit?" She looked at me. "We can practice the dances."

"Uh, what?" Weston asked, scratching his head.

"That's a great idea," Cody said.

Mom scrolled through her phone. "There's got to be some Regency music I can download somewhere."

Cody pulled a piece of paper from his pocket. "I have the list of dances we're supposed to learn and where to find the songs."

He and Mom went into the family room, huddled together, hooking his phone up to the TV so we could watch the videos. I almost said something about "family day," but then I looked over at Weston. I really wanted him to stay.

Weston folded his arms. "Am I supposed to know what's going on?"

I shook my head, smiling. "No. You don't have to dance if you don't want to." I opened the pantry door and pulled out a broom. "This guy will do just fine. I'm sure he's a great dancer."

Weston rubbed the back of his neck, his shy smile creeping onto his face. "I don't mind." He motioned to his Captain America T-shirt. "I'm not really dressed the part, though."

"Oh!" I tossed the broom back in the closet—yeah, it totally missed and fell to the floor, but whatever—and ran to the totes Mom brought down from the attic. "I know I saw ..." Bright orange material caught my eye. I fished out the cummerbund and bowtie and ran back over to Weston. I velcroed them around his neck and waist. "Perfect."

Weston stared at them with his eyebrows inched up. "They're bright orange."

"Grams and Gramps were Harry and Lloyd from *Dumb and Dumber* for Halloween a few years ago." I shrugged. "They keep everything."

"Daphne!" Mom said, catching my attention.

I turned to see that she and Cody had moved the coffee table off to the side, creating an open area for us to dance in the family room.

"Ready?" Mom asked.

Taking Weston's hand, I steered him into the room with them. "Look, I even got Weston dressed for the occasion."

Cody frowned. "Well, now I feel left out."

Mom rushed over to the tote. "We have the baby blue cummerbund and bowtie in here, too."

"How come he gets baby blue, and I'm stuck with this?" Weston motioned to his orange cummerbund.

I shrugged. "I thought it would go good with your reddish-brown hair."

Mom came back over, handing the items to Cody. "Daphne loves things that pop." She pursed her lips. "Why did that not sound right?"

Weston's cheeks were probably about as red as mine.

Chuckling, Cody pressed play on his phone. "Let's dance." He looked at Weston. "Just watch what I do."

He bowed, and Mom curtsied back.

Weston and I did the same, both fighting back laughs.

Then Cody took Mom's hand in hers, very delicately, and they spun in a circle.

It didn't strike me until Weston took my fingers in his that we weren't wearing gloves like they did in the Regency Era. Just a simple touch, but I found myself blushing. Would I do the same with Bentley? I'd be wearing gloves then, so it wouldn't matter.

The whole time we danced, I couldn't help but fight the thought that I wished it were Weston going to the party with me, not Bentley.

CHAPTER TWENTY-FIVE

I'm not sure how Sierra found out, but she was livid about Bentley and me going to the party together. She kept saying something about all his dad's constituents eating it up, loving the formality of it all.

Everywhere I went, her gaze practically burned a huge hole through me like she was freaking Cyclops. Then I snorted, thinking about her with one eye, and suddenly I didn't care.

It was a slightly chilly day out, but not horribly bad for having to wear a tee and shorts in P.E. Everyone around seemed to be freezing, but they had no idea what freezing truly was.

"Talk to me when it's ten degrees," I said to Sebastian as we stood on the field in the middle of the track. "Then, I might agree with you."

"Ten!" Sebastian shuddered. "So not moving to Utah."

"But the snow, man," Dax said, suddenly appearing on the other side of me. "Greatest place to ski."

"Where did you come from?" I asked.

He looked at me like I was crazy. "I've been here the whole time."

No, he hadn't. But whatever. "You've been to Utah?"

He nodded. "My family goes skiing in Park City once a year."

"But you were so shocked when you found out there's less air up there," I said.

Dax's eyes widened in shock. "There's less air in Utah?"

Yeah, okay, the guy really needed to lay off the drugs.

I patted his arm. "Did you know hugs are better than drugs?"

He scratched the back of his head. "Really?"

Sebastian snickered next to me. Then he paused, his lips twisted to the side like he was deep in thought.

"What?" I asked.

He shrugged, looking a little embarrassed. "It's just weird. You seem so nice."

"Um, okay," I said.

Sebastian kicked at the grass, not meeting my gaze. "It's just my sister said you were conceited."

My eyes went wide. "Rosalind said that? I hardly know her." Had Sierra been saying things about me?

Sebastian finally looked at me, a shy smile on his face. "Well, she obviously doesn't know you very well, either."

Ms. Hernandez blew her whistle, bringing all the attention to her. "Listen up! We're dividing into five teams of four today. Because that's how many of you showed up for class." She grunted something under her breath I couldn't make out. "We'll be running four different races, and then a relay race. The team with the best accumulated time will win."

I raised my hand.

"Yes, Ms. Richards," Ms. Hernandez said, nodding her head at me.

"What do we win?" I asked. "A free day?"

When the class shouted in agreement with my idea, she narrowed her eyes at me. "Don't push your luck. You'll get bragging rights."

"Yay!" I mumbled to myself, shaking my hands out like they were pom-poms.

When she split us up, I held back all the swears when I saw it was the same group of guys that welcomed me to the class. I liked Dax and Sebastian. But Trent Dawson was the bane of my existence. Wait, that would make me Batman, not Cap. He was the Red Skull of my existence.

"Alright," Trent said, rounding us together and taking control of the group because his life revolved around P.E. "Powers, you take the one hundred meter. Lopez, you have the two hundred. Richards, the four hundred. I'm taking the eight hundred."

"I'm sorry, you're giving *me* the four hundred meter?" I asked in shock.

"Yeah," he said, looking annoyed that I would even question him.

"That's like a full lap around the track."

Trent clapped his hands together like a little kid. "Aw, hey, guys, look! Richards knows her distances."

"I'm not a runner," I said, grinding my teeth together.

Trent motioned to the other two. "Neither are they. We're obviously not going to win, but I don't want to come in last." He swept his arm toward me. "You're the one who was bragging about having more air or whatever." He sighed. "Let's just get this over with."

"Have you ever thought about giving a TED talk?" I asked him. "You're really inspirational."

He flipped me off before he walked away.

Dax came in last. He wasn't even really trying, and when Trent started yelling at him, Dax started walking.

Sebastian, bless his heart, ran as fast as his short legs could take him. Came in third in his group, but apparently that wasn't good enough for Trent. I said three out of five wasn't bad, so Trent flipped me off again.

Then it was my turn.

I wasn't a runner, this much had already been established. It meant I didn't own a sports bra. All I had on was a cheap bra I found in the clearance section at JCPenney.

Mom said she'd buy me cute bras from Victoria's Secret, but one glance at the price tag, and I hightailed it out of that store. Who would spend that much money on a bra? That would make my girls more spoiled than my feet, and my feet were the ones doing the heavy lifting. The girls were just hanging out and sometimes sweating more than Gramps when he ate spicy food.

I lined up on the track in the fourth lane. That was what I was shooting for. Fourth place. That way, I wouldn't come in last, but it would piss Trent off. Win-win.

Ms. Hernandez shot off her gun like this was the freaking Olympics, and we all took off. The abundance of air was nice. Didn't help the muscles, though. The legs still had to put forth a lot of effort. And the feet. At least my new Nikes were making my life easier.

But then, apparently my girls got mad for trash talking them and wanted to show off. Slowly, one slipped out from my bra. I wasn't enormous, but I wasn't small, either. There was a definite bounce going on. I squished my arm against my boob, trying to stop it from flopping like every soccer player out there.

It slowed me down just a little, but I could survive. I was almost halfway around the track.

But then my other boob didn't want to be outshone. Heaven forbid *that* happen. So, she came out, flapping like the skin dangling from my grandparent's arms.

Pushing my other arm into my other boob, I ran down the track, keeping my focus on the finish line and trying not to think about the fact that I was running like a freaking T-Rex on display at the museum.

Boys loved museums.

Clearance JCPenney bra, you had failed me.

When I finally crossed the finish line, I sprinted to the edge of the track, keeping my back to everyone as I stuffed my girls back where they belonged.

Trent's voice came from behind me. "What was that?"

Doing a quick adjustment of my bra, I took a deep breath before I turned around to face him. "What was what?"

"That form?" Trent looked at my arms. "Who taught you to run?"

"Sue." I pushed past him, trying to create a distance.

Pretty sure Sue was the name of the famous T-Rex every museum wanted.

Trent jogged after me. "You could have won! But you started running like an idiot and came in second place."

I turned to him, my jaw dropping. "I came in second place?"

I'd been so distracted by my spectacle that I hadn't paid any attention to my placement on the track. I just wanted to be done with the race.

"But you could have come in *first*!" Trent had his hands balled into fists.

"I came in second!" I high-fived Sebastian and Dax

before I busted out in a dance, throwing my arms in the air, "On Top of the World" by Imagine Dragons blaring in my head.

"Good job, Richards!" Ms. Hernandez called out, giving me a thumbs-up.

Grunting, Trent threw his hands into the air and stalked off.

After class, I immediately texted Mom: *We need to go bra shopping*.

She responded with a gif of a man tossing glitter into the air.

CHAPTER TWENTY-SIX

*M*om held up a pink sparkling bra, tiny sequins sewn all over. "What about this one?"

I held in a gag. "I'm not trying out for a pageant."

Veronica appeared behind Mom, holding up two bras. She wiggled the blue one. "Classy. Decent amount of coverage." Then she wriggled the pink one. "Simple, but cute."

I twisted my hand back and forth. "Maybe."

Then Taylor came around the corner holding two bras as well: a black lace and a red lace. She turned on the rasp in her tone. "Sexy or sexy?"

Mom snapped her fingers at Taylor. "Neither."

Taylor grinned. "I just wanted to see Mrs. Richards get mad." She disappeared, probably putting them back where she found them.

"Comfort." I tossed another bra into the *maybe* pile. "I want comfort. Support. Protection."

"Are you looking for a best friend or a bra?" Veronica asked.

I slumped onto the bench, resting my chin in my palms. "Maybe this was a bad idea."

Mom sat down next to me, rubbing my back. "After what happened today? We're getting you better bras. I don't care how much it costs."

A worker came up to us, her smile faltering when she saw the pile of bras all around me. "Anything I can help with?"

I glanced at her name tag, which said Effie, before looking at her. "Do you have anything in Care Bears? Or Captain America?"

Effie frowned. "Uh, no ..."

I sighed, blowing the air over my dry lips. "Then, no." I perked. "What about Cherry Coke?"

She smiled. "We do have a cherry one that's adorable."

"But is it comfortable?" I pointed to my chest. "Will it support my girls? This isn't about being sexy, Effie. It's about being practical."

"Ugh." Taylor leaned against a rack of tanks. "You sound like my dad." She picked one up, checked the price tag, and her eyes practically sprang from her sockets. She set the tank back on the rack.

"Let me see what I can find," Effie said, hurrying away.

When she came back, I was pleasantly surprised by her choices. She ushered me into a dressing room, and with each change of bra, the four of them made me come out and model them.

Taylor played "Cool" by the Jonas Brothers from her phone, giving me a soundtrack like I was on the runway or something.

I opened the door and flicked my hip to the side, motioning to the full-coverage cream bra. "I call this *The Granny*."

Taylor and Veronica busted out in a laugh.

Mom shook her head. "That's a no."

Even Effie had pursed her lips in disappointment.

"Next!" I went into the room, coming out with the cherry one Effie had talked about. It was a simple white with red cherries and white lace on the edges of the cups. "This one is pretty nice. Comfortable and soft."

Mom stood, coming over and circling me, tugging on the straps in the process. "This one's a yes."

"For sure," Taylor said, grinning.

Effie clapped her hands together like we'd just made her entire world.

When all was said and done, I had five bras in the *yes* pile to choose from. Narrowing it down would be difficult.

"Okay, Mom, choose one, and Taylor and Veronica choose one together," I said. "I'm not picking."

Mom immediately went for the cherry one.

I turned to Veronica, but she and Taylor were huddled around her phone. Whatever they were looking at had Taylor shocked and Veronica furious.

"I'm going to *kill* her," Veronica hissed.

Mom and I shared a worried glance before we rushed over to see what they were looking at.

Rosalind had posted a picture of me online. I was in P.E., huddled off to the side of the track, my hands stuffed up my shirt. Someone caught a picture of me putting my girls back in place. Certainly didn't help with the rumor of me being conceited. I looked like I was practically fondling myself.

"You've got to be kidding me," I said under my breath.

At first, I thought it might have been Sebastian who took the picture. Maybe Rosalind had asked him to spy on me. But the angle was all wrong, coming from a way different location than Sebastian had been. Plus, he didn't strike me as the type who would do something like this.

"Who's Rosalind? And why would she post this picture?" Mom asked in a tone that said she wanted to hunt her down and give her a good ol' fashioned mom scolding.

"Sierra," Veronica, Taylor, and I said at the same time, an equal amount of venom in her name.

Mom motioned to the picture. "What's the point of posting this?"

"To make me look bad," I said. "Sierra's pissed that I'm going to the Regency ball with Bentley. With his dad running for council, their family can't have any scandals." I rubbed my forehead. "This is a good scandal."

"I'm going to *kill* her," Veronica said.

"That's already been established," I said.

"We just need to figure out how to do it," Taylor whispered.

Effie cleared her throat, and we looked up to see her holding the five bras. "Which ones did you decide on?"

"All of them," we all said in unison.

Now, to figure out how to get even.

CHAPTER TWENTY-SEVEN

*T*he picture didn't have quite the effect that Sierra was hoping for. Yeah, I received some crude jokes from some guys at school, but one glare from Veronica or Taylor cut them off. Apparently, my glare wasn't fierce enough. Taylor had even said it was adorable.

I wore my Grumpy Care Bear shirt—the one with clouds and rain—with a baggy sweater over it, trying to minimize myself. For me, it was too hot for the sweater, but I wasn't about to take it off.

Before I walked into English, I pulled Sierra off to the side. "You're taking this stalking way too far."

She pulled back in fake surprise. "I don't know what you're talking about."

"Do you have someone following me everywhere I go? Or is it you?" I backed away from her. "Either way, it's really creepy, Sierra."

Her nostrils flared. "You're just upset you were caught with your hands up your shirt." Her anger faded into laughter. "What were you doing, anyway?"

"We need to set some boundaries here," I said.

She stepped up close to me. "There are no boundaries, Daphne. This is war, and anything goes in war."

I tilted my head to the side. "That's not really true. Even the military has lines they won't cross."

She rolled her eyes. "You know what I mean."

"Well, since you're not going to stop stalking me," I said, pulling out my phone, and messaging her a playlist labeled *Stalker*, "I created a playlist for you for your stalker stake-outs. Some classics on there. 'Every Breath You Take' by the Police. 'One Way or Another' by Blondie."

Sierra's jaw dropped as she stared at her phone. "You created me a playlist?"

I shrugged. "Thought you could use some inspiration."

"Everything okay?" Bentley's voice made me whip around. There was a struggle in his eyes, trying to stay looking at my eyes instead of my chest. That summed up my entire day.

I folded my arms over my chest, closing off the option. "Everything's fine."

He arched his eyebrows. "You two seem to fight a lot, which is weird because you have a lot in common."

"No, we don't!" we both yelled at the same time, causing Bentley to cringe.

He held up his palms in defense. "Sorry."

It was getting to the point where he wouldn't want to go with either of us to prom. I needed to change tactics.

I pressed my hand to my forehead. "I'm sorry. I'm just so upset about the photo." I patted Sierra's shoulder, and it tensed under my touch. "I took it out on Sierra, even though she said she's going to get Rosalind to take it down."

Sierra's wide eyes turned to me, her jaw tightening.

"That's so nice of you, Sierra," Bentley said.

"So nice," I said, smiling at her.

She lowered her shoulder, moving away from me. "I don't see what the big deal is, but if it upsets her *that* much, well, I'm willing to help out."

What a good Samaritan. Someone needed to get this girl a medal.

"Hey, guys," Weston said, walking up to us. His eyes fought to stay on mine, and I groaned.

I put my arm around Sierra's shoulder and whispered in her ear. "You better watch your back, Sierra." With a smile, I walked into the classroom.

All throughout class, I thought about ways I could get back at her. I could catch Sierra in an awkward pose like she did me, but I wasn't about to stoop to her level. There were other ways of getting even without resorting to low blows.

I mean, if I was going to get revenge, I was going to do it with class.

Sierra's major thing was appearance. She wanted to make sure she looked perfect in public, someone Bentley's parents would want by his side. Which was why she'd shed all the blacks and switched over to the pastels like she was a freaking Kennedy.

"Ms. Winters," Mr. Buckley said, interrupting my thoughts. "You have an announcement to share with the class?"

Sierra bounded to her feet, practically skipping to the front the room. Overkill on the pep, if you asked me.

I twirled my pen in my hand, watching her through a forced smile. I had to play nice. Or, at least look that way.

"As you know, the girls' basketball team is playing our rival tonight," Sierra said, smiling at the class. "We're trying to set record sales, so we want everyone there!"

No, thank you.

I even wrote that on the piece of paper in front of me.

"Afterward, we're having a fundraiser." She made jazz hands toward Bentley, making me squirm. "Bentley's dad, Whitaker Anderson, will be there representing the city council. So, make sure to bring your whole family! There will be photo opportunities!"

That made me pause my drawing of a T-Rex smashing a basketball with its tiny hands.

Photos. Sierra was the junior class president. She'd be taking a photo with Whitaker Anderson. Meeting him and charming him.

"Are you going to the game?" Weston whispered next to me.

I turned to him. "I wasn't planning on it, but maybe I will."

I needed to mess with Sierra's appearance someway. Nothing scandalous that would hurt her or her family in any way.

"Do you want to go together?" Weston asked.

The plan was forming in my head. As much as I wanted to hold it in, a huge smile spread across my face. It would all be perfect.

"That would be great," I said to Weston.

He smiled back, his nose inching up higher than usual. I loved when he did that.

"See you all tonight!" Sierra said.

I watched her walk down the aisle, knowing that smile of hers would be wiped off tonight. I was coming for her.

And she had no idea.

*I*t was amazing how social media spread so quickly. The day had been okay until I went to P.E. All the freshman boys were openly staring at my chest like I might put my hands up there again.

Stupid boys.

"I had nothing to do with it," Sebastian said, his hands held up in defense. "I swear."

I smiled at him. "I figured you didn't. You aren't the vindictive type."

He let out a loud breath of relief, confirming to me that he wasn't involved. He backed away when someone called his name.

"I can take it down for you," Dax said, suddenly appearing at my side, a small section of a sub in his hand.

I jumped a little where I stood. The guy always appeared out of nowhere, like a freaking ninja. "What?"

"The photo." Dax popped the remaining sub sandwich in his mouth and brushed his hands together before pulling me off to the side. "I can take it down from the web."

"Really?" I asked.

Sierra had already said she'd get Rosalind to take it down, but I really didn't believe her. A back-up plan might be smart.

"It's easy," Dax said. "Say the word, and I'll do it."

"That would be freaking awesome, Dax," I said with a huge grin. "Is it possible to delete the picture from her phone, too?

"Yep. What's the girl's name who posted it?"

"Rosalind." I racked my brain, trying to remember Rosalind and Sebastian's last name. "Lopez? I think."

Rosalind and Sierra would be horrified if they knew I hadn't memorized Rosalind's entire back story by now, since, you know, I was supposed to have magically known who she was when we first met. Not to mention, Trent only referred to anyone in P.E. by their last name.

Dax pulled his phone out of his pocket. "She's a cheerleader, right?"

"I think so," I said.

"Cool." He smiled at me. "I'll get it taken care of tonight."

"Do I owe you anything?" I felt like I should at least pay the guy for his services or something.

Dax shook his head. "Nah. It's all good. I love doing this kind of stuff." His eyebrows arched. "You surprised me, Daphne. I seriously thought you'd be the most boring, plain person ever when we first met."

"Uh, thanks?" The guy needed to work on his compliments. "If you see any other embarrassing photos on the phone, feel free to delete them."

"Will do."

Huh. Maybe having to take P.E. with a bunch of freshmen was turning out to be a blessing, not a curse. Well, if Dax actually came through. There was a good chance of him getting high and forgetting to do it.

CHAPTER TWENTY-EIGHT

*V*eronica was lying on her stomach on my bed, her legs kicked up behind her. "Rare" by Selena Gomez played from her phone. "Okay, lay this out for me again."

I was standing in the middle of my room, giving me ample room to move about as I talked. Taylor was plopped in the hammock chair hanging from the ceiling, her feet dangling.

"Okay," I said, pacing the area. "During the basketball game, Taylor will sneak into the girl's locker room, find Sierra's body wash, and dump this in it." I held up a bottle of blue food coloring. "Veronica, you'll stand guard, making sure no one goes in the locker room while she's in there."

Veronica played with the fray on the pillow she was holding in her arms. "Why are we doing all the work?"

I paused my pacing and faced her. "Because *I* can't be spotted doing it. If Bentley finds out, he'll hate me."

Taylor tucked her legs underneath her in the swing. "I don't care if he hates me."

Veronica pushed her finger into her chest. "Maybe *I* do."

I put my hand on my hip. "You care what Bentley Anderson thinks about you?"

She rolled her eyes. "I care about my reputation."

Taylor shrugged. "Don't stand guard. I'll do it with Zander. If anyone catches us, we'll start making out. Problem solved."

"You think Zander would be on board with that?" I asked.

Taylor grinned slyly. "The making out? Yes." When I tossed the bottle of dye at her face, she caught it and laughed. "He won't care. It's not permanent damage. It's a simple prank. He loves those."

Veronica looked at her. "Isn't his family big into April Fool's?"

"Yep," she said. "It's practically a religion in their home."

Veronica turned to me. "And you'll be ..."

"With Weston," I said. "In the stands. Out in public." I pointed at her. "You and DeShawn can sit with us. We can take a selfie of our group and post it online. Everyone will see we were in the middle of the stands, unable to get to the locker room."

Taylor and Veronica shared a look before Veronica spoke. "So, is this like a date with Weston?"

I pulled back in surprise, my cheeks flaring. "What? No!"

"How did he ask you?" Taylor asked.

"He asked if I wanted to go to the game with him," I mumbled, replaying it in my mind. That was how he worded it, right?

"Go to the game," Veronica said slowly. "*With* him."

Dizziness danced across my eyes, so I stepped back, leaning against the dresser, putting my palms on top to brace myself. "That doesn't necessarily mean anything."

Taylor circled a finger around her face. "What did he look like when you said yes?"

Closing my eyes, I pictured the moment. He crookedly smiled, his nose going up in that adorable way. Oh, crap. I popped my eyes open. "What do I do?"

"You go with Weston," Taylor said. "Act cool. No flirting. Just friends."

I rolled my neck. "Act cool. I can totally do that."

Veronica placed her hands over her face. "You're so screwed."

I shimmied, moving back and forth. "I'm covered in cool. It's my special sauce."

Taylor busted out laughing, clapping her hands together.

Veronica hopped up from the bed and placed her hands on my arms. "Daphne, I love you dearly, but if you break Weston's heart, I will kill you myself. That boy is way too nice to be played with."

"I'm not playing with him!" I put my hands on my cheeks, tugging at my skin. "I didn't realize he was asking me out on a date." I lowered my hands. "Maybe I should cancel. Say I'm sick. Stay home. Take all sorts of selfies of me all being sick all night long, so everyone thinks I'm here."

"And miss the Sierra Smurf reveal?" Taylor clucked her tongue. "You can't miss that."

"You know, it's not too late to call off this whole bet with Sierra," Veronica said softly.

"And give her the satisfaction of winning?" I scoffed. "I think not. Not after what her mom did to mine. The Richards women don't back down."

Taylor hopped off the swing and came over to us, wriggling the bottle of food coloring. "Either way, you still need to get her back for the picture she posted of you. I'm going through with my end. You two can do whatever you want." She checked her phone. "Zander's here. I'll see you ladies later." She blew air kisses before she left the room.

I took a seat on the bed. "I don't know how to explain it, but Sierra just gets under my skin. She's all about being fake. Trying to be someone else so people will like her."

Veronica sat down next to me. "She wasn't like that before you moved here. It was like this switch flipped."

"Her mom," I said.

She bumped my arm. "Just like yours."

"I've never backed out on a bet. Ever. Dad always taught me to see things through to the end."

She took my hand. "So, this is about your dad."

"It's about not being bullied around by anyone." My voice came out in a whisper.

"Were you bullied at your old school?" she asked.

It was something I'd never told her about. I thought if I ignored it and pretended to be happy, then all would be well. But it wasn't.

I pushed up from the bed, wiping away some tears that formed at the corner of my eyes. "No. It's nothing. I should get ready."

Veronica opened her mouth to say something, but her phone rang. She frowned at the screen before she declined the call.

"Who was that?" I asked.

"My dad," she said. "He's been trying to weasel himself back into our lives. Mom and Javy might be buying the changes he's claiming he made, but I'm not."

I sorted through the shirts in my closet. "Wait, is he like trying to come back home or something?"

I glanced over my shoulder to see her nodding, twirling her phone between her fingers. "Yep. Mom keeps telling him no, but I can see her resolve slipping."

I pulled out my favorite Captain America shirt and switched into it. "Would it be so bad to have your dad back? I would kill for that."

"Your dad didn't intentionally walk out on your family." She stood, coming over to my jewelry box and sorting through it. "What if he does it again? Do you know how hard it was to pick all the broken pieces of my mom's heart off the floor and try to meld them back together?"

I remembered her calling multiple times a day during those times. It hadn't been easy for anyone in their family. At the time, I'd wanted so desperately to do something to help, but I soon realized the only thing I could really do was be there for her. She just needed a friend, someone to talk to during the trial.

I leaned against my dresser. "Picture your perfect life at home."

She snorted. "Well, for one, Javy wouldn't be so messy. Mom would be home more often. Luciana wouldn't whine so freaking much."

I smiled at her. "But would your dad be there?"

She fiddled with a pair of cherry earrings in my jewelry box. "I mean, I guess. But the old him."

"Did he ever say why he left?"

Frowning, she held out the earrings for me to take. "Wear those. And, no, but I haven't really talked to him."

I took the earrings and put them in. "Maybe start by just hearing him out. Maybe he just had a mid-life crisis or something. Maybe he realized what an idiot he was."

She wiped a tear that was sliding down her cheek. "I think I'm just afraid that if we let him back into our lives, he'll do this to us again."

Putting my arm around her, I leaned my head against hers. "Yeah, he might, but he might not. I'm a firm believer in second chances. I mean, we all do stupid things."

Her arms wrapped around my middle, squeezing me tight. "Fine. I'll talk to him. But I'm only giving him five minutes."

I patted the top of her head. "Ah, look at you. Growing up. I'm so proud."

With a laugh, she shoved me away. She backed toward the door, her eyes softening. "Thank you."

"Always."

I mean, I had no idea if her dad coming back home was a good thing or not. If he had a pattern of this behavior, I'd be saying no in a heartbeat. But the whole him up and leaving was so out of character from him. So opposite of the man I knew growing up.

I did know that if he hurt my best friend again, there would be no forgiving him. I said a quick prayer that Mr. Rodriguez wouldn't let me, or his family, down.

CHAPTER TWENTY-NINE

*W*eston picked me up in his mom's minivan. He wore a blue, black, and white checkered button-down shirt, the cuffs rolled up to just below his elbows. He had the shirt unbuttoned, his Captain America shirt peeking through.

He handed me a bundle of wildflowers when I opened the door. "These are for you."

I took them from his hand, smiling. "They're beautiful."

"They're from my mom's garden." He sputtered it out so fast, it took me a while to piece together what he said. "It's not like professional or anything, I know."

My smile grew. "They're perfect. I'm going to go set them inside."

As soon as I turned my back on him, my smile faltered. He'd brought me flowers. For our "date." What was I doing? I couldn't string this guy along.

But he was *really* cute. And so sweet.

Ugh.

"What are those?" Mom asked, rounding the corner and spotting the flowers in my hand.

"They're from Weston," I whispered.

With wide eyes, she hurried toward me. "What about Bentley?"

"I didn't know this would be a date!" I clamped my hand over my mouth, hoping Weston hadn't heard.

She placed her hands on my shoulders. "Just breathe, Daphne. You've already said yes for tonight, right?"

I nodded, my hand still over my mouth.

"You're going to go to the game with Weston, you're going to be kind, and have fun. Just rein in the flirting."

I lowered my hand. "I'm not that big of a flirt."

She scrunched her face. "You can be when you're not paying attention. Sometimes your excitement comes off as flirting."

"So, don't get excited. Got it."

"Keep your hands to yourself."

I pressed a hand to my chest. "Mom! Yeesh."

She rolled her eyes. "Get out of here." She took the flowers from my hand. "Kind. Friendly. Got it?"

Nodding, I quickly hugged her and then ran out to a still waiting Weston. By the shy smile on his face, he hadn't heard my outburst, so that was good.

But then he opened the door for me, totally respectful-like, and he was making this super difficult.

I just needed to stay calm. Be chill.

"How's Ivy?" I asked as we left my driveway.

"Great." He pointed behind him to the floor behind the chair. "Don't let me forget. She got you a huge bag of Watermelon Sour Patch Kids. I think you're her new super-hero. She keeps asking when you're coming over again." He stole a glance at me, probably watching my reaction.

I couldn't help but smile. "Well, my schedule is pretty full, but I could probably pencil her in sometime soon."

Like, maybe a couple of months from now when the bet with Sierra was over.

He grinned. "Am I included in this scenario? Or just Ivy?"

I made a little box with my hands, even though he was watching the road. "I don't know. I mean, the square they put on calendars is so freaking small. 'Hang with Ivy' will easily fit on there. But 'hang with Ivy *and* Weston?' That's a bit much."

"Just do a w and a slash to shorten with, then an ampersand. That will save some room."

I snapped my fingers. "Oh! I could just draw a Captain America shield with ivy wrapped around it."

He scrunched his nose. "Now I'm thinking about Poison Ivy ensnaring Cap, and that really sucks."

"They aren't even in the same comic universe."

"They could do a crossover."

"If they do that, then Captain America and Wonder Woman need to get together. They go together so perfectly."

Except, Veronica liked Wonder Woman, and the thought of her and Weston dating made me a little queasy.

"Well," Weston said, "as long as you let me hang out with you and Ivy, then I'm fine with whatever."

The queasiness faded, replaced by giddiness.

"Dance Monkey" by Tones and I came on the radio. Weston and I reached for the sound dial at the same time, laughing as we cranked the volume.

"I love this song!" I yelled.

"Me, too!" he yelled back.

We sang out loud—probably off-key—with me dancing like a wild woman. I caught a few people in other cars staring at us, which made me sing to them, making them smile and laugh.

When we pulled into the school and found a parking spot, I hopped out, going around to the front of the van, and playing "Dance Monkey" from my phone, dancing right there in the parking lot.

Weston joined me, and we continued to sing along, our dancing probably as good as our singing, but neither of us cared. I believed this was what true happiness felt like.

"Daphne!" Bentley's voice came from behind me.

I spun around to see him standing there with his mom, dad, and little sister, all looking super polished, like they were fresh off the cover of a magazine.

I quickly stopped the music on my phone and stuffed it in my back pocket. "Hey, Bentley."

Bentley was grinning ear to ear. "Don't stop the dance party because of us."

"I love that song," his sister said, smiling at me. "I love her voice!"

"It's awesome," Weston said, coming to my side.

Bentley motioned between his parents and us. "Mom, Dad, this is Daphne and Weston."

We shook their hands, and I did my best to make eye contact and keep my grip firm, wanting to make a good impression.

His sister cleared her throat. "I exist, too, Bentley."

With a laugh, he wrapped his arm around her shoulders. "This is Adriana."

"Who has excellent taste in music," I said.

She grinned at me.

Mrs. Anderson looked at me. "You were at Zumba, right?" She flicked a finger between Bentley and me. "He's going to the Regency ball with you?"

I tried to keep my smile from faltering, but I didn't do a very good job. I couldn't look at Weston. Didn't want to. His reaction might break me in two.

"That would be me," I said, taking some of my hair and twirling it around my finger, twisting it wildly. I couldn't freak out. Not here.

Shut out the noise, Daphne, I thought.

Mr. Anderson grinned. "Well, at least we know you can dance. Sounds like it's going to be a fun night."

"Speaking of which," Bentley said. "Do we need to practice any dances or anything? I thought we'd just be hanging out, but Adriana is convinced there will be dancing."

She put her hands on her hips. "There's always dancing at balls."

Now I really couldn't look at Weston. I'd practiced the dances with *him*. And we'd done a pretty decent job as a pair.

I was surprised my foot wasn't in pain, because I'd pretty much just shot it repeatedly.

"There's quite a few, actually," Weston said, his voice a little tight.

Bentley put his hands on his head. "Okay, we're definitely going to have to practice. I don't want to screw up."

Adriana clasped her hands together. "Can I be there with you? I'll help set everything up!" She twirled around in her dress. "I do love a good dance."

"Sure," I said, smiling at her. "I'll send Bentley the list of videos."

"This is going to be splendid!" Adriana said.

Mr. Anderson winked at his daughter. "You'll be a terrific host." He nodded at Weston and me. "It was a pleasure to meet you. Enjoy the game."

I awkwardly waved as they walked off, leaving me alone with Weston.

It was like they had sucked the fun right out of our night.

Weston turned to go inside, not looking at me.

I panicked. I couldn't break his heart. Veronica said that.

Like a spaz, I ran in front of him, putting my hands on his chest and stopping him. "My mom and I go to the same Zumba class as him and his mom. Which we didn't know when we picked that one. Cody was there. He brought up the Regency ball and basically invited Bentley to go with us, and Bentley, being the nice guy he is, said yes." I lowered my hands when I realized they were still on his chest.

Why had I said all that?

"So, it just kind of happened. Doesn't really mean anything."

Shut up, Daphne, I thought.

The tension in Weston's shoulders released. "You'll have to take video. I can't picture Bentley doing a Regency dance."

The anxiety in me started to flutter away. "I know. It's going to be epic."

CHAPTER THIRTY

$\mathcal{W}$e found Veronica and DeShawn in the bleachers. They were saving us seats, right in the dead center, as she promised.

I mumbled apologies as I maneuvered through the crowd of people. I reached behind me, taking Weston's hand and guiding him through the maze until we finally got to our seats.

"Good call on the middle seats," Veronica whispered, not hiding back the sarcasm.

I waved my hand. "All those people like being trampled on. Totally fine."

We were squished together, the place packed.

"Why can't we get this kind of turnout at the football games?" DeShawn asked, glancing around. His black hair was cropped close to his head, some slashes carved into the sides, creating a cool design. He had his ears pierced, the large diamonds looking like they were worth more than anything I owned.

"Maybe if you won, they'd come." I slapped my hands

over my mouth, not for the first time that night. I needed a muzzle.

Weston choked on a laugh next to me.

Veronica hit my arm.

"Sorry!" I looked apologetically at DeShawn. "That just came out."

DeShawn surprised me by laughing, his golden-brown eyes lighting up. "You're not wrong."

Both Veronica and I let out breaths of relief. I'd hate to screw anything up between the two of them, even though it was still weird to me that they were together.

I leaned into Veronica. "We need to have a system. If you sense I'm about to say something wrong, pinch me."

"I'd be happy to." She pinched my arm hard. "Like that?"

"Ow!" I rubbed my arm. "Yeah, like that." Then I remembered we needed a photo together. Pulling my phone out of my pocket, I opened the picture mode and handed my phone to Weston. "Selfie time!"

The four of us squished together, all holding up our fingers in "number ones."

The lights in the gym went out, and everyone stomped their feet against the bleachers as the shouts rose.

Right as "Seven Nation Army" by The White Stripes began to play, lights flashed around the gym, creating a strobe effect.

I turned to Weston right as he turned to me. "I love this song!" We said it at the exact same time before we got to our feet, jumping around with everyone else.

The girls' basketball team ran out on the court like this was the WNBA finals or something. Maybe overkill for a regular series high school basketball game, but whatever. It was fun, and everyone loved it.

When the crowd finally calmed enough to sit down, I realized I was holding Weston's hand. When had that happened? Did I grab his hand? Or did he grab mine? And why did it feel so nice?

This was so not good.

Letting his hand go, I reached up and tucked my hair behind my ear, trying to act casual. I had a bet to see through. I'd barely moved back. Honestly, I still didn't know Weston all that well. My hormones needed to chill the crap down.

Too bad every time we scored, Weston and I would high five or hug. Then we started hip bumping, because who didn't love a good hip bump?

At halftime, we were only down by two.

Weston stood, stretching his legs. The bottom of his joggers had ridden up from sitting down, so I reached forward and tugged them back into place.

"Don't like the new look?" Weston asked.

"Hey, if you were going for uber-nerd, you nailed it," I said.

He pumped his fist. "Mission accomplished." He bent down so he was eye level with me. "I'm going to brave the crowd and get a Coke. You want one?"

I pressed a hand against my dry throat. "Yes, please."

"I'll go with you," DeShawn said, hopping up. His muscles twitched under his tight shirt, and Veronica hadn't been kidding about the guy beefing up. I think he'd grown like half a foot as well. He bent down, giving Veronica a light kiss on the lips before he and Weston descended.

"That was completely adorable," I said, batting my eyelashes at Veronica.

Laughing, she shoved my arm. "He's really sweet." She

turned to me, lifting her chin in her way that said she was about to drop a truth bomb. "What. Was. That?"

"It's called a kiss, Veronica. You see, when a boy and a girl—"

"I'm not talking about me. I'm talking about you. Pretty sure you told me your mom specifically said, 'no flirting.'"

I pulled back in surprise. "I never flirted."

"Oh, really?" She cocked her head to the side. "So, the hand-holding, hugging, hip bumping, any excuse to touch the guy, and then smoothing out his pants like you're some long-term couple meant absolutely nothing?"

My cheeks flared. "I was trying to be helpful."

"Helpful is saying, 'Hey, Weston, your pants have ridden up.' But you took matters into your own hands."

I clenched my fists like I could undo it all. So, this was what Mom meant about keeping my hands to myself.

"I told you I like the guy," Veronica said. "If you keep stringing him along, I'm going to give you a good smack-down, and I'm not even kidding." She punched my arm, not being the slightest bit gentle. "There's a preview."

Frowning, I rubbed my arm. "I'm sorry. It just feels natural to act that way around him. He's been a good friend."

Her eyebrows shot up. "Friend?" She turned around, tapping the lady behind us on the arm.

"Yes?" the lady asked with a smile.

Veronica pointed at me. "How long would you say she and the boy that was sitting next to her have been together? Like a guess from what you've seen."

The lady blew air out over her lips, making a raspberry sound. "Oh, I don't know. Six months? A year? The point to where both their parents won't let them be alone for even a second."

My jaw dropped. "What?"

"You two are adorable together," the lady said. "I'm glad my son hasn't found someone to look at like that. I'm not ready to deal with all that crap."

I opened my mouth, ready to chew her out, when Veronica threw her arms around me and held me back, turning me away from the lady.

"Easy, Daph," she whispered.

"She has no idea what she's talking about," I said with a huff.

"I'm going to release you now. You won't do anything stupid, will you?"

I tried to look away, but she put her finger on my chin and turned me toward her. I sighed. "No."

Veronica slowly lowered her arms. "If you don't like Weston like that—which we both know you do—no more touching, young lady."

"Easy peasy," I said.

My phone vibrated, an incoming message from an unknown phone number.

It's done. Pic taken down and deleted. Plus, a couple others, like one of you dancing in a onesie in your bedroom, and one with your pants ripped. You wear Care Bear underwear?

Dax had pulled through. And somehow found my number, which I guess wasn't too surprising given his extracurricular activities.

But, seriously? Was Rosalind freaking stalking me? That was beyond creepy. And she had the photo from the bookstore. Well, not anymore thanks to Dax.

Me: *It's a long story, but, no, I don't usually wear Care Bear underwear. Thank you, by the way.*

Dax: *You should get a restraining order, man. She seems*

*to be obsessed with spying on people. She even has a picture
of two pirates kissing in a car. Girl has issues.*

I froze. Two pirates? She couldn't have been spying on
my mom, could she? I might need to get Dax to delete more
pictures from Rosalind's phone. I mean, what else did she
have?

DeShawn and Weston came back, both holding drinks
and snacks. Weston had a box of Sour Patch Kids and a box
of peanut M&Ms squished between his two hands, which
were holding our sodas.

"Can you grab those?" Weston asked.

"Sure!" I reached up, attacking the situation like a
puzzle. I couldn't touch the guy. His fingers were touching
both boxes on the side. So, I needed to come from the top. I
pinched my fingers over the top of the two boxes and slowly
wriggled them loose, ignoring Weston's stare.

He sat down next to me, our legs touching. Wasn't
much I could do about that. The whole row was squished
together. I was up against Veronica, too. Besides, I wasn't
touching him. He was touching me.

He held out my Coke. I came in from the top again,
making sure our fingers didn't brush. It was a little more
difficult than I thought it would be, but I made it work. I
took a sip and smacked my lips together. It was missing
something.

Reaching into my bag, I fished around for my bottle of
cherry syrup and pulled it out. I squeezed some into my
soda, then stirred it around with my straw.

"That's brilliant," Weston said with a smile.

I held the bottle out to him. "Want some?"

"Yeah." He went to take the bottle, but it was small, so
no way our fingers couldn't touch.

I motioned to his lid. "Take it off. I'll pour some in."

He did as told, telling me when to stop.

"You're being ridiculous," Veronica whispered into my ear.

"Oh, am I?" I narrowed my eyes at her. "You told me, 'no touching.' So, that's what I'm doing."

She answered by rolling her eyes.

Keeping track of all my movements for the rest of the game was draining, and so stupid. I mean, touching someone didn't mean anything. I touched Veronica and Taylor all the time. Didn't mean I was hitting on them. I was just comfortable with them because they were my friends.

I considered Weston a friend. We'd gotten to that point, right?

Thinking about it gave me a headache, so I changed my focus.

I hated to admit it, but Sierra was pretty good at playing basketball. She, like, made a bunch of baskets and had a bunch of rebounds and stuff like that. I was mildly impressed.

For those couple of hours, I forgot she was my enemy. We cheered her on, and the whole team.

Then I remembered what she did to me. That picture she'd snapped and uploaded, trying to make a fool out of me. Then I thought about everything her mom had done to mine. How she had tried to break my parents up, which, if she had succeeded, would mean I wouldn't exist. The thought made me shiver.

And then, when I thought, maybe, just maybe, my resolve was softening, Sierra made the game-winning shot. Pretty cool for her, yeah. But out of everyone in the crowd, her parents, friends, coach, fellow teammates, there was only one person she sought out in the crowd. One person to smile at, wink at, and even blow a kiss to, like she was kissing them goodbye.

Me.

Oh, it was on.

CHAPTER THIRTY-ONE

aylor had sent a group text to Veronica and me with a blue heart emoji and, "Wish I was with you ladies! Have fun!"

She'd put the food coloring in the body wash. The blue heart was the signal.

After the game, the student council went to work, setting up the gym for the fundraiser. Everyone who was staying milled about, talking outside of the gym.

"Man, that Sierra Winters can shoot," DeShawn said, his arm wrapped around Veronica's shoulder.

She reached up, linking their fingers together. Her hand looked so small in his. "I didn't know she was that good."

"She has a scholarship to UCLA," Weston said, sounding surprised that none of us knew that information.

"Really?" I thought back to all my encounters with her, but it wasn't like we did much talking about our lives. It mostly consisted of salty glares, insults, and smirks. Maybe we needed to broaden our communication.

Weston's fingers brushed against mine, so I quickly

folded my arms, pulling them close to my chest. He wanted to hold my hand. I wanted him to hold my hand.

It couldn't happen.

I just needed to get through prom, go with Bentley, then my path would be open to pursue anyone I wanted.

Too bad prom was still months away.

We should have done Sadie's. It was at the end of the month. We could both ask Bentley on the same day, then see who he picks. Maybe I could pitch the idea to Sierra. She probably wanted this to end as much as I did.

A high-pitched scream came from the girl's locker room.

Veronica and I shared a smile, knowing it could only mean one thing. Sierra had used her body wash.

A few women took off toward the locker room, probably to see what was going on.

"Wonder what that was all about?" DeShawn asked.

I snorted. "Someone probably saw a spider."

Weston chuckled. "Probably." He leaned toward me, glancing at my folded arms. "Are you cold? I have a sweater in the car."

I wasn't cold. Maybe cold-hearted. I needed to talk to Veronica. This was all getting out of hand, and it had barely even started.

"Do you mind?" I asked.

He smiled. "I'll go get it."

I snatched Veronica's hand and yanked her away from DeShawn. "I have to go to the bathroom."

As I tugged her toward the bathroom, DeShawn muttered, "Girls are so weird."

"If you have to pee so badly," Veronica said, yanking her hand from mine. "Then go!"

When we got into the bathroom, I rounded on her. "I have a problem."

"*A* problem? Girl, you have a *lot* of problems."

"I like Weston."

"Yeah, I know."

I paced the bathroom, ignoring all the people staring at me. "But I have a family legacy to uphold."

Veronica tilted her head to the side. "I wouldn't go *that* far."

"I just don't want her to win! I'll let my mom down. I'll let my dad down."

Veronica came up to me, putting her hands on my arms and stopping me in my tracks. "You won't be letting anyone down. It was a stupid bet. Just call it off."

"Call it off?"

She nodded. "Call it off. I think even if you talked to your mom, she'd agree."

My heart began to pound away at my ribcage. I hated bullies. Had I become one by what I had done to Sierra? It was just a prank, right? It was just a stupid bet. Not even that big of a deal. Then why did I feel so horrible?

I hated my mind, the way it turned on me, took me to a dark place. A lonely place. I was such an idiot to agree with the bet in the first place. I mean, honestly, Bentley would have never chosen me over Sierra, anyway. I wasn't Bentley Anderson material. I wasn't even Weston Ashworth material.

I was loser material. Weird and quirky. A freak. Those girls at my old school? They were right. I didn't know how to be normal. My brain didn't think in a regular way. I was a hotwired mess, my mind as spastic as my dance moves.

Every gasp for air hurt. I kept reaching for another, like if I piled them up inside, the air would push out all the crazy. It would settle everything down, putting it in its place.

Why was everything spinning? I closed my eyes, wishing it all away. My lips were dry, each breath painful over my skin. Realizing I was on the floor, I closed in on myself, tucking my body into a ball, rocking forward and back, and humming.

Breathe. I needed to even my breathing. Slow it down. In and hold. My scratchy, dry throat craved water. Something cold. Cherry Coke. Those carbonation bubbles sounded nice right about now.

What had I done with the Coke Weston got me? Had I finished it? No, I hadn't. I left in on the stands like a heathen. I hated those people. I mean, honestly, how hard was it to take it with you and throw it away?

I pushed my palms against my eyes, wanting my thoughts to just chill. None of that mattered right now. Breathing calmly, that was what mattered.

How did I do that?

In. Hold. Out. Repeat.

Right?

Shut out the noise.

Happy things. All the happy things. Care Bears and Captain America, saving the world. I pictured them fighting together, the thought making me smile. They'd get along pretty great. I could see Captain America throwing his shield, a Care Bear using a rainbow to change the trajectory, the enemy bursting apart, glitter and sparkles flying everywhere.

I wondered if the Care Bears people would want to do a mash-up with Marvel? I'd watch it. There would be death, but there would be cheer.

My breathing slowed, getting into a better rhythm.

"Daphne?" Veronica's sweet voice broke in, the warmth of her hand seeping through my arm.

I fell into her, her arms wrapping around me and pulling me close. She rocked me in her arms until I finally calmed. She moved her arm, typing something on her phone, but I was too focused on her beating heart to care.

A moment later, DeShawn's booming voice echoed around the bathroom walls. "Ladies, I'm coming in! I'm not a pervert! I'm here for medical reasons only!"

"There's no one else in here," Veronica said through her laugh.

DeShawn came around the corner, lowering his big arms. "Oh, cool." He looked around. "This is where you guys always come to hang out?" His thick lips pulled down into a frown. "I was expecting something nicer. Like couches and snacks and stuff."

"Why would that be in here?" Veronica asked.

He shrugged. "Girls are always coming in here together. I figured there was a good reason why."

My eyes swept past him to see a concerned Weston, holding his jacket in his arms. He was staring at me, hesitant, like he was waiting for my approval or something.

When I nodded at him, he hurried over to me, dropping to his knees. Wrapping his jacket around me, he took me from Veronica's arms and held me close.

He didn't say anything, just held me until I was ready to leave.

CHAPTER THIRTY-TWO

*M*om was waiting on the front porch when we pulled up. Weston jogged around and opened the door for me, helping my shaky self out of the van.

Wrapping his arm around my shoulder, he steered me toward the front of the house. I leaned into him, grateful for the support.

"You're going to want to stop hanging out with me, aren't you?" I said.

"Why would you think that?" he asked.

"Oh, I don't know, every time we do, I have a panic attack and need to be taken home?"

He rubbed my arm. "I don't mind. The time spent with you makes it all worth it."

How I adored this boy. Which was why I needed to call off the bet.

When we got to the porch steps, Mom took me from Weston, wrapping her warm arms around me.

"Thank you, Weston," she said.

"No problem." He smiled at me. "I'll come by tomorrow

and see how you're doing." He pointed at me. "And get my jacket."

That was the second time I'd stolen his jacket from him. Maybe I just needed to keep it.

I mouthed, *thank you*, to him before I went inside.

Mom took me to the couch and sat down with me, pulling me into her arms. "Spill."

So, I did. I told her everything. All about the food coloring, how I really liked Weston and needed to call off the bet.

Mom kissed the top of my head. "You can call off the bet after you apologize to Sierra."

I pulled away, looking at her. "You're okay with it?"

She tucked some stray hairs behind my ear. "Of course, I am. I got too caught up in an old rivalry. You have nothing to do with it." She patted my hand. "And given how you ended up with a panic attack, that's a sure sign that the whole thing was wrong. I'll find a doctor down here you can see. Maybe they could offer some fresh insight."

Someone pounded on the door, causing both Mom and me to jump to our feet.

"Daphne!" Sierra's voice boomed from the other side of the door. "Open up! I know you're in there."

Grimacing, Mom patted my back. "Good luck."

Blowing out a loud breath, I shook out the nerves and went to the door, creaking it open just a bit. I didn't want her to storm the place.

"How. Could. You?" Sierra seethed.

Instead of turning all blue, like I'd intended, she had splotches of blue all over her face and arms, like she had some sort of disease.

I opened the door a little more. "What happened to you?"

"Don't you dare pretend that you weren't a part of this!"

Holding in my laugh was difficult. She looked ridiculous. I had to remind myself that she was blue because of me.

Stepping out on the porch, I shut the door behind me, leaving me alone with her. Probably not my best idea, but we were outside. The doorbell camera could see us, so it wasn't like she could murder me or anything. At least, not get away with it. Man, the whole thing would make for a great Dateline episode.

"Do you know how important tonight was for me?" she asked.

I gave her two thumbs-up. "Congrats on the game, by the way. That last-minute shot was *awesome*." I sang the last word.

"I'm being serious, Daphne." Tears welled in her eyes, and my stomach sank. "I've been waiting for this night forever, and not just because of how much it meant to my basketball career, but it was a chance to get in good with Bentley's family, not to mention my dad was there." Her eyes went wide like she'd said too much.

"Does your dad not get to your games very often?" I asked.

"That's none of your business!" She stepped in close to me, causing me to back into the door. "I will get even. I promise."

I held up my hand, trying to push her away, but she stayed in place. "Listen, about the bet."

"You're going to *lose*."

"Yes, I am."

She opened her mouth, then snapped it shut, confusion crossing over her face.

"I'm calling off the bet," I said. "You can go with Bentley to prom."

She finally backed away from me, folding her arms. "Why?"

I shrugged. "Because this whole thing is stupid. We're fighting our moms' war. I hardly even know you, yet we've been pitted against each other. Maybe we could start over—"

"No." She wiped furiously at the tears on her cheeks. "You are not backing out of this bet."

I circled my hand in front of her, motioning to her arms and face. "I think whatever disease you've caught has gone to your brain. No more bet. You win."

"You *owe* me," she snarled. "After ruining my night. The bet is still on. We will continue to fight for Bentley's affections—"

"That's the thing," I said. "I'm not into him. I like someone else."

She pointed a blue-spotted finger at me. "Don't interrupt me. You are going to try to win Bentley's affections. You're going to take this whole thing seriously, doing everything in your power to get him to ask you to prom. But he's going to pick ME in the end, because I'm the better choice. I'm going to win this fair and square."

"Uh, none of this sounds fair." If I were wearing a Care Bear onesie, I'd be pulling the hood up right about now, trying to find cover. Instead, I had my back up against the front door like a cowering fool, twirling some of my hair around my finger.

"Focus all your energy on Bentley. No more pranks. I want him to pick genuinely off our personalities."

Why was she so adamant about this? "Sierra, I don't want to, and you can't make me do this. There's nothing in it for me."

"This isn't about you!" she screamed.

I shrugged. "I mean, it kind of is, since I'm part of the bet."

She took her phone out of her pocket and pulled up a picture, showing it to me, and my heart dropped to my stomach. The one from the bookstore. My ripped pants, exposed Care Bear underwear, and way too much skin.

"How ..."

"They told me to delete it, which I did. But not before I sent it to Rosalind. She was so right about you."

My lungs constricted, burning. Dax had deleted Rosalind's copy, but Sierra had it, too. Would that moment haunt me forever?

"What do you mean, she was right about me?"

"She kept warning me," she said, "saying how vicious you are behind people's backs."

I scratched my head, so confused. "Okay, I have no idea what she's talking about."

"Stop lying!" Sierra took a deep breath to calm herself before she smirked, satisfaction dancing in her eyes. "If you don't try your heart out to win this bet, we're posting this photo." She paused, her mind reeling. Then, a big ol' smile landed on her face, and I didn't like it one bit. "You know what? New deal. Forget about being asked to prom."

"Okay ..."

"The new bet is to make Prom King and Queen." Her eyes sparkled like it was her most brilliant idea ever. I think she might have officially lost it. Gone cuckoo.

"Basket Case" by Green Day played in my mind, a crowd of people gathering around the band, jumping up and down and banging their heads.

Man, I really missed my dad. It was his favorite band of all time.

"Bentley and me against Weston and you," Sierra's voice cut through the party.

The song shut off like someone had yanked out the power to the speaker. The crowd in my head slowly lowered their hands, glancing around, confused. I had to shove them off the stage, bringing myself back to reality.

"What?"

She put her hands on her forehead. "This is so ingenious." She paced the porch in front of me. "My mom won Prom Queen. Your dad won Prom King. You've already lost Bentley." She smiled at me. "We kissed that day you freaked out at the bookstore. Did you know that?"

Sarcasm dripped from my words. "Weird. Bentley never mentioned it to me. Neither did you. Rude."

"It was after we dropped Weston off." Her head tilted to the side, her smile smoldering like she was reliving the moment. "I've actually liked him for a while. We'd been flirting a ton right before you moved here."

I folded my arms. Taylor had been right about them already liking each other. "Hey! So you went into it knowing you already had a head start?"

"Of course," she said. "Anyway, he doesn't want to go to that stupid ball with you, but he doesn't want to hurt your feelings."

"It wouldn't," I said. "I'd rather go with Weston."

Her lips twitched, clearly not happy with my reaction. "Anyway, I've already won your dad in this scenario."

"That's really weird ..."

She ignored my comment, rattling on, still pacing. "My parents will be ecstatic to know I'm dating Whitaker Anderson's son. And if we win Prom King and Queen? Icing on the cake. Maybe then Mom and Dad will ..." She trailed off, her eyes going wide.

"Your parents will what?" I asked, eager to know where she was going.

"That's none of your business!" she snarled.

Man, she had some anger issues to work out.

"You know," I said, "you could win Prom King and Queen without involving me. I could even help with your campaign." I tapped my lips. "Do people campaign for that? We could probably work up some sweet posters—"

"You don't understand," Sierra said, practically screeching. A part of me wanted to reach forward and hug her. She looked like she could use a big bear hug. "Bentley as my date, my king, is for my dad." She pointed a finger into my chest, poking a little too hard. "Beating you, though, is for my mom. I can make them both proud."

I swatted her hand away from my chest. "Your family has some really weird ideas on how to impress each other. Isn't your scholarship to UCLA enough?"

She paused, taking a slight step back. "You know about that?"

"Weston told me. Congratulations, by the way. That's really awesome."

She sniffed. "My dad didn't quite feel the same way." Her voice switched to a tone that made me believe she was mimicking him. "*As a woman, you can't make a career as a basketball player.*"

"Your dad sounds like a real piece of work," I said.

"No thanks to your parents. I've had to live in misery for seventeen years, thanks to your dad's choice. Now you'll get a tiny glimpse of how I feel." She backed down the steps. "Not a word to your mom, Veronica, Taylor, or anyone else. You need to do this on your own, just like I have to."

"Sierra," I said. "What if I don't want to do this? Cuz, I really don't."

She wriggled her phone at me. "The picture goes viral."

Would that *really* be a bad thing? A photo of my butt forever in the cloud? Okay, yeah, that would be very bad for me and my anxiety.

Maybe Dax would be willing to delete the photo from Sierra's phone as well. He had said he loved doing that kind of thing. How illegal was it? Was that something he could get in trouble for? I mean, he was just deleting some scandalous photos they shouldn't have had to begin with. He was being a hero, really.

"Weston and you have to beat Bentley and me for Prom King and Queen. Good luck with that." Her snooty manner made me pause.

"What's that supposed to mean?"

She put her hand on her hip. "You really think you, Daphne Richards, and Weston Ashworth could become a power couple? Please. I don't think so."

Why couldn't we become a power couple? We could totally be Tim and Faith. David and Victoria. Beyoncé and Jay-Z. Okay, probably not them. But we could become our own epic, unique couple, making waves at our school. We could have our own hashtag. #DaphneandWeston4EVR. Uh, no. #Westne. Nah.

#Daphton. That could work. It sounded like a really cool singer that only needed one name because they were that awesome.

I found myself smiling. This meant I could pursue Weston. We'd win Prom King and Queen, then the photos would be deleted, and all would be right in the world.

Things were suddenly looking up.

CHAPTER THIRTY-THREE

I went to sleep feeling all-powerful, then woke up with so many concerns. One thing I hated was that I was back to being bullied. I thought I'd left all that behind years ago, but I guess bullies were everywhere. No place was immune to them.

But hadn't I said I'd never let it happen to me again? That I'd never let someone have that much control over me? Who cared if that photo got out? Yeah, it was embarrassing. Yeah, I'd never hear the end of it. Yeah, it would be turned into a meme for time and all eternity.

Oh, no. It could be a meme. It would be a *great* meme.

That photo couldn't get out.

Even if Dax got his hands on Sierra and Rosalind's phones, they could have other copies on their laptops or something. They'd be stupid not to have backups. Asking someone to take someone's phone and delete a few photos wasn't *that* big of a deal. Asking them to break into their home and find their laptop to do the same, that seemed to be pushing it too far.

So, basically, I needed to win the bet.

Standing in front of the mirror hanging on the back of my closet door, I bounced on my feet, getting the blood pumping.

"I can do this." I flexed, and, wow, I had no muscles. Nope. Positivity only. "I am strong. I can do anything I put my mind to." I pointed a finger at myself through the mirror. "I'm going to woo the crap out of Weston Ashworth. I *will* win this bet, and do so with grace, dignity, and my sweet dance moves." Reaching over, I grabbed some liquid eyeliner from my makeup bag. "Alexa, play 'Roar' by Katy Perry."

As the song played, I sang along, putting on my makeup. A couple of times, I had to remove my eyeliner and start over, thanks to my crazy dancing sending the liner flying all over the place. I didn't want to look like a circus clown for my date tonight. Because—as previously established—clowns were serial killers.

It was triple date night with Veronica and Taylor. We were watching a movie and playing games over at Zander's house.

Bentley was my original date, but I talked to him after Sierra left my house, letting him know I had feelings for someone else and letting him back out of the date and the ball. He sounded happy for me, so all was well in the end.

Plus, he admitted he had feelings for Sierra. They'd honestly make a cute couple, but only if she went back to being her black and plaid wearing self. Not the pastel Barbie she'd created. I mean, Bentley wore flannel as well. They could be all matchy-matchy.

Wait. That would make them a perfect power couple. I needed to make sure Sierra stuck with her fake Barbie persona. It was obvious how fake she was being, and no one liked fake.

My main goal for the night was to officially become Weston's girlfriend. We couldn't become a power couple if we weren't actually a couple. Then, I could move onto my #DaphtonforPromRoyals campaign.

Back in Utah, I never went on dates. I hadn't really wanted to. Now, I had two dates in one week. Originally, with two different guys, but thanks to a bet to win Prom King and Queen, it was with the same hot guy I had a major crush on. It was pretty much the start of a Taylor Swift song.

"Alexa, play songs by Taylor Swift." If I was going to date like TSwift, I needed to get in the right mindset.

Finally finished with my makeup—I really had to tone down the dancing—I stared in my closet, not sure what to wear. Taylor and Veronica were both getting ready at their own houses, which was truly stupid on my part. I should have had them get ready over here. I needed their input.

Mom was out on a date with Cody. That left one woman in my life whose opinion truly mattered to me.

Sitting down in my swing, I video called Grams.

She answered on the third ring, the background dark.

"Hello?" Grams' voice was shaky like she'd just woken up.

Crap. The time difference. I'd forgotten about that.

A light switched on, lighting up Grams' face. She had total bedhead, her beautiful face clear of makeup.

She squinted at the screen. "Daphne?"

I waved. "Hey, Grams. Sorry to be calling so ..." What time was it there? "Early."

Grams sat tall in the bed, leaning against the headboard. "Is everything okay?"

"I have a date emergency."

Her eyes lit up. "A date? My Daphne? Is he cute?"

I nodded, grabbing some of my hair and twirling it around my finger. "Very. He's really smart, funny, and totally adorable."

Grams wriggled her eyebrows. "Sounds like quite the catch."

"We're watching movies and playing games over at Taylor's boyfriend's house—"

"A group date." Grams nodded her head in approval. "Smart girl."

"I don't know what to wear, and Weston's going to be here soon to pick me up."

"What are your options?"

I smiled sheepishly, still working my hair. "My clothes consist of Care Bears, Cherry Coke, or Captain America."

Grams sighed so loud it rattled the speakers. "Oh, my Daphne girl. What am I going to do with you?"

"Love me forever?"

Grams pursed her lips, deep in thought. Then her eyes went wide, an idea coming to her. "Rompers are back in style, right?"

"Well, yeah, but I don't own any."

"I do. Go to the attic and find my box labeled, 'clothes from the 1970s.' You'll find some rompers in there."

I hopped off the swing. "You really do keep everything, don't you?"

She grinned. "Aren't you glad I do?"

Keeping her on the line, I headed into the attic. I hated going there on my own, so taking a virtual Grams was better than nothing. Her calm voice walked me through it with ease.

Once I found the box, I opened it, peering inside. An old, musty smell hit me, making me grimace.

"There should be a navy-blue one in there," Grams said. "It was my favorite. I'd wear it on dates with Gramps."

"That's so sweet." I dug through the box until I found the romper, pulling it out.

It had short sleeves, a collar, zippered front, and a thick belt around the waist. I pulled back in surprise, though, when I saw how short the shorts were.

"You wore this for Gramps? Did it even cover your butt?"

Grams rolled her eyes. "It was the fashion back then. And it's the fashion now. Don't be such a prude."

Nothing like hearing your grandma call you a prude.

"Are you talking about the romper that zips in the front?" Gramps' sleeping voice came from beside Grams.

She smiled at him. "Yes."

"That one is my favorite." I could hear the smile in his voice. "Especially when you didn't zip it up very far."

I stuck out my tongue. "Seriously? Why? Now I don't want to wear it."

Grams chuckled. "It's fine, Daphne. Wear it. Zip it up as high as you want. You'll look amazing in it, I know it."

"Thanks, Grams. I miss you both!"

"We miss you, too, sweetie," Grams said in a soft tone.

"Love you, Daphne," Gramps said through a yawn. "I'm going back to sleep."

I blew a kiss to Grams and then hung up. I quickly put the box back and hightailed it downstairs, wanting out of the attic.

The romper fit surprisingly well, though it did smell like clothing that had been locked in an attic for years. I almost expected moths to crawl out from the outfit, finally free from hibernation.

Going to my dresser, I snatched my cherry perfume and

spritzed it all over the outfit, hoping that would help. I didn't have time to wash it.

The doorbell rang, and footage of our front porch came up on my phone. Weston was here. My eyes narrowed on the image. Was he wearing a blazer over his Captain America tee? Could he get any cuter? Then he cupped his hand over his mouth, smelling his breath. Yes, yes, he could.

Tucking my phone into my bag, I threw my bag over my body. I quickly put on my tennis shoes and ran to the front door, trying to keep my cool, when Weston's eyes lit up, a huge smile taking over his face.

I completely tossed my cool to the side and threw my arms around him, hugging him tight. I was overjoyed to have him standing on the other side of the door, not Bentley. No offense to Bentley. I mean, he was a great guy.

But he was no Weston.

When I finally released him and pulled back to look at him, I noticed the pink in his neck and cheeks and how his hand trembled on my waist. "Yeah Boy" by Kelsea Ballerini provided the moment's soundtrack, and I couldn't shake the thought that we were so going to win the bet.

CHAPTER THIRTY-FOUR

*Z*ander's parents had a home straight out of the Real Housewives of Orange County. When Weston and I turned into the massive driveway (after being let in through the gates), I got all self-conscious.

I mean, was I supposed to act differently at fancy homes? Be all proper and such? It would be good practice for the ball, but I highly doubted Zander's family talked like they were from the Regency Era.

A scene started in my mind, a bunch of people in Regency clothes dancing to "Rich Girl" by Gwen Stefani, and I found myself moving my shoulders back and forth to the music. I should be the DJ for Cody's friend's party. I'd nail it.

"Yeesh." I stared up at the wide, glass front doors. "Think they're overcompensating for something?"

Weston's laugh was strained. I looked over to see him rubbing the back of his neck, cheeks red, looking at the ground—which, upon further inspection, was smooth, shiny cement with speckles that probably cost more than my car (when Cody first got it).

"You okay?" I asked.

He glanced at me nervously. "I just don't know how to act at places like this. I've never been in a house this nice."

"Same!" When I realized how loud I said it, I clamped my hand over my mouth.

A genuine smile replaced Weston's nervousness. "Should we use accents or something?"

I snickered, but I quickly stopped myself and pretended to be polishing my nails. "No, darling, just act like everything is beneath you, and you've never seen anything so plain in your life."

"Kind of difficult to act that way when I'm standing next to you," Weston said. Then his face turned a bright red.

I loved that his mouth betrayed him like mine always did.

With a wide grin, I threw an arm around his neck, smooshed the side of my head against his, and snapped a picture of us with my cell, wanting to remember the moment.

Weston cleared his throat. "We should probably ring the doorbell or something."

"Oh, yeah." I leaned forward, pressing the button, before turning back to my phone.

The picture took my breath away. I looked beyond happy, my eyes lit up to match my wide smile. Weston, on the other hand, hadn't looked at the camera like I thought he had. Instead of the side of his head up against mine, his forehead was against my temple, his nose pressed against my cheek, his eyes closed like he was breathing me all in.

Weston's hand lightly landed on the small of my back. "Can you send that photo to me?"

I turned to him, our faces close together, and, boy, did

he smell good. I had to work moisture back into my mouth before I could speak. "Sure."

"Dear Future Husband" by Meghan Trainor appeared out of nowhere in my mind, making me blush. What in the what?

The front door opened, the song coming to a screeching halt. The Regency lady in me expected to see a nice butler with a fancy tux, but instead, it was just an average-looking lady wearing pink jeans and a button-down shirt tucked in only in the front.

"You must be Daphne!" She welcomed me with a hug. "Taylor has told me so much about you. I'm Zander's mom." She shook Weston's hand. "Welcome to our home." She waved her hand. "Follow me. The others are already in the movie room."

As we trailed behind her, I tried to casually look around, not wanting to appear like a regular person touring a celebrity's home. With the whole Housewives of Orange County vibe I got outside, the inside took me by surprise. I was expecting fancy. Gaudy. Pretty much screaming, 'please don't sit on or touch anything!'

But it was so casual. Everything was nice, yes, but I instantly felt at home in the mansion. Every room looked lived in and used, clean and tidy, but comfortable.

Weston let out a sigh of relief, barely audible, so I was sure Mrs. Morris didn't hear it.

I glanced over at him, whispering. "I already feel better."

"Me, too," he whispered.

Mrs. Morris looked over her shoulder at me. "How are you liking being back home?"

"Love it." I pointed to her pants. "And love your jeans."

She beamed. "Thanks! Got them on sale at Target! I

should seriously just move into that place, I go there so much." She stopped outside an open door and motioned inside. "Here we are." She peered her head inside. "Zander, sweetie, I'll let you know when the pizza gets here. You kids have fun."

With a wink at Weston and me, she left us in the hall. I moved to go inside the room, but Weston grabbed my hand, keeping me in place.

He was breathing deep. Like, really deep. Just like I did before I had a panic attack. Oh, no. Was he going to have a panic attack? What did I do? Maybe I could stop it. But I could never stop mine. They just came and attacked like crazy, practically consuming me.

I needed to calm him. Reassure him. Tell him to shut out the noise.

His mouth opened, and words tumbled out of his mouth all in one heap, taking me a moment to process all of it. "WouldYouLikeToGoToSadieHawkinsWithMe?"   He closed his eyes, pursing his lips like he was scolding himself.

"What?" I stuttered. I mean, I'd heard what he said. It was just, girls asked guys, right?

"Sadie Hawkins." He sighed, then took a deep breath. "I thought maybe we could go together. If you'd like. We could both wear our Captain America shirts and belts."

His question caught me off guard. Sadie Hawkins. It was in a couple of weeks. Veronica and Taylor hadn't really talked about it. Were they going? I think they would have said something if they were. Maybe we could all go together.

Weston and I would look awesome in our Cap gear. It would definitely help the #DaphtonforPromRoyals campaign.

Time ticked by, and I realized I'd been silent for too

long. Weston slowly nodded, like he was accepting my answer, but I hadn't even given one!

He moved to go into the room, a slight frown on his face, when my instincts finally kicked in, and I lunged for him, trying to stop him from entering the room so I could give him my answer.

"YES!"

My outburst shocked him, causing him to stumble. Since I was already lunging for the guy, like he was about to be shot and I was going to take the bullet for him, we tripped over one another and fell to the ground, landing with a thud on the carpet.

Veronica and DeShawn rushed over, helping us to our feet.

"Are you okay?" Veronica asked.

DeShawn smoothed out Weston's blazer, then patted him on the shoulder. "Digging the look."

"Uh, thanks," Weston stammered.

Both Weston and I were bright red. At least, it felt like I was. My cheeks and neck were on fire—a raging inferno of 'why was I such an idiot?'

What was wrong with me?

"Oh. My. Gosh." Taylor swept me into a hug. "I love your outfit!"

Zander and DeShawn moved quickly, guiding Weston away from us and talking to him about things that guys talked about. Whatever that was. But whatever they were saying had Weston at ease, slipping back into his smile.

"Thanks," I said to Taylor. I tugged on the bottom of the romper, wishing the shorts were longer. "It's Grams'."

"Like, real vintage?" Veronica asked. She took a sniff. "Why does it smell like an old-folks home?"

I fiddled with the zipper in front. "I just pulled it out of the attic."

Taylor reached forward, tugging the zipper down way too low for my liking.

I zipped it right back up, higher than I had it to begin with, ignoring her frown.

Veronica put her hand on my arm. "So, what was *that* all about?"

"Uh, he asked me to go to Sadie Hawkins with him." I glanced over at the guys, who were by the soda machine—they had a freaking soda machine? Weston caught my eye, and we shared a smile.

"And that required you to maul the guy?" Veronica held up a hand. "Wait. He asked you? Isn't is supposed to be the other way around?"

Taylor shoved her on the shoulder. "He got Daphne excited. It was kind of adorable." She squeezed my arm. "It doesn't matter who asked. I'm happy for you."

Veronica smiled. "Me, too."

"Daphne," Weston called from the soda machine. "They have Coke and some cherry syrup. Want me to make you a Cherry Coke?"

"Yes, please!"

Taylor lifted her phone, turning it to selfie mode and squishing next to Veronica and me. "Smile, ladies!"

After a quick photo, Taylor rounded all the guys up with us, the six of us squished together in the frame. Weston's arm wrapped around my back, and he pulled me closer to him, his head pressing up against mine. I noted how nicely I fit in the crook of his arm.

"I already saved us some seats." Weston reached out like he wanted to hold my hand, but he hesitated, so I offered it to him. Taking it, he steered me toward the middle of the theater room. He motioned to our seats, our sodas already set in the cup holders, a blanket on each chair. A bag of Watermelon Sour Patch Kids sat in one of the chairs. "Best seats in the house."

I quickly went for the seat with the candy, snatching them up before plopping onto the seat. "I call this seat."

Weston grinned, taking the chair next to me. "I figured you would."

Reaching into my bag, I pulled out a king-size bag of peanut M&Ms, tossing them to him. "I heard those were your favorite."

I'd texted Ivy to see, and also to check in on her. She was adjusting to her new life quite well. It was just such a shock at first, which it was for every girl.

As the movie started, I scooted to the left side of my chair, putting myself closer to Weston and setting my arm on the armrest. Weston leaned to the right, his arm pressing up against mine. I opened my hand, my palm resting up, letting him know it was there for the taking.

Halfway during the movie, he finally took my hand, interlocking our fingers. I tried so hard to contain my smile, but then I shot a sideways glance at him, noticing his huge smile, and I let mine fly free.

Now, all I had to do was secure my status as his girl-friend by the end of the night, and I was one step closer to winning the bet.

CHAPTER THIRTY-FIVE

*M*y wish didn't come true. Weston had dropped me off, walked me to the door, and we stood there in awkward silence before he finally gave me a quick hug, said goodnight, and practically sprinted back to the van.

But that didn't quite mean anything. Maybe he wanted to take things slow, which would normally be a good thing. Maybe I could tell him about the bet, then he'd understand how dire the situation was.

Although, we still had a couple of months until prom. Plenty of time to secure our power couple status.

Tonight was bonfire night, which was another opportunity for Weston and me to make our mark on the world.

DeShawn picked us all up in his SUV, Veronica in the passenger seat, Weston and me on the middle row, and Taylor and Zander snuggled up in the back.

Despite my best efforts to make it a onesie party, since Sierra had taken over the planning of it, that idea had been squashed. Taylor and Veronica wouldn't even let me wear one to the bonfire.

A huge moving truck had finally delivered the rest of our stuff from Utah. Taylor and Veronica raided my winter supplies, borrowing thick jackets, beanies, scarves, and gloves for the night like we were heading into a snowstorm.

All I needed was a hoodie, and I was good to go. These people didn't know the true meaning of cold.

"Oh, my." Veronica looked over her shoulder at me. "Have you seen Sierra's post today?"

Shaking my head, I pulled up Sierra's social media page on my phone. Staring at me was an adorable picture of her and Bentley with the caption, "*Hot date with this guy!*"

"They make a cute couple," Taylor said.

I shot a glare at her from over my shoulder.

She shrugged and mouthed, "*What?*"

Didn't she understand the importance of #Daphtonfor-PromRoyals? Nope. Because Sierra said I couldn't mention anything to Taylor or Veronica. Really, what difference would it make if they knew? Knowing Sierra, she told Rosalind about our change in the bet.

Rosalind. She'd be there tonight. I needed to keep my cool around her, even though I wanted to grill her about stalking me. It would be kind of fun to take Dax's advice and file a restraining order.

I'd need to find a time to talk to Veronica and Taylor. Make them see the importance of Weston and me making things official. Or, at least, make people *think* we were official. I mean, that lady behind us at the basketball game thought we were a couple. Maybe I could convince everyone at school that we were a couple as well. And hope no one said anything to Weston.

The fire was roaring by the time we got to Huntington Beach. Sierra and Bentley must have gotten there way before everyone else to get things set up. Honestly, I was impressed. The fire was big and steady. There were tons of hot dogs, chips, soda, plus everything needed to make s'mores. People were milling about, way more than I expected.

"Did she invite the entire junior class?" Taylor asked as we walked through the sand to join them.

Well, if she wanted everyone's votes for Prom King and Queen, then, yeah, Sierra would.

"I thought this was just a small gathering," Weston said, a nervous quiver in his voice. Huh. Why was he nervous? He'd seemed fine at the basketball game, and that place was packed.

Reaching over, I took his hand in mine, interlocking our fingers. The tension in him seemed to relax, and he smiled over at me.

"Daphne!" Sierra jogged over to us, all smiles and fake appearances, dragging Bentley along with her. Man, if I didn't know she hated me, I'd think she was actually excited to see me.

They stopped in front of us, and she snuggled into Bentley, making a show of it.

"Bentley brought a karaoke machine," she said, putting her hand on his chest. I watched his reaction, seeing if he thought Sierra being super affectionate was weird. He squirmed a little, clearly uncomfortable, and I held back a smile.

"We're having a competition," she said. "Best couple to perform gets an iTunes gift card! You and Weston *have* to sign up."

Weston tensed next to me, and I wasn't sure why. Did he not like karaoke? Did he not like the thought of us being labeled a couple? We were still getting to know each other, but it was obvious he liked me. Right?

He released my hand, tucking his into his jeans' pocket. Huh. Maybe not as much as I thought. I could have misread everything. Or maybe all my panic attacks had put him off. They were a lot to take in.

Taylor shimmied. "Well, then you should all just forfeit because Zander and I are going to kick your trash." They high-fived each other, then moved in for a long kiss.

Okay, then.

DeShawn draped his arm around Veronica. "What do you say, babe? Should we join in on the fun."

Babe? Had they reached that level of their relationship?

"Only if I get to choose the song," Veronica said, smiling up at him.

Sierra squealed. "This is going to be so much fun!" She pointed behind her. "Rosalind has the sign-up sheet. You can't pick the same song as another couple. So, if there's a song you're dying to sing, you better hurry over there."

Taylor and Zander pried apart from each other, then hurried over to Rosalind. DeShawn was hot on their heels, tugging Veronica along. I loved that they were as competitive as me.

Weston didn't budge, though. His focus was on the ground, his foot kicking the sand around.

Sierra leaned into Bentley. "We're doing 'You're the One that I Want' from *Grease*."

Of course they were. She was even dressed like Sandy, pre-makeover.

I smiled at Bentley. "You chose the song, didn't you?"

He laughed. "Uh, no. That was all Sierra."

Her smile faltered for a second. "I thought you were fine with the song?"

"I am!" Bentley cleared his throat. "I'm going to go get a drink. Do you want anything?"

Sierra shook her head, frowning as she watched him walk away. Her fake smile came back, though, when her focus came back to Weston and me. "You're going to sign up, right?"

I glanced over at Weston, who was still staring at the sand like it was the most interesting thing in the world. I looked at Sierra and shrugged. "I have an Android. No iTunes."

She scoffed. "Who doesn't have an iPhone?"

I raised my hand. "Me. I just said that."

"I don't, either," Weston mumbled.

I smiled at Sierra. "Will you excuse us?"

Taking Weston by the arm—he wouldn't pull his hands out of his pockets—I steered him away from the large group of people, stopping him when we were out of hearing range. With the sea breeze going, it wasn't too far.

"You okay?" I asked.

Nodding, he rubbed the back of his head. "Yeah. I just, uh, I'm not really a karaoke person."

"No biggie," I said.

Yeah, it would have been good for our #Daphtonfor-PromRoyals campaign to sing a song as a couple, but I'd never seen Weston so uncomfortable before.

I glanced over my shoulder at everyone around the bonfire. Rosalind caught my eye, a sneer on her face. She made a show of turning to Sierra and Bentley, making them cuddle so she could snap a picture of the two of them.

So, Sierra had told Rosalind the change in the bet. Of course, she would. A part of me wanted to march right over and sign Weston and me up for karaoke. I'd pick "10,000 Hours" by Dan + Shay, and Weston and I would nail it.

But then I looked back at Weston, who was currently staring out at the sea, watching the waves, and my competitive nature took a back seat. Mostly because I shoved it back there and duct-taped it shut.

"Do you want to go for a walk?" I asked him.

He blew out a breath of relief. "Yes, please."

Stuffing my hands in my hoodie pocket, I moved away from the group, going closer to the shore. Weston walked next to me, his hands in his pockets, his focus on his steps. The sand became more packed the closer we got to the water, making it easier to walk on.

Pausing, I bent down and took off my shoes and socks, holding them in my left hand. The sand was cold under my toes, but I welcomed it. It had been a while since I'd been to a beach. I'd missed it.

"Aren't you cold?" Weston asked, looking down at my feet.

"Nah," I said. "This is nothing."

We walked for a bit in silence. I didn't want to push anything or make him talk if he didn't want to. Something was bothering him, but I figured if he wanted to talk about it, he would. I didn't mind silence. It was time to think. To reflect.

Which got me thinking about my dad, and I just started talking.

"My dad *hated* the beach. He wasn't a fan of all the sand getting everywhere. Not to mention, he had the most sensitive skin ever. It's where I got it. We burn so easily." I stared up at the night sky, the clouds covering up the stars. "I'm probably getting burned right now."

Weston chuckled next to me. "I'm the same. Redheads and sun don't really go together well."

"Dad was ecstatic when we moved to Utah. More of a mountain man. We'd go on hikes all the time."

"Did you go camping?" Weston asked.

I nodded. "Oh, yeah. It was Dad's favorite thing to do. He *loved* campfires. Roasting marshmallows and making s'mores. He'd always tell ghost stories before bed, and I'd pretend to be so tough, but then I'd wake up in the middle of the night from a nightmare and end up crawling between my parents in the tent."

"Is that where you get your love of horror books? Your Dad?"

"Yep. I have a love-hate relationship with being scared. Like, the books, movies, and TV shows scare the crap out of me. But I love it and always go back for more."

Weston's hand suddenly grabbed mine, holding on loosely. "I have social anxiety."

I turned to him, startled. "Really?"

"I can do fine for a bit. Like at the basketball game."

"It seemed like you were having so much fun."

He looked eagerly at me. "And I was. I had a blast with you. But, I was lost in the crowd, you know? The focus wasn't on *me*."

"I get that," I said. "I hate being in front of people or knowing there are a lot of people staring at me."

"Exactly." He licked his lips. "Last night at Zander's, I was nervous at first, since I'm still getting to know DeShawn and Zander. And Taylor. But having you by my side made it so much easier. Your presence is always so calming."

I bumped our arms. "I feel the same about you."

He rubbed the back of his neck. "Tonight, well, it was the third night in a row that I've done something social."

I interlocked our fingers. "You're nursing a social hangover."

"Yeah. Is that weird?"

"Not at all." I stopped walking, turning to face him.

"We can just hang out, the two of us tonight. Veronica can text me when it's time to go."

His hand landed on my waist, pulling me closer to him. "As nice as that sounds, I am hungry."

"We can swoop in, steal some hot dogs, and swoop out, like pelicans in the night."

"I don't want to take you from your friends."

"They'll understand, trust me. They know all about my anxiety." My eyes went wide. "Not that I'm going to tell them about yours! I can say it was mine or something."

A smile landed on his lips—his crooked, nose inched up, adorable one. "I don't mind Veronica and Taylor knowing. I really like them."

"Hey, me, too!"

He took a step closer to me. "Thank you."

I squeezed his hand. "Weston, you can talk to me about anything. No judgment here. I mean, I had a freaking panic attack in the middle of a bookstore. After I ripped my pants and practically exposed myself to you."

"About that. Are we ever going to talk about the Care Bear—"

"Nope. Not happening."

He nodded. "Got it." He lifted his other hand, lightly placing it on my cheek, his thumb caressing my skin.

I smiled at him, letting him know he could kiss me. At least, I hoped that was what he'd read out of it. I could move in for the kiss myself, but I didn't want to spook the guy.

His nose brushed against mine, and, oh boy, it suddenly got way hot out here. My heart raced just thinking about his lips on mine.

With the perfect moment lighting up the night, "Young and in Love" by Ingrid Michaelson ran through my mind. I didn't want the night to end. This overwhelming feeling of finding your perfect person. The ability to talk to someone about anything and everything, no judgment attached. It was a rare, uncut gem, and I had it in my grasp.

Weston closed his eyes, his lips centimeters from mine. Closing one's eyes during a kiss was typical. I knew that. But a part of me wanted to keep watching and make sure it was really happening. That I wasn't just dreaming or imagining it.

"Weston!" Bentley's voice broke through the night, ending our moment. "Daphne!"

It was too dark for Bentley to have seen what we were about to do. No way Bentley would intentionally break up a kiss between Weston and me.

But it still sucked.

With a small sigh, Weston took a step back from me, removing his hand from my waist, leaving the spot cold.

Bentley jogged up to us, smiling. "I just wanted to make sure Weston was okay." He ran his fingers through his hair. "You know you don't have to do karaoke, right? I have no idea why Sierra is pushing it so much."

"Yeah, I know," Weston said. "I think we'll sit this one out." He looked at me. "If that's okay."

"Yep," I said.

Bentley opened his mouth like he wanted to say something, but then snapped it shut.

"What?" I asked.

He sighed. "Nothing. I just." He sighed again, deeper and longer. "Sierra's acting kind of weird. And her new ... look ... is kind of throwing me off."

"It's so not her," I said.

Bentley threw up his hands. "It's not! But when I mentioned something, she scowled at me."

Weston sucked in a sharp breath. "Never comment on a girl's clothes, man."

I chuckled.

Bentley looked at me. "Do you think you could ask her about it? Make sure she's okay? I just don't know why she changed her look. I liked it the way it was."

I pointed a finger into my chest. "You want *me* to talk to her?" I bit back a laugh. That sounded like a terrible idea.

"She seems to really value your opinion," Bentley said. "She talks about you all the time."

Her talking about me didn't surprise me. But the fact that Bentley was acting like the things she was saying weren't mean or anything was beyond weird.

No way Sierra would listen to me.

"Yeah, sure," I said. "I'll see what's going on."

Honestly, I was dying to know myself. Maybe I could get her so mad, she'd yell the truth at me. It was probably the only way it would happen.

"Thanks," Bentley said. "You guys coming back? There's so much food."

Weston patted his stomach. "I'm starving."

"Me, too," I said.

When Bentley turned around, heading back to the firepit, I looked over at Weston. "You sure you're okay going back?"

Nodding, Weston took my hand. "As long as you're with me, I'll be fine."

"I'll smother you like a burrito."

He broke out in a laugh, causing me to do the same.

My, oh my, I *really* liked this guy.

CHAPTER THIRTY-SIX

*M*r. Buckley wore a royal blue suit, the tee underneath a light pink. He grinned at the class for a second before he put on his super serious face that made me want to crawl under my desk and hide.

"I have a project for all of you," Mr. Buckley said, the sternness in his eyes not lightening. "Something fun." His tone and grave face told me otherwise. "You'll split into groups of four and prepare a skit together. You can pick any scene from the book of your choice, old or new, and act out the scene."

There were some murmurs around the classroom, everyone taking it in. It actually sounded pretty fun to me. Aside from the whole getting up in front of the class and having everyone stare at me thing.

"You'll perform the skit this Friday in class," Mr. Buckley went on. "I want each of you dressed in character." He folded his massive arms together. "And since I'm in a good mood today"—it was slightly terrifying that he considered this a good mood—"I'll let you choose the groups." He glanced at his watch. "You have five minutes."

He went to his desk, ending the conversation.

Bentley reached over, tapping my arm. "We should be a group. Sierra, me, you, and Weston."

Zander glanced back at me. "Hey, you and Weston should join us." He motioned to his friend sitting next to him.

I liked the option of *not* being with Sierra, but she shot me this look like working with her and Bentley would somehow help with the bet. At least, that was what I read from the two-second smirk. It was amazing how much Sierra could say with just a look.

"She's with us already," Bentley said.

Zander arched an eyebrow at me, waiting for my response. He was probably used to Taylor, who would never let a guy dictate her life like that. She'd choose whatever team *she* wanted, not caring about others' feelings, even if it meant being in a different group than him.

"You're with us, right, Daphne?" Sierra asked, all light and airy like we were BFFs.

I had a feeling working with her could be disastrous, but I couldn't turn down the challenge in her eyes.

I licked my lips, turning to Zander. "I'm going to join their group, but thanks."

Mr. Buckley had us rearrange our desks so we could brainstorm.

"What scene should we do?" Bentley asked, all smiles. He sat next to Sierra with me across from him and Weston next to me.

"There's always *Romeo and Juliet*." Sierra set her hand on Bentley's arm. "We can be star-crossed lovers, you weeping over my dead body. Then I wake to find you dead and kill myself."

"So, we're going for something light and happy," Weston said.

I turned to him. "*Lord of the Rings*. You can be Samwise. I can be Frodo." I looked at Sierra. "You can be Gollum. We can fight over the ring until you plunge to your death in the flaming hot lava."

Both Bentley and Weston chuckled. Sierra, on the other hand, didn't find it funny. Huh.

"What's the one they made a movie of?" Bentley asked.

I took a strip of my hair into my hand, twirling it around my finger. "That doesn't really narrow it down for us. I mean, what books *haven't* they made into a movie?"

Bentley snapped his fingers. "*The Giver.*"

Sierra sighed. "*Boring.* Let's stick with *Romeo and Juliet.*"

"Who would Daphne and I be?" Weston asked.

Sierra waved her hand. "The cousin or priest or something."

"Attention!" Mr. Buckley belted out. "*Romeo and Juliet* has been taken!"

Sierra growled, taking us all by surprise. She quickly covered it up with a smile. "We need to act quick before all the good stuff is taken."

Bentley raised his hand. "My vote is *The Giver.*"

"*Lord of the Rings*," Weston said with his hand raised.

Sierra's eyes lit up. "*Gone with the Wind*! Such a great kissing scene."

Sierra knew the classics, impressing me. I was expecting her to suggest *Twilight* or *The Fault in Our Stars.*

"I think we should do something funny," Weston suggested. "What about *Diary of a Wimpy Kid*?"

Sierra scrunched her face, not liking the option. She wanted something romantic. Something where she and

Bentley could showcase their amazing relationship. We needed a book with multiple couple options. If Sierra and Bentley were going to do a romantic scene, so were Weston and me.

My cheeks flared, everything in me warming up. I snatched a notebook from my desk, using it to fan myself. I wasn't sure if I *could* do a romantic scene with Weston in front of the entire class.

"What's that other book they turned into a movie?" Bentley asked. "*Divergent* or something like that."

"What? No!" Sierra said. "The ending of that series was *tragic*."

"Uh, so was *Romeo and Juliet*," I said.

"That's totally different," Sierra said.

"Was it?" I asked.

Mr. Buckley clapped his large hands together, getting everyone's attention. "You have two more minutes to decide, otherwise I'm choosing for you. Also, *Twilight* and *The Fault in Our Stars* have been taken."

I held in a snort.

"*Princess Bride?*" I said.

"One of us can be Westley, the others the three men that abduct Princess Buttercup?" Weston said. "We can reenact the scenes where Westley fights each one of them."

Sierra rolled her eyes. "He said *one* scene. Not three." Her eyes lit up. "What about *The Hunger Games?*"

"You have a weird idea of funny," I said.

"*Harry Potter* is taken," Mr. Buckley announced. "One minute."

"Well, we need to hurry and pick something!" Sierra said. "Otherwise, Mr. Buckley will pick for us, and who knows what he'll give us?"

"Maybe we should let him choose," Bentley said. "Make our job easier."

Weston nodded in agreement.

My mind reeled, trying to figure out what to do. We were overthinking the whole thing. We needed to simplify.

What costumes did Grams have? The Regency Era, of course. I could find enough for everybody. Probably. Plus, the book I was thinking of had two endless love stories in it.

"Ten seconds!" Mr. Buckley said.

I smiled at my group before shouting out, "We're doing *Pride and Prejudice!*"

Mr. Buckley nodded, accepting our book.

Then I raised my arm, waiting on him to call on me. "Instead of doing one scene, can we act out the entire book in five minutes?"

Others in the class chimed in, saying it would be funny to try to cram an entire book in five minutes. Plus, the faster we moved, the less likely I would get nervous. Same with Weston.

Mr. Buckley grinned widely before switching to his serious face. "Five-minute storylines it is."

Weston held up his hand to high-five, which I happily did.

CHAPTER THIRTY-SEVEN

I invited Sierra, Weston, and Bentley over to my house after school, but with Sierra's basketball practice, we had to move it to the evening.

Since I had a bunch of costumes, plus every version of *Pride and Prejudice*—movies and books—I figured it would be a good place to meet. Mom was a fan of anything Jane Austen, which she passed on to me. Mom had finished with my dress for the ball this weekend, so we had spent Sunday night in our dresses, watching *Northanger Abbey*, and munching on snacks. I told her we needed to make it a monthly tradition to dress up like characters from a movie and watch it. She was totally on board.

Bentley sat on the couch, throwing his arm up and resting it on the back. Sierra took the spot next to him, cozying into him like they were some long-term couple. He seemed a little surprised at first, but then his natural smile came, and all was right in the world.

Weston took a seat on the loveseat, resting his arm on the back like Bentley had his arm. Then, he lowered it, setting his hand in his lap. His arm went back and forth a few times, clearly not sure how to sit.

"Anyone want something to drink?" I asked from the kitchen.

"Cherry Coke will be great," Weston said with a smile.

Bentley looked over his shoulder at me. "Do you have Dr Pepper?"

"You're in luck," I said, opening the fridge. "That's what my mom drinks."

"I'll have a Dr Pepper, too!" Sierra said.

Of course, she would. Bentley could have requested goat milk, and Sierra would have wanted the same.

I brought the four bottles of soda into the family room and divvied them out. I plopped down next to Weston.

"Where should we start?" Weston asked.

He'd come a little early, so I had him get some totes down from the attic, ignoring his jabs at my being afraid.

I pointed to the totes on the floor. "Well, we can go through costumes, or figure out the skit."

"Skit first," Bentley said, pulling out a notebook from his backpack sitting on the floor. "We gotta figure out our characters before we pick the costumes."

"So, I'm assuming you all know the story of *Pride and Prejudice*?" I leaned forward, grabbing the book and a notepad I'd placed on the coffee table.

"I've seen the movies *and* read the book," Sierra said with way too much pride.

"I've seen one movie," Weston said. Then he snapped his fingers. "Oh, and the *Pride and Prejudice and Zombies* movie."

"Best version!" Bentley said with a huge grin. "I've seen practically every movie version thanks to my little sister. Did you know they have a 1940s version?"

I nodded. "That's my favorite one!"

Bentley and I were sharing a smile, and he opened his mouth, probably to say something about the movie, but Sierra quickly cut in.

"Obviously, I'll be Elizabeth Bennet," she said.

"Why, *obviously*?" I asked. It honestly made sense for her to be Elizabeth, me to be Jane. It was what I assumed would happen. But the way Sierra said it made me squirm. I mean, Elizabeth and Mr. Darcy were more likely to be crowned Prom Queen and King than Jane and Mr. Bingley.

She pointed to her head. "Brown hair. Duh." Sierra swept a hand to me. "And since you have blonde, you should be Jane."

"I know the story like the back of my hand," I said. "*I* should be Elizabeth."

Bentley cut in before I could list out my reasons. "Does it really matter? With all the characters, we're each going to have to play multiple characters."

Sierra shook her head. "I'm *only* being Elizabeth. She's the main character so she'll be in, like, all the scenes. Plus, she has a nature similar to mine."

"Stubborn?" I said. "Hard-headed?"

Tightening her jaw, Sierra glared at me, her nostrils flaring. It took her a couple of seconds to compose herself. "She's a strong, independent woman." She folded her arms. "You are like Jane, humble and reserved."

The way she said it didn't sound like a compliment.

Bentley smiled at me. "You should be flattered. Isn't Jane considered the prettiest of all the Bennet sisters?"

Oh, I couldn't stop the smile that came to my face. Sierra was *not* happy with that comment. Her hand flexed in and out of a fist as she tried to rein in her anger.

"Yes, she is," Weston said, his nose inching up as he smiled at me.

Though I didn't want Sierra to get her way, I was so happy with Bentley and Weston's comments that I agreed to be Jane. In reality, I was probably Mary. No way I was going to say that out loud.

Sierra placed her hand on Bentley's arm. "He'll, of course, be Mr. Darcy."

"What's with all the 'of course's?" I asked.

"He's handsome, rich, and has dark hair." Sierra motioned to Bentley. "It doesn't get more obvious than that." She smiled softly at Weston, trying to appear kind, but I could see the struggle behind her eyes. "Weston and Mr. Bingley have similar manners. I think he'd make a great Mr. Bingley."

He would. Honestly, I liked Mr. Bingley more than Mr. Darcy. That was who I would choose.

I wrote down all the character names on my pad of paper, then wrote our names next to the ones we'd play. "Okay, what about Mr. and Mrs. Bennet?"

Bentley raised his hand. "I'll take Mrs. Bennet. Weston can have Mr. Bennet."

I chuckled at the thought of Bentley portraying the single-minded Mrs. Bennet, writing their names down as I did.

"Mr. Wickham?" I said.

"Guess that should be me," Weston said. "Since he has scenes with Mr. Darcy."

I looked at Sierra. "Are you really *only* going to be Elizabeth?"

"Yes," she said.

I sighed. "Then I guess I'm Caroline Bingley, Charlotte, Kitty, Lydia, and Mary." I bumped arms with Weston.

"Wanna be Mr. Collins? Can't have Bentley proposing to her as two different guys."

Weston sat tall, smoothing out his shirt, his nose sticking up in the air. "It would be my honor to serve the Bennet family so admirably. There's not a character finer than I."

I laughed so hard, I snorted, falling into Weston, making him laugh as well. When I looked over at Sierra, she was glaring at us. Then a smirk crossed her face that made me uncomfortable and left a bad feeling in the pit of my stomach.

The doorbell rang, so I pulled out my phone to see who it was. We weren't expecting anyone.

Kimber Winters paced on the porch, looking frazzled. She moved like she was going to open the front door and just walk in, but she stopped herself and went back to pacing.

Mom appeared in the hallway, shuffling toward the front door and muttering like she was giving herself a pep talk. Totally didn't blame her.

With a deep breath, she smoothed out her hair and then opened the door, smiling at Kimber. She opened her mouth to say something, but Kimber pushed past her, rushing into the house and frantically looking around.

"Sierra!" her mom screamed.

Sierra stood from the couch. "Mom, I'm right here."

Placing her hand on her chest, Kimber let out a breath of relief. "Oh, thank goodness. I got your note about being over here and I ..." Her voice trembled, causing me to roll my eyes.

Mom put her hand on her hip. "And you what, Kimber? Thought we were torturing her or something?"

Kimber scoffed. "Being in your home is torture in and of itself."

I glanced over to notice Bentley and Weston sharing a confused look. They had no idea how much our moms hated each other. Or why.

"We're working on a school project." Sierra motioned toward Bentley, like knowing he was there would calm her mom.

When Kimber set eyes on Bentley, she did calm. Man, she had issues. No wonder Sierra was all messed up and so determined to carry out the bet. This small part of me suddenly wanted to let her win the bet.

Then Kimber looked in disgust at my mom, and I changed my mind.

Weston leaned close to me, whispering in my ear. "What's going on?"

I kept my voice low. "Short story? My mom is Elizabeth Bennet, my dad Mr. Darcy, and Mrs. Winters is Caroline Bingley."

Weston mouthed, "*oh*," as his eyebrows furrowed, trying to process what I said.

Kimber stood tall. "While I'm here, I wanted to let you know that Friday is Sierra's birthday, and we'll be having a party at our house. With the DJ, the music *may* get a little loud, so don't call the cops on us."

Bentley laughed. "Wouldn't that be your husband?"

Kimber and Sierra both tensed, but Bentley didn't seem to notice. I hadn't seen her dad at all since we'd moved in. I wasn't sure if he was living there or not.

"Her birthday is *on* Friday?" Mom asked, glancing over at me.

Kimber rolled her eyes. "That's what I said."

Why on earth was Mom looking at me so funny? Then the realization hit me. I quickly pulled up the calendar on my phone, checking the date.

"That's *my* birthday," I said, not hiding the shock in my tone.

Sierra turned to me, her eyes going wide. "We have the same birthday?"

"Apparently," I said, double-checking the calendar to make sure I hadn't read it wrong.

"That's awesome!" Bentley said.

No, it really wasn't.

Weston eyed me, probably wondering why I hadn't mentioned it before now. My dad went all out on birthdays. He'd bring me breakfast in bed, shower me with presents all day long, bake and decorate the cake himself, and take me anywhere I wanted. Ever since he passed, I hadn't wanted to celebrate my birthday. Mom and I hardly talked about it. Veronica and Taylor never brought it up unless I did, which was never. So, it usually came and went without much fanfare.

Mom lifted her chin, her eyes ready for war. "Well, we're having a party, too, and who knows how late it will go."

Uh, we were?

Kimber sniffed. "Yes, well, I guess it won't be a school night for your boy toy, so he can stay up a little later."

I gasped. So did Sierra.

Mom, though, she balled her fists, looking ready to maul Kimber.

I quickly ran over, pushing my mom back right before she could lunge, creating a safe distance between them.

Sierra stood next to her mom, glowering at her, which surprised me. For the briefest of seconds, Kimber looked ashamed. It was gone just as quick, though.

Bentley and Weston had both stood from the couches, looking clearly uncomfortable and totally confused.

Kimber laughed. "It was a joke, Laura. Lighten up." She put her arm around Sierra, her eyes on me. "Well, I hope someone still comes to your party. Most will probably be over at our place."

Bentley cleared his throat. "We can have a joint party at my place."

All of us turned to him.

He grinned. "We have a huge room dedicated to parties. The DJ can set-up in there. All of Sierra and Daphne's friends and family can come, and that way no one from school has to choose what party they want to attend."

"That's really not necessary," Mom said while Kimber said, "We wouldn't want to intrude on your family."

I felt Sierra staring at me. We locked eyes, and for the moment, our rivalry disappeared. I could tell in her eyes that she was upset by her mom's comment. I was embarrassed by my mom's reaction. It was a moment of realizing how stupid they were being.

It made sense, combining the parties. Although we didn't have one planned. That was a spur-of-the-moment decision by Mom to make Kimber mad.

I'd never been to Bentley's home, but from what I'd heard, it was a mansion. There would be so many people there and so much space, Sierra and I could probably avoid each other all night if we wanted to.

It meant finally acknowledging my birthday, but I couldn't avoid it for the rest of my life. Might as well approach with style, just like Dad did.

"I'm fine with that if you are," I said to Sierra.

She nodded. "Yeah, I think that would be good."

"What?" Kimber asked, a mixture of shock and anger.

Mom rubbed my arm. "Are you sure you want that,

sweetie?" Her tone held a worry that went beyond just having to share a party with Sierra.

I took a piece of my hair and twirled it around my finger, wanting the whole moment to end. "Yeah." I looked at Bentley. "I mean, if your parents are okay with it."

He was all smiles. "They will be." He rubbed his hands together. "This is going to be epic!"

Well, that was one word to describe it, but probably not the one I would choose.

CHAPTER THIRTY-EIGHT

*T*uesday morning, I was in a good mood, despite my upcoming combined birthday party with Sierra. I figured it would be a good time to flaunt how fun #Daphton was, with our love of songs and dancing. Bentley and Sierra, on the other hand, would just be showcasing how incredibly boring and polished they were, no imaginations whatsoever.

Plus, I'd had a delicious bacon, egg, and cheese bagel for breakfast, with a Cherry Coke on the side. Things were looking optimistic.

Veronica happened to park right next to DeShawn, so the second we got out of the car, they were all cuddles and gooey-eyes, which I was still getting used to, but it was definitely growing on me. The only thing that mattered to me was that he treated my best friend with respect.

He had his arm wrapped around her shoulder, his grin as bright as I was feeling inside. He looked over Veronica's head at me. "Hey, it's the birthday week girl!"

"Birthday week?" I asked.

DeShawn's grin somehow grew. "Why only have a day when you can have a week?"

Veronica smiled sheepishly at me. "Sorry. I tried to tell him you don't make a big deal of your birthday."

"It's okay," I said. "I've been thinking about it, and Dad would have wanted me to go all out. I think I need to focus more on making him proud than wallowing in the past."

She squeezed my arm. "I like that idea."

DeShawn's gaze went passed me, locking on someone else and lighting up. "Weston, my man!"

Weston came into view, and my morning got even better. He immediately high-fived DeShawn, sporting his adorable smile.

"Nice clutch ace last night," DeShawn said. He glanced over at us. "Our team would have lost if it weren't for him."

"Are we supposed to know what you're talking about?" Veronica asked. She had her fingers intertwined with his hand that hung over her shoulder.

"Game talk," Weston said, his gaze on Veronica. Then he high-fived DeShawn again before taking off into the school.

He hadn't glanced in my direction once.

Huh.

Veronica frowned at me. "Is everything okay between the two of you?"

I shrugged. "I thought so."

"He's probably thinking about that hottie he met last night," DeShawn said, wriggling his eyebrows. "Melted his brain." He bumped Veronica's hip. "Girls do that to a guy."

When both Veronica and I stopped walking, his smile faltered. So did his steps. Probably because his arm was still around Veronica, and their interlocked hands yanked him back.

DeShawn threw up a hand in defense. "His words, not mine. I have no idea if she really is hot. He seems to think so. He wouldn't shut up about her in the chat room last night."

Anger filled Veronica's eyes at the same time my stomach crashed into the ground. I placed a hand over my mouth, worried my bagel breakfast sandwich might make a reappearance.

DeShawn let go of Veronica and cautiously backed away. "I'm not the one who said she was hot! I swear!"

Veronica rolled her eyes. "That's not why I'm mad."

He blew out a breath of relief, his hand rubbing the top of his head. "I thought I was a dead man there for a second." He scrunched his eyebrows. "Why *are* you mad?"

Veronica motioned to me. "He's supposed to be into Daphne, not some stupid *hottie*." She put her hands on her hips. "How did they meet?"

DeShawn swallowed, clearly uncomfortable with the conversation. "Maybe we should forget I said anything."

"How did they meet, DeShawn?" Veronica asked.

"Some online chat room," he spat out.

I hadn't moved from my spot. It was like my feet were cemented to the ground, one with the asphalt, but so not in a romantic way. Weston had met someone else? We had just flirted last night at my house.

At least, I thought we were flirting. Was I wrong?

"Oh, good," Veronica said, her hand on her chest. "So, it's probably just some fifty-year-old pervert preying on the young and innocent."

I wasn't really sure how that would make the situation any better.

"They exchanged pictures. They have a mutual friend that introduced them." DeShawn licked his lips, his eyes going wide when Veronica snarled. "I really need to stop talking. I think I'll see myself out of this conversation." He took off before either of us could stop him.

Not that I would have stopped him. I was welded to the ground.

Veronica placed her hands on my shoulders, her eyes softening. "Breathe, Daphne."

Breathe? Had I stopped breathing? Oh, no. A panic attack had come on. When had that happened? The moment I found out the guy that I was falling for had found someone else? Yeah, that was probably it.

Maybe DeShawn was wrong. Maybe it was all a misunderstanding. But Weston hadn't even so much as glanced at me.

"There's no way he moved on that quickly." Veronica twisted her lips in thought. "I know how much he likes you."

"Not anymore," I whispered.

She lowered her hands. "Let me talk to him during math and find out what's going on."

*W*hen Veronica joined us for lunch, I knew it wasn't good news. Her eyes were a mix of sorrow and anger. So much so that Zander and DeShawn excused themselves the second she showed up.

"What's going on?" Taylor asked, clutching the sandwich in her hands so tight, I worried about its survival.

Veronica's nostrils flared. "He met someone else. Said he was 'smitten.'" She growled. "And here I was worried about Daphne breaking his heart. Not the other way around. I'm going to kill him."

"Your kill list is really growing," I mumbled, twirling some of my hair in my hand. "I'd hate for you to go to jail over a stupid crush."

"This is beyond a crush," Veronica said. "We all know how you feel about him. It's painfully obvious."

I arched an eyebrow. "Painfully?"

Veronica rolled her eyes. "You know what I mean."

Taylor wiped some breadcrumbs from her skirt. "This makes no sense whatsoever. No one switches crushes overnight."

I scoffed. "Says the girl who had a new crush every week in middle school."

"Weston isn't a girl in middle school," Taylor said. "That's totally different."

I pressed a shaky hand to my stomach. Having your crush actually crush you was the worst feeling ever.

Veronica snapped her fingers in front of my face. "You just need to remind him how much he likes you."

Taylor nodded. "Definitely."

Veronica huffed. "I'm so sick of the men in my life letting me down."

"Uh, oh," I said. "Did you end up talking to your dad?"

"Huh?" She tucked some hair behind her ear. "Oh, yeah. We hung out on Sunday."

Taylor frowned. "It didn't go well?"

Veronica pulled a bottle of water from her bag and took a sip. "It went really well, actually." She smiled softly at me. "I'm glad I took your advice." She pointed the water bottle at me. "Doesn't mean I'm dropping my guard, though. I'm sure he'll disappoint me soon enough."

The bell rang, and I sighed. Weston sat next to me in English. Though I wanted to, I couldn't avoid him.

Maybe Veronica was right. I needed to keep on fighting.

I couldn't give up because of some girl he chatted with once. That was ridiculous.

When I walked into our English class, Weston was on his phone, not paying attention to anyone around him. I handed Bentley and Sierra a rough outline of the skit.

"I put that together last night," I said to them. "Tweak it all you want and give it back."

Sierra scrolled the pages, looking impressed.

"Sounds good," Bentley said.

I turned to Weston, setting a copy of the skit on his desk. "I put that—"

"I heard what you told them," Weston said, his focus still on his phone. I'd never seen him so attached to the thing. Maybe he *was* a girl in middle school.

"Good." I took a deep breath. "Have a good night last night?"

He finally looked up at me, his face neutral. No adorable, crooked smile. But it wasn't swimming with hate or disgust like he couldn't stand me. Just indifference. "Played *Rainbow Six Siege* with the guys."

"That's right," I said, smiling. "What did DeShawn call it? A clutched ace or something?"

"Clutch ace." His eyes went back to his phone, a small smile forming on his face when he read a message on the screen. "Oh, by the way, I can't do Sadie Hawkins anymore. Sorry."

Wow. He'd met some random girl last night, talked with her for a few hours, and now he was canceling dates because of it? That was ... intense.

DeShawn had said a mutual friend had introduced Weston and the girl. My gaze immediately went to Sierra. Had she done this? Set him up with someone else?

Even if she had, she couldn't force him to like her. I mean, the heart wanted what the heart wanted.

My heart wanted Weston.

I sank back in my seat, fighting off the tears. I wouldn't cry. It was just a stupid crush. I'd get over it in time.

I found my gaze wandering back over to Weston. Everything we'd been through flashed through my mind. All the flirting. Our date. The little moments we'd shared. Him opening up to me at the beach. Our *almost* kiss that same night.

It hit me hard. I wouldn't be getting over Weston Ashworth anytime soon.

Though I wasn't one to listen to music in class, I popped in an earbud, using my long, wavy hair to hide it. I scrolled through the playlists on my phone until I found my Grumpy Grooves. Taking a deep breath, I pressed play, letting "Someone Like You" by Adele take me to my sad place.

CHAPTER THIRTY-NINE

*a*s soon as I got home, I put on my Grumpy Care Bear onesie, ready to mourn. It was something I was good at, mourning. I'd figured it out after my dad passed. I'd spent so much time faking happy, telling people I was okay when inside, I was a pile of mush.

A couple of months after his funeral, I'd taken a day to really mourn. Shut off my phone, locked the doors, surrounded myself with a bunch of junk food, got down on the floor, and sobbed until nothing was left. In the end, I felt good. It was my way of releasing.

Okay, so Weston and I hadn't ever been official, and he wasn't, you know, dead. But he was pretty much the guy of my dreams, and he'd found another girl. If I wanted to mourn, by golly, I'd mourn.

I stopped in the middle of the family room, staring down at the coffee table. "Sorry, Grams and Gramps, but I'm going to ruin your HGTV vibe for this dreadful occasion. Surely, you'll understand."

With a heave of effort, I pushed the coffee table off to

the side—seriously, did the manufacturers use the biggest, densest tree they could find to construct the thing?

Then, I grabbed all the snacks from the kitchen, setting them in a body-shaped circle on the floor. Lastly—but most definitely not least—I grabbed a six-pack of bottled Cherry Cokes and a bunch of straws.

After creating a long straw chain and setting the bottom into a bottle of Cherry Coke, I laid down in the middle of the living room, grabbed a Hostess Cupcake from the box to my left, ripped open the package, threw the plastic over my head, and stuffed the entire cupcake into my mouth. The cream oozed out, smearing onto the corners of my mouth.

How had Weston gotten over me *that* quickly? It had to have been some kind of world record, which totally would have impressed me if it hadn't been *me* on the receiving end. My biggest crush basically crushed me like a can of Cherry Coke in his perfect hands.

I swallowed. "Alexa, play Kelly Clarkson's *My December* album."

I picked up the end of my straw chain and took a huge gulp of Cherry Coke, the bubbles welcoming against my tight throat. It was already constricting, waiting for me to cry like a fool.

Who was this girl? And was she really *that* amazing? I swore, if she had better dance moves than me ... No. I couldn't think that way. That was impossible.

Reaching out, I grabbed the next thing I could get my hands on—a package of gummy bears. I opened the bag and stuffed a whole bunch of the little dudes in my mouth.

"Sorry, guys," I said, my words mumbled as I ate. "It's nothing against you. I'm just having the worst day of my life." I sniffed. "Okay, not the *worst*. Nothing can top my dad dying. But you get the idea."

More bears fell to their demise as I shoved as many into my mouth as I could. The leftover cream from the cupcake mixed with the gummies, adding a nice touch.

I fished out a white gummy bear—best flavor—and stared into his non-existent eyes. "I'm datable, right? Yeah, I got some quirks, but who doesn't? He's only known this girl a day. A day!" I popped the gummy into my mouth. "She's probably gorgeous. Like, drop-dead, in a totally different league than me, gorgeous." I threw up a hand. "Of course he'd land someone like that. Weston's the hottest guy I ever met."

The tears started to trickle out. Down my cheeks, the warm water landing in my ears.

Then it hit me: I was going to lose the bet to Sierra. #Daphton couldn't win Prom King and Queen if there was no #Daphton!

I grabbed the entire gummy bear bag and dumped it over my face, some landing in my open mouth, others bouncing off my nose, chin, and cheeks, and falling to the ground.

My picture would go viral. I'd become the Care Bear Underwear Girl, which was a total mouth-full and not clever at all.

Why? Why, why, why?

"Daphne?" Mom's face came into view above me. "What on earth are you doing?"

"Weston left me for a gorgeous model!" The words spewed out, along with pieces of gummy bear.

Mom stepped back, her face scrunched in both confusion and disgust. "What?"

I finished off the food in my mouth before speaking again. "It's over. Me and Weston." Although it never really began.

Mom frowned. "Why?"

"He met someone else." I pulled the hood of my onesie over my face. "I'm just going to go die now, thanks."

Rustling sounded next to me—probably Mom clearing a path—then she sat down and pulled the hood so I could see her.

"Are you sure? That guy likes you. I know he does." Mom reached across me and snatched up a Hostess Cupcake.

"He's moved on, Mom. I've lost the bet. I've lost Weston. Really, what's the point of going on?"

Mom rolled her eyes. "A little dramatic, no?"

I shrugged. "Maybe."

She took a delicate bite of the cupcake, like a normal person.

"How does someone move on so fast? I mean, we almost kissed the other night, and then, bam! He's canceling our date to Sadie Hawkins."

Mom's jaw dropped. "You almost kissed, and you didn't tell me?"

Red worked its way onto my face. "Oops."

She pointed her cupcake at me. "You're supposed to tell me these things." Her voice softened. "He really canceled your date?"

I nodded.

Mom licked her lips, looking out the window. "This doesn't make sense. It seems out of character for him."

"Maybe I never really knew him," I said in a whisper.

"Oh, sweetie." Mom finished off her cupcake and then laid down beside me, linking our arms. "I'm sorry this happened. Relationships suck, don't they?"

"Yup."

She sighed. "Why does life have to be so complicated?"

"I wish I knew."

"Well, tonight, we'll do whatever you want," Mom said, turning to face me. "We can watch movies, play games, lay here on the floor until we fall asleep. Your choice."

"Just you and me?" I asked.

Mom nodded. "Of course. Just me and my Daphne girl. Did you turn off your phone?"

"Yep."

Mom reached into her pocket, pulled out her phone, and then turned it off. "Me, too. I'm all yours tonight."

A night of Mom and me consuming all the junk food and watching sappy Hallmark movies was just what I needed. It was the perfect way to mourn the loss of a potentially amazing relationship.

The doorbell rang, followed by Alexa's voice. *Cody Brooks is at the door.*

Mom pulled back a little in surprise. "I didn't know he was coming over." She wiped some tears that had fallen from my eyes, kissed my cheek, then stood to answer the door.

I so wasn't in the mood for Cody. I wanted a night of just Mom and me, eating our feelings away. Well, *my* feelings.

"I brought Chinese!" Cody said from the doorway.

I groaned. He'd brought us dinner?

Then, I sat up. He brought dinner. My stomach rumbled, wanting something other than sugar.

Cody marched into the house, giving a shocked Mom a light kiss on the lips before he went into the kitchen and began pulling plates from the cupboards. Three plates, to be exact.

He looked over at me, his smile falling. "You okay, Daphne?"

"Bad day," I mumbled.

His smile came back. "Well, some food will cheer you up."

I slowly rose to my feet so he could see Grumpy on my onesie. "Cheer my stomach? Yes. Cheer *me*, though? Uh, no."

Cody chuckled. "It doesn't do any good to wallow. Just makes things worse."

Mom went to Cody's side. "Did we make plans?"

He shook his head as he took boxes from the plastic bag and set them on the counter. "Thought I'd surprise the two of you. I got orange chicken, Mongolian beef, chow mein—"

Mom cut him off. "That was really sweet of you, Cody, but now isn't the best time. Daphne needs some space."

Cody scooped some orange chicken onto a plate. "What happened, Daphne? It couldn't have been that bad."

I folded my arms, getting annoyed by the guy. "It's really none of your business."

Cody looked at Mom like he was waiting for her to scold me. But Mom nodded. "I think this is something best left between Daphne and me." She placed a hand on his arm. "But it was really nice of you to bring dinner."

Cody set the box down and rested his palms on the counter, his gaze settling on my junk food body outline on the floor. "You ladies are going about this all wrong! My sisters always do the same thing, and it just makes things worse. You need to put yourself in a happy mood. The right mindset."

"I'm in exactly the right mindset I want to be, thank you very much," I said, lifting my chin into the air. "I want to *wallow* tonight, so *wallow* I will."

Mom offered me a soft smile. "It's her coping mechanism."

"Not a very good one," Cody said, giving me the scolding look that Mom hadn't.

I pointed at him. "Dude, you're not my dad! Back off."

Cody sighed. "Now, Daphne, let's not use angry words."

Mom put her hand on her hip. "My daughter will use whatever words she wants. My daughter knows how to handle her own emotions."

Cody motioned to me. "She keeps having panic attacks. That's not a sign of handling her emotions well."

"When did you become a doctor?" I asked.

He rubbed his forehead. "This is coming out all wrong."

"Ya think?" I said.

He opened his mouth, but Mom cut him off. "Cody, I think it's time for you to leave. I'll call you tomorrow, okay?"

He pushed away from the counter. "Enjoy your dinner, ladies." He turned and left the kitchen, heading for the front door.

"Oh, we will!" I said.

Mom shot me a look, telling me to shut it. When he closed the door, Mom came to my side. "Speaking of doctors, I have an appointment set up for you next week. It was the earliest I could get."

I tugged on the hood of my onesie. "Thanks. I think it's overdue." I swallowed the thick lump in my throat. "Sorry for yelling at Cody like that."

Mom pulled me into a hug. "He overstepped. I'll talk with him tomorrow and get everything straightened out. He was only trying to help."

"I know," I said, holding her tight. "But it's—"

"None of his business." I could hear the smile in her voice. "I know." She pulled back. "Ready to pig out?"

I pushed up the sleeves of my onesie. "I was born ready, baby."

CHAPTER FORTY

The rest of the week hadn't gone any better. Weston hardly talked to me. Rarely made eye contact. He'd even unfriended me on every social media site, taking me by surprise. I mean, we couldn't even be friends? I thought we'd gotten along so well.

My Grumpy Grooves playlist accompanied me everywhere I went, casting an ugly, dark cloud over the whole dismal thing.

We were in English, waiting for class to start. Mr. Buckley's desk had been moved off to the side, all the students' desks pushed back, so there was enough room up front to perform the skits.

Weston stood nervously off to the side, wringing his hands together. I knew this whole thing was difficult for him, getting up and performing in front of the class. I went to him, putting my hands on his shoulders so he would look at me.

"We can do this, Weston," I said, trying to convince me as much as him. "Just shut out the noise."

"Shut out the noise," he repeated, nodding as wildly as a freaking bobblehead.

"We're in this together," I said.

He let out a breath of relief. "Together." Then his eyes went wide, like he suddenly remembered he didn't want to be my friend.

Would that honestly kill him? Being my friend? I mean, we had so much in common and hanging out with him was fun.

He shrugged away from me, turning his attention to his phone. Man, he was a bundle of nerves. Was he that scared to perform? It would be over in five minutes. His phone buzzed in his hands, startling him, even though he'd been looking at the screen. It flew from his hands, landing with a thunk on the carpet, right next to my feet.

Bending down, I picked it up, handing it back to him. But it had been enough time to see he had a text from someone named Mercy. And this Mercy person was excited to see him tonight.

Tonight. It was my birthday party. Was he not coming anymore? What had I done to upset him *that much*?

I'd had this hope that I'd be getting a birthday kiss from Weston, especially after our almost kiss. But that obviously wasn't going to happen now.

The bell rang overhead, making both Weston and me jump where we stood.

Mr. Buckley must have seen how flustered we were because he picked us to go first. With all the prep for our birthday bash, and the growing doom inside me, we hadn't even practiced. We'd just passed the script around, getting it to a place we could all agree on. The skit was going to be interesting, to say the least.

Sierra stood in front of the class. "Ladies and gentlemen, we present to you, *Pride and Prejudice.*" She hurried off to the side, keeping a wide distance from me, like she might catch a disease from being near me.

Weston, dressed as Mr. Bennet in a brown vest and white cravat, sat on a chair, reading a book, his right ankle lifted and resting on his left knee.

Bentley, dressed as Mrs. Bennet in a pale Regency dress and a white bonnet, came running in. He spoke in a high-pitched squeaky voice. "Mr. Bennet! Mr. Bennet! Netherfield Park has been let at last! You must go there at once and introduce yourself to a Mr. Bingley, letting him know about your five wonderful, *single* daughters."

Weston smiled over the book at his adoring wife. "It's already been done, my dear. Hopefully, we'll have a daughter off our hands by the end of the season."

"Oh, Mr. Bennet!" Bentley squealed. He ran off to the side.

Weston stood, moving the chair out of the way. He quickly donned a brown suit coat and a top hat.

Sierra (as Elizabeth in a green Regency dress), Bentley (still as Mrs. Bennet), and I (as Jane in a blue Regency dress) strutted toward Weston (now as Mr. Bingley).

"Oh, you handsome man!" Bentley sang. "You must marry ... uh, I mean, dance with one of my daughters." He shoved me toward Weston. "This is Jane. My eldest and most beautiful. I think you'll find her to your liking." He curtsied, and then ran off to the side, changing over to Mr. Darcy's black suitcoat and top hat.

I smiled at Weston, but he just bowed while I curtsied before we did a few steps of a dance, Weston looking everywhere but at me. When we finished, he moved like he couldn't get away from me fast enough. Pushing the negative thoughts from my mind, I ran over to get into my Charlotte costume, a pink floral dress, while Bentley went to chat with Weston.

"Why aren't you dancing?" Weston asked him. "There are so many young ladies here to choose from. Surely, one must catch your eye."

Bentley snorted, holding onto the lapel of his jacket and sticking his nose in the air. "I rarely dance with anyone below my station. There's no one here worth my time."

Sierra and I linked arms, walking in circles near the guys, chatting away.

"What about Miss Elizabeth Bennet?" Weston said, pointing at Sierra. "She seems favorable."

"Hardly," Bentley said. "I'm just really not feeling her vibe."

Sierra glanced over her shoulder at him and glared, though he did not notice, as he still whispered with Weston.

I patted Sierra's arm. "What do you think about Mr. Darcy?"

"That odious thing?" Sierra spat. "Please. I'd rather listen to Mary play the piano for twenty hours straight than spend one second with *him*."

We rushed off, Weston switching to Mr. Bennet, Bentley changing to Mrs. Bennet, and me changing back into Jane's dress. Sierra, of course, stayed as Elizabeth because she'd refused to be anyone else.

I was breaking out in a sweat like I was in Zumba class with all the running around I was doing. At least it was keeping my mind occupied. Well, for the most part.

"Mr. Bennet," Bentley said in his high-pitched voice, "we need to send our darling Jane to Netherfield Park. Mr. Bingley won't fall in love with her if he can't stare at her beautiful face."

"Well, yes, Mrs. Bennet," Weston said in a deep voice.

"That would be a pity. Everyone should have the chance to gaze upon our beautiful Jane." Those last words were strained, like he didn't want to say them.

Ouch.

"Oh, Mr. Bennet!" Bentley slapped Weston with a handkerchief, then turned to me. "Jane, dear, take a horse at once to Netherfield Park."

I snatched a stick horse from the ground, straddled it, and trotted across the room while Weston and Bentley changed back into Mr. Bingley and Mr. Darcy. They looked to be sweating as bad as I was. Sierra, on the other hand, looked so cool and poised.

As I "trotted," Sierra threw some water at my face for a rain effect, going a little too far with the amount. I sputtered as water ran down my face, making it hard to see. I tripped over my own feet, stumbling to the ground.

I scrambled back to my feet, glaring at Sierra. She was sure making it easy to hate her again. She just answered with a shrug as I hurried over and switched to a burgundy dress so I could portray Miss Caroline Bingley.

Bentley and I stood in the "parlor," chatting away. Weston "opened" the door for Sierra and led her into the room with us.

Scoffing, I put a hand to my chest, taking in her outfit. "What on earth happened to you? I daresay, Miss Bennet, you look like a pig fresh out of a mud pit." I turned to Bentley, setting my hand on his bicep and gently squeezing, my smile sly. "Don't you agree, Darcy?"

He harrumphed. "Did you walk the whole way here, Miss Bennet?"

Sierra smoothed out her dress. "I do love a good stroll on a beautiful day like this."

I choked back a laugh, but it evaporated when I saw

Bentley wasn't laughing. He was really embracing his Mr. Darcy character. He looked entranced by Sierra, who stared at him, a smile sliding onto her lips.

I cleared my throat. When Bentley and Sierra continued to stare at each other, I looked over at Weston to see if he noticed, but he was checking his phone, which was totally out of character for him. There was more to this scene, but it obviously needed to end.

"Your sister is all better, Ms. Bennet," I said. "Take her home. Next time, she should really consider a carriage."

Grabbing Sierra by the arm, I yanked her over to the side.

"Ow!" Sierra ripped her arm from me. "Settle down."

"If you'd stop gawking, I would," I snarled.

A few people near us snickered, reminding me that the skit needed to continue.

We rushed through it, switching back and forth between characters, stumbling over one another and our lines. But we finally got to the final scenes.

Weston (as Mr. Bingley) came back to Netherfield and visited me (as Jane). He was unbelievably shaky, like really selling his role. I thought he might pass out.

Weston nervously licked his lips, his eyes on a piece of paper on the floor. He read from the script, his voice monotone. "Jane, from the moment I met you, there was a spark I couldn't deny. You're everything I want in a wife." Swallowing, he got down on his knee. "You're the most beautiful lady I have ever laid my eyes upon. Will you marry me?"

Yeesh. Was a fake proposal to me *that* awful?

"Uh, yeah," I quietly said.

"Great." He immediately jumped to his feet, shook my hand like we'd just made a business arrangement, then moved away.

Bentley (as Mr. Darcy) got down on one knee, facing Sierra. "Miss Bennet. Elizabeth. I haven't stopped thinking about you since the moment we met. You drive me wild, yes, but in a good way. I love that you challenge me and push me to think differently. I will only ask this one more time. If you say no, I'll be out of your life forever. If you say yes, you'll have my heart unconditionally. Elizabeth Bennet, will you marry me?"

Tears formed in Sierra's eyes. Like, actual tears. Were they real? Or part of the acting?

Sierra put a hand to her lips, covering up her smile. Then, she finally lowered her hand to speak. "Yes!" She threw her arms around his neck, hugging tight.

The class broke out in applause.

Sierra leaned back and looked into Bentley's eyes, and I felt like I was intruding on a very personal moment. Again. She pressed her lips against his, kissing him softly.

The applause in the room shut off quickly, everyone gasping. That so hadn't been in the script. But neither had a lot of things we'd said.

Mr. Buckley had to clear his throat for Bentley and Sierra to break apart. They got to their feet, eyes locked, and bowed before the crowd.

I tried to take Weston's hand so we could join them in front of the classroom, but he left the room, not looking back.

My stomach sank. I suddenly didn't care about the bet anymore. I just wanted to know what I'd done to make Weston hate me so much.

CHAPTER FORTY-ONE

I twirled in my knee-length silver dress, the gauzy material poofing out. The rhinestones on the top half sparkled in the light, making me grin.

"I feel like I'm going to prom," I said, checking myself out in the mirror behind my closet door. "Dad would love that we're going all fancy for my birthday." Talking about it had made it easier than I thought. I'd been going about my birthdays all wrong.

Mom smiled widely. "He'd be wearing a tux and probably would have ordered a limo for the night."

I faked frowned at her, my fist on my hip. "You didn't get a limo?"

She rolled her eyes. "No, Your Majesty." She tugged a curl out from my up-do, letting it fall against my cheek. "Any way I can talk you into heels?"

I glanced down at my white sneakers. I'd replaced the laces with silver ribbon to match my dress. "Mom, these are my dancing shoes. People can't enjoy my sweet moves if I'm tripping all over the place."

Mom shrugged. "Sounds entertaining to me."

I shoved her arm, making her laugh.

She wore a simple red sundress, nothing as fancy as what I was wearing. We'd seen pictures that Sierra had uploaded of her dress for tonight when she'd gone shopping for it. A pale pink evening gown with pinned-on fabric roses on the top half, like she was in the Miss Teen USA pageant. Totally not suiting her, but perfect for the Kennedy vibe the Anderson family had going.

Mom had dragged me out of the house and bought me my own extravagant dress for the party, even though I told her it wasn't necessary.

Mom looked at me, her head tilted to the side, sizing me up. "Something's missing." With a snap of her fingers, she ran out of the room.

"Okay, then," I said.

My phone buzzed, an incoming video call from my grandparents. Plopping down on my bed, I accepted the call, smiling brightly when I saw my grandparents grinning back at me.

"Hey, Grams and Gramps!" I said.

"Happy birthday, Daphne!" they said in unison.

Gramps cleared his throat, then counted to three. They started singing the happy birthday song in total, perfect harmony. I so hadn't gotten their amazing singing genes. I took after Dad's side of the family, off-key, and totally okay with it.

I clapped my hand against my arm when they finished, still holding onto the phone. "Thank you!"

"You're looking fancy," Gramps said.

I pulled the phone back so they could see more of the dress. "Apparently, turning seventeen is the new sixteen. Can't just have a simple party."

They chuckled.

"Well, you look beautiful," Grams said.

Mom hustled in the room, sitting down next to me. She wrapped a chain around my neck, clasping the necklace together.

I looked down to see a diamond staring up at me, all shiny and perfect. "Whoa."

Grams gasped. "Is that the necklace Ian gave to you?"

Mom smiled. "Yep. Thought it would be perfect for tonight, and I was correct."

I fiddled with the diamond. "You know it's just a birthday party, right? I'm not getting married or anything."

"You better not be getting married!" Gramps yelled.

I waved a hand at the screen. "You know I wouldn't get married without you here. But I am thinking something extravagant, like Vegas and Elvis." I used the best Elvis impersonation I could muster. *"Love me tender, love me true."*

Gramps turned to Grams. "Maybe we should turn this into a ten-year trip?"

"Gramps, relax," I said. "I'm not getting married anytime soon. I don't even have a boyfriend."

"What happened to that Weston guy?" Grams asked. "Did my romper not do the trick?"

I blinked back some tears, not wanting to talk about him. "Uh, that didn't go anywhere."

"Probably better this way," Gramps said, popping a lozenge into his mouth. "Daphne doesn't need to rush into anything. Take your time. Date different guys."

Grams looked over at him, her eyebrows raised. "I seemed to remember you talking marriage just a week after we met."

Gramps scoffed. "Times were different back then!

Besides, I knew you were the one once I saw you in that romper."

I scrunched my face. "You two are disgustingly adorable."

Mom sighed. "Makes me miss Ian."

Grams kissed Gramps on the lips before turning back to the screen. "How are things going with Cody?"

Mom and Cody had a long talk the night after he brought us dinner. He apologized for the way he acted, saying that thanks to raising his three younger sisters, being a 'Dad figure' got the best of him. Mom and I understood and said we were sorry as well.

He and Mom took the rest of the week off, giving Mom time to just focus on me, and them time to weed through their feelings for each other. Tonight would be the first night they'd seen each other since Dadageddon.

Mom smiled. "Good. We've been having a lot of fun together." She shrugged. "He's just not Ian. No one ever will be."

I wrapped my arm around her. "And that's okay." I blew out a deep breath. "I really hate to admit this, but I kind of like Cody. He's a nice guy."

Gramps huffed. "I'm not sure if I like this. My girl dating without me there to supervise."

"Dad, I'm a grown woman," Mom said.

"You'll always be my little girl," he said. "My baby."

Mom put her hand on her chest. "Aww. I miss you guys so much."

"We miss you, too, sweetie," Grams said.

"Don't worry, Gramps," I said. "I'll keep a close eye on her. I've been meaning to set up some cameras in the front room."

Gramps nodded, satisfied with my comment. "Good. Good."

Mom slapped me upside the head. "We don't need surveillance in the house. Nothing is happening."

"Coming from the lady I caught making out on the couch," I said.

Grams gasped. "You didn't!"

"Yep," I said.

"Can we install a system with speakers?" Gramps asked. "That way, next time Laura is making out, I can chime in and tell them to cut it out?"

I broke out in a fit of laughter as Mom scowled at us. My family was just what I needed to cheer myself up.

"Can we please stop talking about making out?" Mom asked. Her frown turned into a smile when I wouldn't stop laughing. Wrapping her arm around me, she kissed me on the temple. "Just remember this conversation when you want to make out with ... someone."

My laughter abruptly stopped. She was thinking about Weston.

"That won't be happening," I said, trying to keep my voice even. I wasn't going to let it ruin my birthday or my party.

Mom went to say something, but the doorbell rang. She looked down at her phone. "Cody is here." She waved to her parents. "Love you!" She pushed up from the bed and left the room.

"You'll keep an eye on her, right, Daphne?" Gramps asked.

"Of course." I sighed. "And I was serious. I like Cody. He's been really great to Mom. And to me."

Grams' eyes went wide. "Wow. I'm surprised you're admitting that."

"Me, too."

She grinned. "Well, I'm glad she's happy. Wish we could be there for your birthday party."

"Your present is in the mail," Gramps said. "It's going to be a few days late. Let us know when you get it."

"Will do." I blew them kisses. "Love you!"

"Love you!" they sang in unison, and, boy, I missed them.

Mom giggled in the front room, my cue to go. Grabbing my newest sling bag creation—silver with rhinestones to match my dress—I hurried out into the front room.

Cody smiled when he saw me. "Happy birthday, Daphne!"

"Thanks," I said.

His smile turned sheepish. "I know I already apologized, but I'm really sorry about the other night. I wasn't trying to be your dad."

"I know," I said, holding onto the strap of my bag. "It's all good."

He held out a box covered in magenta wrapping paper. "This is for you."

With a grin, I snatched it from his hand, ran to the kitchen, set the box on the counter, and ripped open my present. Inside were six bottles of my favorite cherry syrup. "This. Is. The. Best!"

Cody laughed. "I'm glad you like it."

"I do," I said, turning to him. I went up to him, holding out my arms for a hug.

Cody pulled me into him, giving me the biggest bear hug. "You're an amazing young lady, Daphne."

I grinned when we released each other. "You're not so bad yourself." I motioned between him and Mom. "But I never want to catch the two of you making out on the couch again. Or anywhere for that matter."

Cody blushed. "Deal."

I shimmied. "Now, let's go get our party on."

CHAPTER FORTY-TWO

*T*he difference between Zander's home and Bentley's house was crazy. To start, Bentley's was almost twice as big. I knew his parents both came from money, but this was insane. The large fountain in the front was practically bigger than my house. Marble lions circled the inside, water spraying from their mouths.

The valet attendant took Cody's keys, offering him a slight bow before getting in the car and driving off. Cody offered Mom and me a slight quirk of the eyebrow that I read as, "They have a freaking valet?"

The double doors in front were open, so Mom, Cody, and I walked in. Jazz music drifted from somewhere to the right.

We stood in the grand entryway, taking in all the gold and marble. It was like Oprah and Queen Elizabeth had helped design the freaking palace, everything ornate. The large vase next to the front door looked worth more than *me*.

"Mr. and Mrs. Anderson agreed to have the party here?" Cody asked, looking up at the glass chandelier.

"They're brave," Mom said. "Letting a bunch of

teenagers invade the place."

"Oh. My. Gosh." Ivy's voice rang out behind us.

I turned to see her and Weston in the doorway, Ivy's jaw practically on the ground as she took in the house. Weston was busy checking out his phone. So, he did come to my party.

Ivy's gaze found mine. "We're so underdressed!" She looked down at her tee and jeans, a frown on her lips.

"No, you're not," I said, rushing over to her and pulling her into a hug. "Just the birthday girls dressed up."

She looked over at my mom. "She's wearing a dress."

Mom waved her hand. "This old thing? Found it at a thrift store years ago."

I introduced Mom and Cody to Ivy, before Mom steered Ivy toward the party, chatting away and melting the tension in Ivy's shoulders. Cody trailed behind them, glancing around at everything as he did.

Weston took a tentative step toward me. "Uh, happy birthday." He rubbed the back of the neck and pointed to the right. "Sounds like the party is this way."

He took off, leaving me alone in the entryway.

Okay, then.

The ballroom was packed. Yes, they had a ballroom. Yes, it was something straight out of a historical drama. Yes, I glanced around, expecting the king and queen to be sitting on their thrones, gazing out at all their minions.

Instead, Mr. and Mrs. Anderson stood at the front of the room, greeting and chatting with people like this was some sort of political event.

I expected to see a DJ since Kimber had said they hired one, but a live band was on the opposite end of the room, playing jazz. As much as I loved music, this so wasn't my jam.

Sierra and Bentley stood next to his parents, Kimber and a man I took to be Sierra's dad on the other side of Sierra. With her ball gown and the way they were talking to everyone, you'd think it was their wedding reception.

The tension between Sierra's mom and dad was painfully obvious. I writhed in my dress like there was a snake slithering through it, which was way more welcome than whatever was going on with her parents. A little bit of sympathy pinged in my heart, but I squashed it since we were sworn enemies.

Bentley and I locked eyes, and he gave me a look I couldn't quite read. He didn't look all that happy, though.

I went to the refreshment table up against the far wall, staring at the ginormous marble lion statue in the middle. Above its head was a large bowl, bubbly cream-colored liquid cascading down all the sides, landing in a pool at the lion's feet. It was hands-down the gaudiest drink fountain I'd ever encountered. Couldn't they just have set some bowl on the table, filled it with punch and a ladle, and called it good?

Someone was staring at me. I could feel it. I scanned the room until I spotted Sebastian and Rosalind standing near the dessert table. Sebastian waved, then moved like he wanted to come talk to me, but Rosalind pulled him back, hissing something at him.

His gaze went to the ground, clearly upset, but he obeyed his sister.

Why was everyone acting so odd? And why did Rosalind hate me so much?

"This is so weird," Taylor said, appearing beside me. She had a champagne glass in her hand, filled with the sparkling cider. After topping it off under the fountain, she twirled it in her hand. "Couldn't they just have red solo cups and some soda?" She adjusted her black, leather jacket, clearly uncomfortable.

Zander came up beside Taylor, putting his arm around her back, looking just as out of place as he tugged on the top of his floral tee. "Have you checked out the food?"

A waiter passed by, offering us what looked to be coconut shrimp. We all shook our heads at him, and he left with a disgusted glance like we were beneath him.

"Yeesh," I said under my breath.

Veronica and DeShawn were suddenly on the other side of me, both looking like they would like to be anywhere but here.

"This is, uh ..." DeShawn rubbed his chin. "Quite the party."

I groaned. "This is *awful*. Seriously. There should be pizza rolls, not sushi rolls."

Zander patted his stomach. "That sounds so good."

Veronica put her hand on my arm. "Maybe we should just go. We can go grab some burgers or something."

Taylor nodded. "Fully agree. It's your birthday, Daphne. Let's have some *fun*."

I took in all the guests. Besides those that knew the Anderson family, everyone else looked bored out of their minds. We'd invited so many people. Even Taylor's and Veronica's families had come.

Javy sat in the corner, drawing on his arm, while his sister, Luciana, twirled in circles around him. Veronica's mom stood nearby, talking with someone I didn't know.

A few of Taylor's brothers, plus their parents, were chatting with Mom and Cody, all of them clearly out of their element.

Mom must have sensed me staring, because she turned her focus to me, a frown on her lips.

Then, I saw Weston talking—no, flirting—with some beautiful girl. Probably Mercy. She put her hand on his arm, laughing at something he said.

This was all so ridiculous. The only reason I agreed to this stupid party was to help win the bet—which had sounded fun. I mean, the whole blackmail thing sucked but trying to win Prom Queen was adventurous.

But with Weston out of the picture as Prom King, I'd lose the bet. Which meant I had to get the photo of me deleted from Sierra and Rosalind's phones.

In the meantime, it was my birthday, and I intended to have fun. That was what my dad would have wanted. And maybe I could corner Weston at some point and demand some serious answers.

I smoothed out the front of my dress. "I'm going to go talk to Bentley first and see if we can't get this place livened up a bit. His parents were so kind to throw the party, I don't want to just walk out." Another waiter passed by, holding a tray of escargot, and I dry-heaved. "At least, not yet."

Snatching an empty champagne glass next to the fountain, I filled it with sparkling cider, downed it, and shoved the empty glass into Veronica's chest—she just happened to be the closest person to me. Head held high, I weaved through the guests, heading for Bentley. His arm was linked with Sierra's, the two of them chatting with some really old dude with an impressive white handlebar mustache.

I swore relief danced in Bentley's eyes when he saw me.

I spoke softly, not wanting to interrupt the old dude. "Can we speak in private for a second?"

"Uh, Sierra, I'll be right back." He placed his hand on my elbow and steered me out of the ballroom like he couldn't get out of there fast enough.

CHAPTER FORTY-THREE

*A*s soon as we entered the hallway, Bentley threw his head back and let out a long breath, his whole body relaxing. He pulled at the top of his tux. "This is awful, isn't it?"

I leaned against the wall, crossing my ankles. "It's not the ideal birthday party, but, I mean, the place looks nice."

He lowered his head, looking over at me. "I'm sorry, Daphne. When I asked my parents if we could host a party here, I didn't expect my mom to take it into her hands and hire caterers and everything." He ran a hand down his face. "Although I should have. It's what she does."

"You doing okay?" I asked. "You looked a little ... I don't know, annoyed or something in there."

He checked over his shoulder, and then steered us farther down the hall. "It's Sierra. Have you had a chance to talk to her yet? About the wardrobe change and stuff?"

I'd had so many things on my mind, I'd completely forgotten he'd asked me to do that. I scrunched my nose. "Yeah, I totally forgot. Sorry."

He sighed. "She just hasn't been the same lately. I miss

the old her." He fiddled with his bowtie, clearly annoyed with it. "She's acting weird in front of my parents, too. All uppity, like this is normal life for her." With a grunt, he finally ripped off the bowtie, shoving it into his pocket. Then, he undid the first few buttons of his shirt. "I hate tuxes. I hate this whole party."

"You need to liven it up a bit," I said.

He quirked an eyebrow as he undid the buttons on his cuffs. "Any suggestions?"

"Is there any way we can change the music or something?" I offered. "Maybe get some pizza rolls up in this joint?"

"I like the sound of that," a deep voice said from the side of me.

I turned to see Whitaker Anderson loosening his bowtie with one hand, the other resting in his pants' pocket. He smiled softly at me. "Apologies, Daphne. My wife doesn't know the meaning of subtle."

My face reddened, not wanting him to think I was complaining. I stuttered out the next words. "This is totally fine! I mean, the band is, you know, like live, and the food is, you know, um, fancy and stuff."

Bentley snickered next to me, so I punched him in the stomach, causing his laughter to grow.

Mr. Anderson placed a soft hand on my shoulder. "Well, you're the birthday girl. What would you like?" The gesture, and the gentle tone of his voice, reminded me of my dad, and I had to blink back tears.

I took a shaky breath. "If it's not too much to ask, maybe get rid of the band? Play some pop music we can dance to?" I bit my lip. "And, for the food, maybe snacks that don't require living things to die?"

"Hey, that coconut shrimp is amazing," Bentley said,

pointing his finger at me. He shrugged. "The escargot I could do without."

Mr. Anderson retrieved his phone from his pocket. "I'll make some calls. We can get the other ballroom set-up immediately. Get a DJ and some of those pizza rolls you were talking about." Putting his phone to his ear, he turned away, already talking to someone about food teenagers would actually eat.

I looked at Bentley, my jaw practically on the floor. "The *other* ballroom? How many do you people have?"

"Just two," he said, smiling. "Sometimes so many people come to his shindigs that he likes to have a back-up place for the overflow."

I snorted. "Next, you're going to tell me you have a fancy library like in *Beauty and the Beast*, complete with a rolling ladder."

He stared at the marble floor. "Uh, it's down the hall, on your left."

My eyebrows hitched up. "Really? I might have to check that out later. I've always wanted to ride one of those ladders."

Sierra glided out of Ballroom One with a smile so light and airy, I waited for the birds to show up, chirping at her shoulder like a freaking Disney movie.

She paused at our sides. "What's going on?" She set a hand on Bentley's arm. "You've been gone so long."

Bentley checked his watch. "It's only been a few minutes."

"Good news," I said. "Mr. Anderson is setting up a real party in the other ballroom." I held up two fingers. "They have two!"

Sierra frowned. "What's wrong with this one?"

I started to laugh, but then realized she wasn't joking. I

cleared my throat. "Hey, if you like it, then that's great. My party will have a DJ and edible food." I shimmied. "Plus, my sweet dancing."

Sierra plastered on a smile, but her jaw twitched in anger. "Well, good luck getting people to go to your childish party."

Bentley pointed at the open ballroom doors. "You're actually enjoying that, Sierra?"

Her smile faltered. "Yeah, of course. It's so refined and—"

"Snobby?" I said, nodding. "Agree."

Bentley chuckled, causing Sierra's cheeks to turn pink. She looked desperately at Bentley. "I thought you liked this lifestyle."

He shook his head. "That's my parent's lifestyle, not mine." He huffed. "Well, it's my mom's. Dad would enjoy Daphne's version of a party."

Sierra went speechless, her mouth moving like she was trying to find something to say, but nothing came.

Then, she suddenly stomped her foot. "I wore this stupid dress for *nothing*?"

Bentley and I shared a confused look.

Sierra motioned to the pale pink dress. "I thought this is what you wanted."

"Why on earth would you think that?" Bentley asked.

I slowly backed away, wanting out of the conversation. I didn't need to be around to witness the argument. I had a feeling it wasn't going to end well.

The problem was, my sneakers kept squeaking against the marble, making it difficult to walk out unnoticed.

Both Bentley and Sierra whipped their heads toward me.

I came to a screeching stop, then used my thumb to

motion behind me. "I'm just gonna see myself out." Then I spun and ran, heading into the foyer and out of their sight, silently cursing my squeaking shoes.

Mr. Anderson stood in the open doorway, staring out at the sunset, still on the phone. He glanced over his shoulder when he heard my shoes declaring my presence—okay, maybe Mom had been right about not wearing tennis shoes. He smiled at me before he ended the call and came to my side. "Everything is set. DJ is on her way, and the food is being prepped in the kitchen."

"Whoa! You don't waste any time, do you?"

He laughed, sounding like Bentley. "It helps to have connections."

"But the food? Do you guys have a grocery store out back or something?" Honestly, it wouldn't have surprised me if they did.

He leaned in close, like he was telling me a secret. "Between you and me, I was hoping this would happen. Had my kitchen staff make sure there was soda, chips, ice cream, pretty much the works, on hand."

No grocery store, but a kitchen staff. What a life. I'd make them stock up on Cherry Coke and Watermelon Sour Patch Kids. Lifetime supply, always available.

"Even have pizza rolls." He stood straight, rubbing the back of his neck. Another Bentley trait. Like father, like son. "Now, I have to go break the news to my wife."

"Thank you, Mr. Anderson," I said. "You didn't have to do any of this, so I'm beyond grateful."

He grinned. "Happy to help. Bentley told me about your father. I'm sorry to hear of his passing. He must have been one amazing man to raise a daughter like you."

Tears pricked at the corners of my eyes, and I flicked them away. "He was the best. And he loved birthdays."

"Then let's make sure you have a party he'd be proud of." He moved toward the ballroom. "Oh, and please call me Whitaker. Anyone who wears sneakers with a fancy dress is a friend in my book."

I now fully understood why the public loved the man so much. He was friendly and easy to talk to. Not stuck-up at all.

I did a little dance in the foyer before I ran into Ballroom One to tell my friends and family the good news.

CHAPTER FORTY-FOUR

*T*hirty minutes later, my family and friends were in Ballroom Two, getting our groove on. It had been a pretty even split, those that came over to my party, and those that stayed at Sierra's. Sierra had seemed disappointed that so many switched over, but I cared nothing about the numbers. I just wanted to make sure those with me were having a good time. From the laughter and smiles all around me, the party was sure not disappointing.

Taylor, Veronica, and I stood near the refreshments, each holding a red Solo cup of Cherry Coke.

Taylor held up her cup in a cheer. "To Daphne, for coming back to California and gracing us with her amazing presence."

"And her *sweet* dance moves," Veronica said, lifting her cup.

"Hear, hear!" Taylor said.

We clinked our plastic cups together before each taking a sip.

Ivy ran up and threw her arms around me. "This is the

best party *ever*!" She dropped her arms before jumping up and down with a squeal. "I got a guy's number!"

"Wait, what?" I asked, shaking out some Cherry Coke that had jumped out of the cup and down my hand because of Ivy's bear hug. "Who?"

With a wicked grin, she pointed to a guy on the center of the dance floor, his charisma stealing everyone's attention.

"Javy?" Veronica looked at Ivy, lifting her hand in the air, setting a bar. "Might want to aim higher."

Ivy's enthusiasm faltered, a frown forming. "Why? He's super hot!"

Veronica grimaced. "Is he?"

Laughing, I pushed her away from us, then smiled at Ivy. "It's her brother. I adore Javy, but just so you know, he's a lady's man. The girls at his school love him."

Ivy sighed, her hands clasped under her chin. "I can see why."

Man, I hoped Weston didn't freak out when he heard. I glanced around but didn't see him anywhere. I turned back to Ivy. "Where's your brother?"

Ivy went pale, her eyes searching the floor.

Taylor and Veronica shared a look, neither of them looking like they wanted to say anything.

"What?" I asked.

Veronica threw her hands up. "I can't right now. I'm too ticked off about it." She turned around, going to the middle of the ballroom and joining her brother on the dance floor.

Ivy was hot on her heels, like she couldn't get away fast enough.

Taylor put her hands on my shoulder, her eyes full of so much sympathy, it killed me. "Listen. Um. Here's the thing." She pursed her lips, thinking.

"Just spit it out."

Taylor squeezed my shoulders. "Weston stayed at Sierra's party. With that other girl."

Usually, when I heard his name, heat flooded me. This time, though, cold air washed over me, making me shiver. Goosebumps broke out on my arms. Taylor started rubbing my arms.

I tried to say something, but nothing came out.

"He was acting really weird," Taylor said. "Veronica has even asked him again what's going on, but he just said he was interested in someone else. End of story."

Shrugging away from her, I hurried out into the foyer, hitting Weston's number the second I entered. Yeah, he was only in the other ballroom, but I didn't want to talk to him with a whole bunch of witnesses.

Voicemail.

Did I leave a message? Demand an answer?

No. I'd probably end up blubbering like a fool.

Instead, I texted him. *My party isn't the same without you. You and Mercy are both welcome.*

Okay, Mercy wasn't really welcome, per se, but I still wanted to be the guy's friend, even if that meant him having another girl in his life.

I paced the foyer, waiting for a reply.

None came.

Me: *I hope everything's okay. I hate not having you here.*

That probably sounded super desperate, but oh well. It was how I felt.

Even though I knew I shouldn't, I checked out Sierra's Instagram, wanting to see if she posted any photos.

My stomach sank all over again, a dread in me I hadn't felt for the longest time.

Sierra had uploaded a ton of pictures, which wasn't

really the problem. Of course, she was going to make it look like it was the best party ever.

It was the pictures of Weston and Mercy that got to me. Dancing together, laughing, her kissing him on the cheek with him blushing.

Wow. He'd really gotten over me fast. Unless he never liked me that way to begin with.

But Weston *had* liked me, right? He'd told Veronica. He'd flirted with me. Asked me out on a date. Brought me flowers. Almost kissed me. Thanks, Bentley, for totally ruining that moment.

If he got over me quickly, then so be it. I couldn't stop him from liking another person. But that didn't mean shutting me out of his life.

Why couldn't he be friends with me? Did he have to be so rude? Especially on my birthday. This was the first party I'd had since my dad passed, and I wanted it to be memorable.

I wouldn't stop thinking about Weston until I knew what was going on. I wanted answers. And I wanted to end everything with Sierra once and for all.

Even if that meant the most embarrassing picture of me gracing the world forever.

Gathering up every ounce of courage I could muster, I balled my fists and stormed into Ballroom One.

CHAPTER FORTY-FIVE

I frantically searched the room until I found Weston and Mercy dancing near the jazz band, all formal like some old couple. His right hand was on her waist, her left hand on his shoulder, while their other hands clasped together as they swirled around.

At the sight of them, my courage faltered, so I swooped in, not really thinking my actions through. I had to confront him while I had at least an ounce of courage left in me.

Coming up behind Mercy, I tapped her on the shoulder until she looked over at me.

"Mind if I cut in?" I asked. I didn't wait for a response. I grabbed Weston and practically yanked him away from her, dragging him off to a corner.

"Daphne." Hearing my name on Weston's lips tormented me. How had I fallen for this guy so hard and so quickly?

And how had he gotten over me so fast?

He stood in front of me, a pained look in his eyes. When I took a step closer to him, he stepped back, holding out his hand.

"Please, stay there," he said.

Okay. I was done.

I folded my arms. "What's going on?"

He ran his shaky fingers through his hair. "Nothing. I ... uh ... I met someone else." His eyes were on the ground, unable to look at me.

"And that requires you shutting me out of your life completely?"

He finally looked up at me, so much sorrow in his eyes. "This is *killing* me, Daphne. Just, please, leave."

An acoustic version of "Killing Me Softly" by the Fugees strummed in the back of my mind, providing a tragic feel.

"No." I rushed to him, planting myself in front of him before he could react. "Weston, I like you. A lot."

Swallowing, he checked over his shoulder, like he was searching for someone. Probably Mercy. I placed my hands on his cheeks and forced him to look at me.

"If you don't feel the same, then fine," I said, still holding his face. "But you can't deny that we're great friends. We have so much fun together! Why can't we be friends? Did I do something to upset you?"

His soft hand landed on one of mine, holding tight. "Trust me, I want to. It's just, things are complicated right now." He closed his eyes, taking a deep breath. "Being this close to you and not ..." He sighed, his eyes opening back up. A tiny tear ran down his cheek, landing on my hand, the warmth contrasting with the coldness radiating in my heart.

I moved closer, resting my forehead against his. "Talk to me, Weston. Please."

"I can't," he said, so shaky and soft. Pulling back, he pressed his warm lips to my forehead before dropping his hand and stepping away from me. "Just know, this is not how I wanted things to go." He looked me straight in the eye. "You have to stay away from me." Stuffing his hands in his pockets, he backed away. "I'm so sorry, Daphne."

With that, he turned and left the ballroom, Mercy running after him, but not before shooting me a dark look. I shot it right back, twofold.

That hadn't given me the answers I wanted. Clearly, something was keeping him away from me. An easy guess would be Sierra. But what had she said to him that would cause this reaction?

Someone tsked behind me, causing me to twirl around. If I hadn't been in such a foul mood, I would have loved how my dress poofed out with the spin.

Rosalind stood there with her arms folded, nose in the air, a look of triumph in her eyes. She wore a floral jumpsuit that looked amazing on her. I was about to say as such when she spoke.

"That's too bad things didn't work out with Weston," Rosalind said. "Crazy that, of all the girls he could fall for, it's Sierra's cousin."

"Mercy is Sierra's cousin?" Had she set them up? I sought her out, only to find her looking in confusion at Rosalind and me.

Rosalind checked her nails. "Small world, right?" She sighed, looking completely bored with the conversation. "You're going to lose the bet. No one would blame you for raising a white flag."

"So you can upload that picture of me? No, thanks."

She pursed her lips. "Speaking of pictures, some photos that were on my phone have been deleted. You wouldn't know anything about it, would you?"

"Why would that even matter? I know you guys have other copies."

Her mouth twisted into a cruel smile, making me shiver. "Oh, I have *so* much more than that. Photos and videos of you that you definitely wouldn't want anyone to see. Same with your mom. Veronica. Taylor. So much I could use."

"You're stalking *all* of us? Why?"

Her nostrils flared. "I'm not stalking anyone!"

"Says the girl that has secret photos of everyone I love."

"You have secret photos?" Sierra suddenly came into view, her confused gaze on Rosalind.

The smugness in Rosalind's eyes faltered for a fraction of a second, then she was back to full-on diva mode.

"It's called insurance," Rosalind said.

"Insurance for what?" Sierra asked.

Rosalind scoffed like she was completely surprised Sierra would ask such a question. "For the bet." Her eyes narrowed on me. "She *can't* win."

Sierra shook her head. "This is not how I wanted to win. You know that, Rosalind."

I turned to Sierra, hands on my hips. "You blackmailed me with a photo from the very beginning! It was all your idea!"

Sierra pointed to Rosalind. "It was *hers!*"

"How convenient," I snarled. "Someone for you to blame it on instead of taking responsibility for your own actions."

Sierra rolled her eyes. "You sound like an old person."

Kimber approached us, putting a hand on Sierra's and Rosalind's shoulders. "Girls, maybe you should talk about this outside?"

"Maybe we should talk about your daughter and her stalker best friend blackmailing me!" I said, my hands flexing like they wanted to throw something.

Rosalind stomped a foot. "I'm not a stalker!"

I smirked. "Fine. Show Mrs. Winters your phone. Since she won't find any photos of my friends and family on there, you won't mind."

Rosalind took a step toward me, the smugness in her eyes almost blinding. "She already knows about them."

"What?" Sierra asked, looking between her mom and Rosalind.

Kimber blushed. "Honey, we were just looking out for you."

Sierra folded her arms, a brilliant shade of red hiking up her neck, about to invade her entire face. "I told you I could handle this myself. I don't need help from either of you!"

Kimber tsked, taking a soft step toward her daughter. "Oh, honey. You haven't been the same since your dad moved out. Rosalind and I just wanted to fix things for you. Make life better."

"How is stalking Daphne going to make my life better?" Sierra seethed. "How is blackmailing her going to fix anything? You and Dad are done, Mom! He's not coming back!" She waved her hands around. "Me winning some stupid bet isn't going to magically bring our family back together."

I leaned toward her. "I think you're forgetting that you blackmailed me, too."

She hissed at me, causing me to step back.

"Yeesh! Sorry." I motioned to all of them. "The three of you are all the same. You're obsessed with how people view you. You have to feel superior to everyone around you in order to be happy."

"I do not!" Sierra snapped. "And I don't care what people think of me!"

I pointed to her pale pink frou-frou dress. "You look like

a freaking Barbie doll! What happened to the cool Sierra I met when I first moved here?"

She opened her mouth, ready to yell, but then she took a step back. "You thought I was cool?"

I nodded. "The plaid-wearing, red lipstick, friendly girl I met? Yeah, she was cool." I tugged on one of the flowers on the front of her dress. "This girl, though. She's far from cool."

Sierra slapped my hand. "Don't touch my dress!"

"Why?" I cocked my head. "Afraid of ruining your perfect Kennedy vibe you have going on?" I marched over to the bombastic fountain and filled a champagne glass with the cider before going back over to Sierra. "And if this were to suddenly spill on your dress, you wouldn't care?"

Sierra's eyes went wide. Then, she lifted her chin. "No. I wouldn't."

With a grin, I tossed the cider at her, watching it spray all over the front of her dress.

Sierra gasped, spreading her arms wide, staring down in shock at her ruined dress.

I went up and yanked off two of the flowers protruding from the fabric, tossing them on the floor when I was done.

"What are you doing?" Sierra screeched.

"Fixing your dress," I said. "You look ridiculous. You can thank me later."

"Thank you?" Sierra's hands balled into fists.

"You're welcome," I said.

She growled. "I wasn't ... ugh! You're insufferable!"

"Hey, thanks!" I folded my arms. "Can we end this now, please? There are pizza rolls in Ballroom Two waiting for me to consume them."

Cold cider suddenly rained down on me, covering my right side. I turned to find Rosalind holding two empty champagne glasses, smiling triumphantly at me. She set the glasses on a table and pulled out her phone, smirking. "I think I'll post a picture right now."

"Don't you dare," I snarled.

Rosalind's eyes held a challenge. "Try and stop me."

I could never turn down a challenge. I needed to be the lion, not the cub, and make Taylor proud.

In my head, I cranked up "My Body" by Young the Giant, getting myself in the right mindset.

With a roar, I ran at Rosalind, wrapping my arms around her middle and pushing her backward. Rosalind shrieked, pounding weakly at my back, surprised at my attack.

"Say you won't post the photos, and I'll back off," I said, still driving her back.

"No, you freak!"

Freak. The same thing my bullies used to call me because I sang and danced everywhere I went. It flooded me with bad memories. All of them circling around me, taunting me, pushing me.

This ended now.

Releasing her, I snatched a tray of escargot from a nearby waiter and started pelting Rosalind.

"Delete the photos!" I said before I threw a round of escargot at her.

Rosalind threw up her arms to block her face. "Stop!"

"I'll stop when you delete the photos!"

She lowered her arms. "I can't delete anything with you throwing things at me!"

Taking the last snail from the tray, I threw it at her, hitting her smack in the nose.

She squealed, flailing her arms around. "It touched me!"

"What's going on?" Mom came into view, staring at the four of us in shock.

I pointed at Rosalind. "She's blackmailing me with a bunch of not-so-nice photos of me, you, basically everyone I know and love." Then I pointed at Sierra. "So is she!"

"It's one photo!" Sierra said.

I scoffed. "Is that supposed to make it any better?"

"What photos?" Mom asked, worry dancing in her eyes. "What does she have?"

Kimber stepped forward. "Ones that would make Ian turn over in his grave."

Mom and I gasped at the same time. Mom went in front of Kimber, glaring at her with a hatred I'd never seen on her before. "Don't you *dare* say his name or bring him into this." She heaved with anger, and I worried she might throw a punch. I wasn't sure if I'd stop her if she tried. I kind of wanted to punch Kimber in the face myself.

Kimber snarled. "We all know he made the wrong choice back then."

Mom shook her head, pointing at Sierra and me. "You look at those beautiful girls and say that again."

The hatred in Kimber's eyes dimmed as she glanced over at Sierra.

Sierra had shrunk back, clearly embarrassed by her mom.

This whole thing had gotten way out of control. I held out my hand to Rosalind. "Let me see your phone."

"No!" Rosalind said.

"Stop being such a brat, and do the right thing," I said, still holding out my hand.

"Give her the phone, Rosalind," Sierra said, stepping up beside me. "Or I'll take it from you."

Surprise flashed on Rosalind's face. "Sierra, I was doing this for you."

Sierra shook her head. "You were doing this for my mom. And yourself. Now, hand over the phone."

"Where's the birthday girl?" Mr. Winters' voice boomed from the right, making us all look at him. He came toward us, completely oblivious to our argument, with a huge smile on his face, and holding a large cake in his hands. He started singing *Happy Birthday* in a rich baritone, but when no one joined him, he trailed off, looking around the quiet room.

"Not now, Dad," Sierra said, still glaring at Rosalind. "Seriously, hand over your phone. Now."

Rosalind wriggled her phone. "You want it, come and get it."

Sierra and I exchanged a glance before we lunged at Rosalind, our arms outstretched. With a squeal, Rosalind ran to the side, right into Mr. Winters and the birthday cake. It splattered against her, chunks of cake flying everywhere, smacking into Sierra and me right as we got to Rosalind. With Rosalind still squealing like a pig, freaking out about the cake all over her, Sierra and I scrambled to get the phone from her hands.

As soon as my hand wrapped around the phone, I yanked it from Rosalind's grip and stepped back. My foot landed on a chunk of cake, my shoe sliding over the frosting, and sending me spiraling down, the phone flying into the air. A searing pain radiated through my cheekbone as my face smacked into the side of the lion fountain, making it tilt to the side. Sparkling cider poured down on me, drenching me through, as I landed with a thump on the marble floor.

Sierra and Mom both hurried over, pulling me away from the spilling fountain.

I pressed a hand to my cheek.

"You're bleeding!" Sierra looked over at someone, but I closed my eyes, trying to stop my world from spinning. "Bentley, go find some towels!"

The sound of his shoes striking marble echoed throughout the ballroom as he scampered away.

It took a second to regain my bearings, everything finally coming to a stop. I opened my eyes to see Sierra and my mom staring at me, concern in their eyes.

"Sweetie?" Mom moved the wet curl that clung to my face, covering my eye. "Can you focus on me?"

"Um, hello!" Rosalind motioned to her cake-covered body. "I'm here, too!"

"You're not the one who hit your face!" Sierra snapped. "She could have a concussion."

"But my phone!" Rosalind whined, bending down and picking up the remnants of her shattered phone.

Sierra rolled her eyes. "You can get a new one. Chill out."

Bentley came running back into the room with Sebastian on his heels, both of them holding towels. Sebastian just tossed one at Rosalind—who caught it against her chest, her jaw hanging wide—before he came to me, wrapping a towel around my body. I clutched onto the towel, grateful for even the slightest bit of warmth.

Bentley pressed another towel to my cheek, holding it in place. "This cut looks really bad."

Mom nodded. "She's going to need stitches. Help me get her up."

Together, Mom and Bentley got me to my feet, through the speechless crowd, and out of the house. Cody stood on the curved driveway, watching as the valet drove his car up to the front.

Cody held open the back door, so Mom and I could climb in before he got into the driver's seat and drove off.

I'd given Cody a hard time for acting like such a dad. But the fact that he moved so quickly, knew to get the car as soon as he saw me fall, and didn't say a word, made me grateful for his fatherly ways.

CHAPTER FORTY-SIX

I sat on the hospital bed, wishing I wasn't in a slopping wet dress. Especially one covered in blood.

Mom checked her phone. "Veronica and Taylor are going to get you a fresh set of clothes."

"Thank goodness," I said.

Cody looked at the gash on my cheek and whistled. "Looks like the fountain won this round."

"Feels like it, too," I mumbled. To say my face was sore was a grave understatement.

Bentley stood off in the corner, fuming. Sierra kept a wide distance, standing closer to me.

Bentley and Sierra had followed us to the hospital, and by the way he was reacting, Sierra had spilled the beans about the bet. I had a feeling he'd eventually get over it. It was just a lot to take in at the moment. He hated bullies as much as I did.

Mom's phone rang. "It's my parents. I'm just going to step outside for a sec." She looked at me. "You okay?"

I smiled over at Sierra, and she returned the gesture. "I'll be fine."

Mom hesitantly glanced between us, but finally left the room, answering her phone in the process.

A nurse opened the curtain, joining us near the bed.

Sierra and I shared a quick glance. The guy was *hot*.

"Looks like you had a rough night," the nurse said, taking in my dress before turning his attention to my cheek. "I'm Dexter. Daphne, right?"

I nodded. "You're not a serial killer, are you?"

Dexter chuckled. "No. Even if I was, I would kill other serial killers. So, unless you're a serial killer yourself, you're safe."

"Whew," I said. "Good thing I'm not a serial killer." I sighed. "My mom won't let me watch the series."

Dexter smiled. "That's probably a good thing. That show is ... intense." He cleaned up my wound. "You in pain?"

"A little," I said. "But not unbearable." I stared at all the blood on his gloves, becoming light-headed. "Not good with blood, though."

Sierra took my hand. "So, you'd be a horrible serial killer."

"Poison," I said, closing my eyes. I so didn't want to watch whatever Dexter was doing. "No blood involved."

"Should I be worried you answered that so quickly?" Sierra asked, sarcasm in her tone.

"Maybe a little." I squeezed her hand. "Neighbor."

"So, what happened?" Dexter asked.

I sighed. "A questionable bet, a scandalous photo, a stalker, and a lion fountain."

Dexter laughed. "Sounds like the start to a good horror story."

Sierra put her other hand over our clasped hands. "I'm so sorry, Daphne. This whole thing got out of hand. I've just been upset since my dad moved out."

"I heard your mom say that," I said. "When did that happen?"

Sierra sighed. "A couple of months ago. Before you guys even got here."

"That's why you wanted to win the bet so badly," I said, everything coming together. "In hopes of your parents getting back together."

Dexter put his hand on my chin, stopping me from moving. Oh, yeah. The guy was sewing up my face.

"Mom never got over your dad choosing another girl," Sierra said.

"That was *so* long ago." I still wouldn't open my eyes. Pretending like a needle wasn't frolicking through my skin was the best way to go.

"I know," Sierra said. "She really loved your dad. Like, a lot. More than she's ever loved my dad."

I had no idea her feelings had been that strong.

"Oh." I blew out a breath. "Us moving in was probably a trigger. Your dad moves out, then the lady who took her first love moves in next door and has a daughter with sweet dance moves."

Sierra chuckled. "And that daughter looks *exactly* like Laura did when they first went through this whole thing." She squeezed my hand. "I took everything out on you because I could. But I shouldn't have. My parents' problems aren't your fault. I think I need to accept the fact that they aren't going to stay together."

"I'm sorry, Sierra," I said. "If you ever need someone to talk to, I'm right next door."

"You know, your likable personality made it *really* hard to hate you through all of this."

"I'll try to rein in my awesomeness around you."

Sierra laughed. "Never rein yourself in around me. I like you just the way you are, Daphne."

I finally opened my eyes. "Aww, we had a moment." I tried to look over at Bentley, but Dexter held me in place. "Bentley, you were witness to this special moment."

He came into view, a soft smile on his face. "I don't think I'll ever understand girls."

Dexter grinned. "You won't."

Bentley and Sierra shared a small smile, and I hoped that meant everything would work out between them. With Sierra back to being herself, the two would go great together.

Veronica and Taylor ran into the room.

"What happened?" Veronica asked.

"Daph, are you okay?" Taylor asked. Then her gaze went to Dexter, and her smoldering smile landed on her face.

Sierra stood, grinning at me. "Think that's my cue to leave. I'll come by tomorrow, Daphne, and see how you're doing."

Bentley patted my leg. "Happy birthday, Daphne."

"Thanks, Bentley."

He and Sierra left, and I couldn't help but notice he put his hand on the small of her back as they went out the door.

Taylor put her hands on her head. "My mind is officially blown."

Veronica gawked at the door. "Tell us everything. Now."

"I'm going to stop you right there," Dexter said. "I really need Daphne to stop moving so much."

I held out my hand to Mom as she reentered the room. She rushed to my side, taking the seat Sierra had vacated, her warm hands wrapping around mine. This obviously wasn't how I wanted to end my seventeenth birthday, but having my friends and mom with me meant the world.

I glanced back at Cody, who offered me a warm smile. Huh. I even liked having him here. Go figure.

*S*ierra texted me later that night after I'd gotten home from the hospital, taken a long, hot shower, and changed into my Cheer Bear onesie, hoping to fill myself with cheer.

Sierra: *Photos and videos are deleted. All of them.*

Me: *Positive?*

Sierra: *Yep. I've never seen this side of Rosalind before. It's kind of creepy.*

Me: *Kind of? The girl was stalking me and a whole bunch of other people.*

Sierra: *Okay, fine, totally creepy. How are you feeling?*

Me: *Sore. My cheek hurts. I have a headache. But I'll live.*

Sierra: *Good. By the way, Rosalind admitted to blackmailing Weston. Said she'd upload all those pictures if he didn't pretend he wasn't interested in you.*

My heart swelled. That was why he'd shut me out. It wasn't that he didn't like me. He was trying to protect me. Seriously, the guy couldn't get more amazing.

But that still didn't change the fact that he had Mercy in his life now. Even if it had started as a way to prove he was over me, I'd seen the uploaded pictures. The ones of them flirting. Her kissing his cheek, causing him to blush. You can't fake that.

Sierra: *I talked to Mercy. She said she likes Weston, but she could tell he was hung up on someone else. Once I explained everything, she understood. She's going to back off of him.*

For some reason, that didn't make me feel all that better. I didn't want to be his seconds. I wanted him to choose me. To want me.

Me: *Thanks.*

Sierra: *By the way, I ended up enjoying that playlist you sent me.*

Me: *The stalker one?*

Sierra: *Yep. You have really great taste in music. Anyway, good night. Happy birthday!*

Me: *Happy birthday to you, too! Night.*

I checked the time. Almost midnight.

I thought back to my interaction with Weston inside Ballroom One. He'd looked so pained. So torn. No matter how he felt, the guy deserved to know the truth.

Not caring about the time, I texted him.

Me: *The photos are deleted. The ones Rosalind had.*

I went to toss my phone to the side when I saw the little dots dancing across the screen. Weston was already replying. Then the dots stopped. Then they started again. Then stopped.

Okay, this guy was killing me.

Suddenly, my screen lit up. He was calling.

I cleared my throat before I answered, trying to sound calm, even though my heart was about to burst out of my chest. "Hey, Weston."

"Are you serious?" he asked, so much hope in his tone.

"Supposedly." I grabbed some of my damp hair, twirling

it around my finger. "Even if she has some secret photos somewhere, I don't care anymore. I'm done with her and anyone else trying to ruin my life."

Weston blew out a loud, long breath. "You have no idea how happy this makes me." Pause. "I'll be there in ten."

He ended the call.

Be here in ten? He was coming over? I glanced down at my onesie, debating what to do. Did I change? I couldn't get back in my fancy dress. It was ruined from the cider shower —and bleeding on it.

I touched my cheek before I hopped out of my hammock chair, running to the mirror behind my closet door.

I was a total mess. My right eye was black and blue, all the skin swollen. No makeup. In a Care Bear onesie. A bandage covering the stitches on my cheek. Hair still drying from my shower, all wavy and out of control.

But this was me. I didn't care what those other girls or Rosalind said about me. I wasn't a freak. I wasn't weird. I was Daphne. A little quirky, yeah, but that was what made me fun.

If Weston couldn't accept me like this, then what was the point?

CHAPTER FORTY-SEVEN

*a*fter pulling my hair back in a ponytail—I didn't want to give myself the opportunity to twirl it—I snuck outside, sitting down on the porch steps.

It was a little chilly out, but with my onesie, it kept me nice and warm. Seriously, they were the greatest creation ever.

When Weston's van pulled along the curb, I went to stand, but dizziness overcame me, so I plopped back down. My head was still woozy from the hit.

Weston got out of the van, coming around to the sidewalk, pausing when he saw me sitting there. The streetlamp let me see his gorgeous face and that adorable crooked smile. He held something in his hand—I think a couple of bottles of soda—but my focus couldn't peel away from his face. He came closer, his smile fading when he finally saw my face, his eyes going wide.

He rushed forward, dropping to his knees in front of me, setting the bottles down, and resting his hand on my good cheek. "What happened?"

I pressed my fingers against my bandage. Oh, yeah. "Guess you didn't hear?"

He shook his head. "No. I was with ..." He trailed off, his hand leaving my face, but I quickly grabbed it, putting it back against my cheek.

"Mercy," I said. "You can say her name."

Closing his eyes, he sighed. "I never actually liked her. Not like *that*."

I smiled. "I saw the picture of her kissing your cheek." I squeezed his hand. "Can't hide a blush."

His eyes shot open. "Yeah, I went red. In embarrassment, not, like, in happiness or anything."

I didn't know why, but I loved how frazzled he was acting. It reflected what I felt on the inside.

"I couldn't believe how forward she was being," he muttered. "I just met her."

I went to lower my hand, realizing that I, myself, was being a little forward, having him so close to me, his hand on my face.

But Weston freaked out again. "I'm not talking about you! You can be forward all you want. I mean. That's not!" He mumbled something under his breath, making me smile.

Scooting over on the step, I patted the spot next to me, which he happily took, relief flashing in his eyes.

I needed, no *wanted*, to get everything off my chest.

"I made a totally stupid, questionable, and ridiculous bet." I spewed the words out so fast, I was surprised they didn't send Weston flying backward.

"What?" he asked.

I took a deep breath and then dove in, going all the way back to the beginning, telling him all about my mom, my dad, and Mrs. Winters. I divulged everything about my bullies in elementary school, calling me a freak and weirdo, and my inability to stand up for myself back then. I told him about the bet with Sierra, Rosalind's involvement—including the blowup at the party—and how it had been killing me, because I hadn't been expecting so much collateral damage.

"The thing is, I like Bentley," I rattled off, staring at my hands. "He's been a good friend, but there was never that spark, you know? I mean, we touched and nothing. Then I barely touch you, and I'm like totally freaking out, sparks flying everywhere. I worry they'll set everything around me on fire. Or me. *This girl is on fire!*" I sang that last part, because I can't dial myself down when I'm cranked up. "The whole bet was stupid. I wasn't expecting to fall for you during the whole event. It just happened. You're just unbelievably perfect and beyond gorgeous. And that smile? Swoon."

I went to grab some of my hair to twirl, but then remembered I'd pulled it back. So, I settled on twiddling my thumbs. "Your taste in music is amazing. I love that I can sing and dance in front of you, and you don't look at me like I'm a freak. I mean, you'll join me, which is awesome. You're like the guy of my dreams."

I leaned back, placing my palms on the porch. "From the moment we practiced those dances in my living room, I knew I wanted to go to the ball with you and not Bentley. And don't even get me started on the date." I scoffed. "Veronica told me to stop flirting with you, but I didn't realize I *was* flirting. It's just natural around you. Hormones, am I right?"

I glanced over at Weston, only to see him staring at me with his jaw hanging wide open. What was his problem? It was just a bet. Nothing to get worked up over.

Then I clamped my hand over my mouth, realizing I'd

laid my feelings for him out there, not even batting an eye while doing it. I had said that stuff OUT LOUD.

I was the one with the problem.

I froze, not sure what to do. Did I go into the house and lock the door? Curl into a ball on the porch, assuming the fetal position? Tell him I was just joking and to disregard everything I'd said? Only, then I'd be lying to him again.

Maybe I just needed to move on. Pretend the whole thing was normal.

I smiled at him. "Would you like to go to the ball with me tomorrow night?" I glanced at my watch, seeing it was already after midnight. "Well, tonight, technically. I know it's totally last minute, and you don't have to dress up. I mean, I am. And my mom and Cody are as well, but you don't have to. Will that be weird? Going on a double date with my mom and her twenty-four-year-old boyfriend?"

His lips moved like he wanted to speak, but nothing was coming out. Crap. I'd broken Weston.

I had to stop myself from pulling the hood of my onesie over my head and slinking away. Yet my mind kept spinning, my mouth unable to stop.

"I mean, there's always the bright orange cummerbund. Maybe Bentley would let you borrow his suit. Although, he's taller than you. But I guess my mom could pin the legs up or something." I snapped my fingers. "Duh! The Mr. Bingley outfit you wore for the skit. He's my favorite. Seriously, if I had to choose between him and Mr. Darcy, there would be no hesitation on my part. I'd snatch Bingley right up." I pulled my legs into my chest, wrapping my arms around them. "I'm still talking out loud. Why can't I stop?"

Closing my eyes, I took deep breaths, feeling the panic attack coming. I'd told Weston that *I fell* for him. That was pretty much the equivalent of saying, "I love you." And now he'd lost his ability to speak. I had turned him mute.

The deep breaths weren't working. I wheezed, grasping at every breath I could. The fire sprang to life in my lungs, spreading like a wildfire throughout my body. Sweat broke out on my neck and forehead. Plus, like every other part of my body.

I found myself rocking where I sat, squeezing my legs so hard against my chest like I could squeeze the panic attack out of me.

My lips. So dry. Same with my mouth. I needed water. An extra freaking large Cherry Coke. Chapstick would have been good, too. Maybe a new personality. Or a muzzle for my yapping mouth.

Maybe it wasn't too late to move back to Utah. Yeah, the house had sold rather quickly, but we could find somewhere else. Or live with Aunt Shannon until we found a place.

A warm hand landed on my cheek, and I peeled my eyes open to see Weston kneeling before me, holding two bottles of Cherry Coke. What?

Slowly lowering my legs, I stared into his calm eyes, everything coming into place.

Weston. Cherry Coke.

I fell for him all over again.

Snatching one of the bottles from his hand, I twisted off the cap and started chugging. The sweet, cold, bubbly liquid against my throat was just what I needed. It flowed like a river through me, something beautiful and magical. My hand reached out, fumbling to find the other bottle. When I finally got it, I pressed it against my neck—still drinking the other one—and let the cool plastic do its work.

My heart slowed, but still raced way too fast.

When I finished the bottle, Weston took it from my

hand. I kept the other one against my neck, still needing to cool down.

Weston placed a hand on my knee, looking me straight in the eye. "Breathe, Daphne. All the happy things. Cherry Coke. Your family. Friends." He smirked. "Me." When I sucked in a sharp breath, my breathing intensifying, he quickly shook his head. "Nope. Not me. Sorry. You weren't ready for that." He scrunched his face, thinking. The sight alone brought my heart rate back down. Calming me.

His fingers drummed along my knee, though I wasn't sure he was aware he was doing it. "Mr. Bingley? Care Bears. Uh. Let's see. Captain America, obviously. He's the epitome of cool and collected."

I nodded my agreement, making him smile. Our eyes locked, and his nose inched up, that adorable crooked smile taking over his face. Instead of sending my heart skyrocketing like I thought it would, an immediate calm wove through me.

I set the bottle on the porch and then turned back to Weston, wrapping my arms around his neck. With his arms around my back, he pulled me closer, hugging tight.

My heart steadied, finding the same rhythm as his. We breathed together, holding one another close, and man, this moment was perfect.

Weston lightened his hold on me so he could pull back and look at me. "Yes."

I furrowed my eyebrows, my arms still around his neck. "Yes, what?"

He smiled. "Yes, to the ball. I'd love to go with you."

I grinned madly before my cheeks flared. "I really said all the stuff in front of you, didn't I?"

He slowly nodded, then pressed his forehead against mine. "It's okay, though, because I feel the same way."

"Really?"

"Really."

I interlocked my fingers behind his neck, tugging him lightly. Just enough to say, hey, kiss me already, but without being *too* forceful.

Every moment with Weston had been intense. Suddenly blazing hot, difficult to breathe, not being able to think straight. But when his warm lips met mine, all the noise around us shut off, an instant peace. It was just him and me, our lips moving in a harmony *way* better than our singing voices, and just as beautiful. Everything about it felt right. Perfect. Just the way it was supposed to be.

Songs switched around in my head, like it was trying to find the right song for the moment. "Dibs" by Kelsea Ballerini. Static. "At Last" by Etta James. Static. "The Way You Make Me Feel" by Michael Jackson.

Static.

My mind finally settled on "10,000 Hours" by Dan + Shay. Perfect.

Something inside me lit up, not in a fire way like I'd be sweating in seconds, but in a clarification way. A moment of all the stars in my mind aligning.

Weston was *the one.*

My parents always said they had an instant connection. Something raw and real. They knew they'd spend the rest of their lives together, even with stupid Kimber ... uh, whatever her maiden name was ... trying to interfere.

It would sound crazy to anyone, but I'd found my Ian. I wasn't sure if Veronica or Taylor would understand. I mean, we were seventeen for crying out loud. Mom might possibly understand since she went through the same thing, but I'd hold this nugget of information to myself for a long time.

Although, maybe I could make some bet on it. I'd totally win.

Okay, no bet.

Weston pulled back, a soft smile on his face. "What song was playing in your head while we kissed?"

I ran a finger along his jaw, making him shiver and me smile. "What makes you think there was a song playing?"

He chuckled. "There's always music playing in there." He twisted his lips in thought. "I went through a whole bunch. 'All of Me' by John Legend. 'If I Can't Have You' by Shawn Mendes." He shrugged. "I finally settled on '10,000 Hours' by Dan + Shay."

Not containing my smile, I kissed him again, my hands on his cheeks. He really was my person.

"Daphne." Mom's voice rang out from the doorbell system, startling Weston and me.

I looked over my shoulder at the camera. "I'm getting my birthday kiss, woman!"

Weston choked on a laugh in front of me.

"Technically, your birthday is over," Mom said through the speaker.

"Yeah, okay, fine." I sighed. "Just one more minute."

"Sixty seconds, starting now." She sounded like a robot.

I turned back to Weston. "Guess that's my cue."

Weston stood, helping me to my feet as he did. He patted his pockets, his eyes going wide in concern.

"What?" I asked.

He grunted. "In my rush to come over, I forgot your birthday present."

"I thought the Cherry Cokes were my present."

"Those were emergency backups in case you had a panic attack." He took my hands in his. "I'll bring your real present tomorrow, promise." He leaned in, softly kissing me on the lips. When he pulled back, he wore a shy smile that made my heart flip. "Will you be my girlfriend?"

"YES!" I threw my arms around his neck with so much force, he stumbled backward down the walkway, but luckily saved us from crashing to the ground.

"I need to start bracing myself for your hugs," he said through his laugh.

I kissed him repeatedly on the cheek. "Yeah, you do."

"Ten seconds," Mom sang.

My eyebrows shot up. "Do you think something will explode if I don't get inside in time?"

"I don't want to find out." He leaned back, kissing my non-stitched cheek. "Goodnight, Daphne."

"Night, Weston."

I hurried inside to find Mom standing in the entryway.

"Speaking of stalkers," I said.

Mom rolled her eyes. "Hey, if you're going to spy on me, I'll do the same." She grinned. "Did I hear the word 'girlfriend'?"

"You were listening, too?"

Mom put an arm around my shoulder. "Just a little bit."

"Well, yes, you did."

She hugged me tight. "I'm happy for you. I really like him." When she released me, her face turned serious. "But if I ever catch Weston over here after midnight again, I'll ground you for the rest of your life."

"Yeesh. Got it. No late night rendezvouses. For *either* of us."

She backed toward the hallway. "What do you think he got you for your birthday?"

I clasped my hands together, doing a little shuffle in my steps. "I don't know, but I can't wait to find out!"

Mom blew me a kiss. "Night, my Daphne girl. Love you."

"Love you, too, Mom."

She stood in the hallway, arms folded, eyebrows quirked. She really wanted to make sure I made it to my bedroom. Alone. What kind of girl did she think I was?

"Get your mind out of the gutter, young lady!" I said.

I ran to my bedroom before she could retaliate, leaving a laughing Mom behind me.

CHAPTER FORTY-EIGHT

*a*s much as it pained me to admit, not only did I like Cody, but his friends were freaking awesome. They welcomed Weston and me with open arms, acting like we'd all been friends for years, and it wasn't weird to have two teenagers there.

It put both Weston and me at ease within minutes of showing up for the party.

I straightened out Weston's cravat. "You look so hot."

He held onto the lapel of his blazer, lifting his chin a little. "I daresay, I do look smashing tonight."

Laughing, I pushed his shoulder. He caught my hand and pulled me close to him, arm wrapped around me, whispering in my ear. "And you look positively radiant."

That was it. I was investing in a misting fan, because, boy, oh boy, it was hot in the room. I hoped that thrilling feeling would never leave. The overwhelming hormones of having the guy so close to me, saying and doing flirty things. It was the perfect high.

We all lined up in the family room of the guy hosting

the party. The ladies curtsied while the men bowed before we began our dance.

As we followed the steps—only messing up a little bit—I couldn't contain my smile. I loved that Weston was willing to dress up and do dances from the Regency Era with me. How many boyfriends would agree to that?

Then, my smile doubled at the thought of him being my boyfriend.

Weston came close to me, my gloved hand touching his bare hand as we danced to the music.

"Would you really choose Mr. Bingley?" he asked, his eyebrow arched.

"Definitely." I twirled around him. "Mr. Darcy has *nothing* on him."

I spun away from him, moving to my next partner, who happened to be Cody.

"Ah, young Miss Richards," he said with a British accent. "How are you doing on this fine evening?"

I had to bite back my laugh. Not that he was bad at the accent or anything, just the ridiculousness of the whole situation.

"Wonderful, thank you," I finally said. "I have been enjoying the weather we've been having."

"Much better than snow, I presume?" he asked.

I nodded. "Much. Have you been? In snow?"

He shook his head. "I usually go on holiday somewhere warm."

I circled away from him, passing Mom on my way back to Weston.

"We're taking Cody with us on our next trip back to Utah," I said to her. "The guy has never been in snow!"

Huh. The thought of Cody going on a vacation with my mom and me didn't bother me. I mean, no way they'd sleep in the same room. Probably not even at the same place if I had my say. But I liked how nicely he fit in my family.

By the huge grin on Cody's face, you'd think I'd made his night. In fact, Mom's smile was just as big.

After the dance ended, Weston took me out to the porch swing in the front of the house. It was a tad chilly outside, but not too bad. I snuggled into Weston to keep warm, though. He had his arm around me, holding me close.

"Having fun?" I asked.

"A lot more than I thought I would." He fiddled with the lace on the sleeve of my dress. "I wasn't too sure about a Regency ball at some random dude's house."

I snickered. "Well, you better get used to it. I have a feeling Cody will be inviting us to more costume parties in the future."

He kissed the top of my head. "If you're there, then I'm in." He pulled a square box from his pocket, wrapped up in Care Bear paper. "Your birthday present, as promised."

Shimmying, I snatched it from his hands, then carefully opened the package, trying not to rip it too much.

"Are you one of those people who keep wrapping paper?" he asked, amused.

"No, I would just feel terrible if I decapitated a Care Bear or something." I set the wrapping in my lap, then took off the lid.

It was a necklace, a Captain America shield on a silver chain. I picked it up, running my finger over the front. "I love it."

"Check the back," he said.

I turned it over to see an engraving. *I'm with you until the end of the line.*

"Weston," I whispered. "This is absolutely perfect."

He kissed my cheek. "So are you."

I held the necklace out to him. "Will you put it on me?"

"Of course." He wrapped it around my neck, clasping it together.

I looked at it, hanging against my chest. "Totally goes with the Regency dress, doesn't it?"

He laughed. "Totally."

Putting my hand on his cheek, I rubbed my thumb across his freckles, something I'd wanted to do the day we met. Thank goodness I'd kept my hands to myself back then, because how weird would that have been?

He spoke in a low, reverent tone. "I am, you know. With you until the end of the line."

"Same."

He kissed me softly, one hand on my neck, the other on my waist. I kept my hand on his cheek, wanting to feel his warmth.

"Do we have to go back inside?" he whispered.

"I'm not in a hurry," I said.

With a smile, he kissed me again, pulling me close to him, while "Speechless" by Dan + Shay serenaded the moment in my mind.

EPILOGUE

The flashes from Cody's camera blinded me momentarily, making me stumble over a fake vine running along the gym floor. Thankfully, Weston was right there, arm already hooked with mine, keeping me from face-planting as we walked into prom.

As I blinked away the spots dancing across my vision, Cody came up next to us, showing us the picture he took with his digital camera. In addition to all his other amazing skills, the man was a wonderful photographer. I hadn't found a flaw in him yet, but I'd never give up, no matter how long he and Mom stayed together.

"Turned out perfect," Cody said, smiling wide.

He'd caught both Weston and me in a moment of awe as we entered the gym, seeing how the entire place had been transformed into a beautiful garden. Large, fake, weeping trees surrounded the perimeter, their vines running across the ground—total trip hazard, but whatever. Different style fountains canvased the area, adding a serene feel. Strings of lights hung from the ceiling and trees, giving the whole thing a romantic vibe. Flowers, benches, and fake stone paths filled the space, with a large opening in the middle for dancing. There was even a small, wooden bridge crossing over a fake pond, blue shimmering paper beneath it.

Mom saddled up next to Cody, beaming at the screen. "Look at you two. So adorable."

She had on a navy knee-length dress, Cody with a matching navy suit and tie.

Mom's eyes lit up as she took in the background behind Weston and me. "Oh, go stand in front of that tree."

Without waiting for a reply, she ushered us to the tree, making sure we were in the correct position. She adjusted the silk bottom of my magenta evening gown, then made sure the lace halter top was smoothed out.

She eyed my Captain America necklace. "Any chance you would take ..."

"Nope," I said, cutting her off. "It stays on until I die."

Weston looked fake offended. "You aren't going to be buried with it? Harsh."

I rolled my eyes. "Bad phrasing. It's never coming off, okay?"

Face all business, Mom took a stray curl of mine and set it against my cheek, right above my faint scar. "Make sure you smile with your teeth."

I pushed her hand away. "Mom, I know how to smile."

"I know, but you always look so beautiful with your big smile." She moved onto Weston, straightening out his magenta bow tie. "This white suit with the bright pink was a brilliant move. Makes it pop."

Weston grinned at my mom, his crooked lips making me want to kiss him.

"It was Daphne's idea," he said.

"Laura," Cody said as he pointed the camera at us, adjusting the lens. "Out of the frame."

"Just a second!" she hissed, getting on her tiptoes and fluffing out some of Weston's hair.

I sighed. "Mom, this is prom, not our wedding."

Weston snickered, causing Mom to glare and his laugh to cut off abruptly. With her eyes narrowed, she stepped back so Cody could take pictures of us.

I had my arm wrapped around Weston's waist, my other hand holding onto the lapel of his jacket. "I told you that you look hot tonight, right?"

He smiled, facing the camera. "Yep. Almost as many times as I've told you that you look gorgeous." He pressed his warm lips against my cheek, Cody's flash going off in the background.

"Us next!" Taylor said, rushing over and pushing us out of the way. She yanked a confused Zander along with her until they were in front of the tree. She wore an emerald green halter top dress that went to just above her knees, plus her black leather jacket that was so perfectly her.

Zander had on a light-gray suit with a green tie to match her dress. Taylor threw her arms around him, kicking up her leg behind her.

"Make sure my booties are in the picture!" Taylor said to Cody. She dropped her smile, turning on her sexy smolder for the camera. Zander had a brooding thing going on that made them look like a couple on the cover of a magazine.

Veronica and DeShawn came next, looking all debonair and cool. Veronica's long, maroon dress hung nicely around her curves, the striped back showing some of her smooth skin. DeShawn wore a maroon suit, his muscular build and sure stance looking like he was at the NFL draft. Which, with his talent, that day would probably come in a few years.

Sierra and Bentley came last, and my heart swelled. Seeing Sierra back in her black with red lipstick made me happy. Her black dress was two pieces, a long, silk skirt and the black top with long, sheer sleeves. Bentley looked like James Bond with his classic black tux, one hand on the small of Sierra's back, the other tucked in his pocket.

Mom took the liberty of fixing everyone's hair and clothes, making sure the pictures were perfect.

Weston pressed his lips against my ear. "She's not going to follow us around all night, is she?"

"I sure hope not," I said.

Mom and Cody had signed up to be chaperones, which I had mixed feelings about. Having Cody there to snap candid pictures throughout the night was going to be priceless. But having Mom at my prom had the chance of being all sorts of awkward.

I patted Weston's chest. "We better keep the making out to a minimum."

He grinned. "I make no promises."

A flash made us whip our heads to the right. Cody narrowed his eyes at the screen, a small smirk on his lips. "What were you two talking about? You both have a mischievous look in your eyes."

"Nothing," Weston and I said at the same time.

"Jinx!" I quickly counted to ten. "You owe me a Cherry Coke."

He rubbed the back of his neck. "You count way too fast. I'm not even sure you said all the numbers."

Mom took Cody's arm and steered him away from us. She smiled at me as they backtracked. "Just pretend like we aren't here. You two have fun!"

Sierra scoffed behind me. "How can we pretend they

aren't here?" Her glare fixed onto her mom standing near the refreshments. "I can't believe our moms did this to us."

I patted her arm, fake consoling her. "This was a chance for them to work through their differences and whatever other crap they said to us."

Mom and Kimber had been slowly working on their relationship, seeing as they were neighbors and their daughters were now friends. It had been rough, with lots of snarky comments and burns, but their hatred for each other had chipped away, revealing the possibility that they could be civil to one another. They'd helped plan prom, making a surprisingly efficient team. It probably helped that they wanted to limit the time they were around each other.

It also helped that Sierra's parents had finally filed for divorce. I mean, divorce sucked, but everyone in their family had seemed happier since the papers were signed. Sometimes fresh starts were needed.

Bentley draped his arm around Sierra, smiling at Weston and me. "Twenty bucks says Sierra and I win Prom King and Queen."

"No bets!" Sierra and I shouted.

Bentley grimaced. "Yeesh. Okay." His smile came back. "But we're so winning."

He leaned down, kissing a grinning Sierra on the lips. They really did go well together. And it had been nice that we could double date with them, everyone now with the person they were meant to be with.

"What a Man Gotta Do" by the Jonas Brothers started playing from the speakers. Weston and I turned to each other, shouting at the same time, "I love this song!"

We ran out onto the dance floor, immediately finding the groove. Out of the corner of my eye, I could see Cody snapping pictures, and I did my best to ignore him, focusing on having the time of my life with Weston.

The others came over and joined us, the eight of us creating a circle as we danced. Laughter bubbled up inside as I watched everyone let loose, none of us caring how we looked.

When it came time to announce Prom King and Queen, we lined up, facing the front of the room.

"We so got this," Bentley said.

"Of course we do," Sierra said.

Everyone at school had loved them together, becoming the power couple I worried they'd become.

Weston wrapped his arms around me, pulling my back into his chest and whispering in my ear. "But they don't have what we do."

No, they certainly didn't. Weston and I had something special. We eased into each other's lives naturally, making the perfect blend. I'd never been so happy in my life.

Kimber and Mom were standing on the stage, for once being next to each other without looking like they wanted to kill the other. They were actually smiling. Like, genuine smiles.

"And the Prom King and Queen are," Mom started, doing a little shimmy with her shoulders.

Kimber opened the envelope like this was the freaking Oscars or something. She grinned madly, and my heart sunk.

Bentley and Sierra had won.

Sierra squealed next to me as she and Bentley moved toward the stage.

"Taylor Thomas and Zander Morris!" Kimber shouted into the microphone.

Bentley and Sierra skidded to a stop, spinning around to look at the other couple in shock.

Taylor threw her body around Zander as he lifted her off the ground and spun around, both of them shouting in glee.

"What in the what?" I whispered.

"Oh, look at that," Veronica said next to me, the sarcasm obvious. "Another couple in the universe besides you guys. So weird."

I shoved her on the arm, making her laugh.

As I watched Taylor and Zander get crowned, I couldn't help but smile. They really were an adorable couple, well-liked at school, and had been together for a year, which is like eternity in high school. It made sense.

Weston dropped his arms from around me, then took my hand, pulling me away from the group.

"Where are we going?" I asked.

He smiled over his shoulder at me. "It's the first time tonight your mom and Cody have been distracted. Thought we could take advantage of the situation."

"I like where your head is at, Mr. Ashworth," I said.

"Thank you, Ms. Richards."

He led me over to the wood bridge tucked into the corner of the gym, surrounded by the pond and fake trees. The twinkling lights hung down all around us, setting the perfect mood.

When we neared the center of the bridge, Weston suddenly dropped my hand, his face going pale.

"Are you okay?" I asked.

He nodded vigorously, his head bopping up and down. "Totally fine. Cool." He cleared his throat. "There's just been something I've wanted to say you but didn't know how, and haven't really had the chance, and life has been crazy with school and family and everything. The timing has never been right. But we're here now and it's, like, all romantic and stuff with the trees and lights and crap, and I just need to get this off my chest before I explode."

He sucked in a sharp breath, then suddenly spewed, "I love you!" He blew out a long breath of relief. "Oh, man, it feels so good to say that. I love you. Like, a lot." He put his hands on top of his head, clasping his fingers together. "Whew. I feel like this huge weight has been lifted off my shoulder, you know? I should have said that forever ago and saved myself all the stress." His face went red. "Unless you don't feel the same. Then, that would suck. Maybe don't say anything if you don't. We can just pretend this didn't happen and go back out onto the dance floor or something."

I'd already known that I'd fallen in love with Weston, but this moment just confirmed it. He was my other half.

Throwing my arms around his neck, I looked in his eyes. "I love you, too. Like, a lot."

His nose inched up with his crooked smile, and I wanted to remember the moment forever. Being in his warm embrace. Knowing I'd found my forever, and together, we could conquer the world.

A loud click of a picture being taken sounded to the right. I looked over to find Cody peering out from behind a tree, holding his camera up, a smile on his face.

"Just ignore me," he whispered.

Well, at least he'd captured one of the most amazing moments of my life before he went and made it all awkward.

"Let me see," Mom said, coming out from behind Cody. She put her hand on her chest as she stared at the screen. "Aww. You two. So cute." She twisted her lips to the side in thought as she looked over at us. "Daphne, turn to the side.

And then, Weston, come up behind her, interlocking your fingers, both of you looking at the ground."

I threw my head back and groaned. "Seriously, Mom, stop. This isn't a photoshoot."

Weston took my hand, shaking his head as he steered me off the bridge and away from my crazy mom.

"Did I overstep?" Mom asked from behind me.

"A little bit," Cody said. "But they'll get over it."

Weston tugged me close to him. "You're lucky I love you."

I grinned up at him. "Say it again."

Coming to a stop, Weston set his warm hand on my cheek, his thumb caressing my skin. "I love you." He closed the distance between us, his kiss the perfect melody of my soul.

ACKNOWLEDGMENTS

A monster shout-out to everyone at Monster Ivy Publishing for their continuing awesomeness. Working with them has been a dream, and I've grown so much as a writer thanks to the ideas and edits that come from them. Cammie, I LOVE the cover so much—it's perfection. Mary, thanks for the texts as you read. Hearing someone be as excited about my book as I am gives me all the feels.

Chad, thanks for putting up with my quirkiness through all these years of marriage. Like Daphne, I'm constantly singing and dancing (and not very good at either), no matter where I am, including in public. I just love music. If it's not playing somewhere around me, it's playing in my head. It just always takes me to my happy place. Chad, you are, and always will be, my Weston.

To all my middle school and high school friends, thanks for always sticking by my side and being the best of friends a girl could have. Kayla, Evelyn, Jenny, Michelle, Candis, and Kacie, I'm not sure I would have survived those years without you!

To my secret water-polo-playing-and-swim-team-dude

crush who was the inspiration for Bentley, thanks for being you. No one knew about my crush, even my best friends, because you were so out-of-my-league-it's-never-going-to-happen that I kept that nugget of information to myself. Besides, I'm a Daphne and you're a Bentley. And I needed a Weston (and scored big time with him).

A big thanks to my cats, Harper and Aviendha, for keeping me company through the edits. You girls light up my life.

A special thanks to my Father in heaven for giving me the courage to push through my anxiety and continue writing. Telling stories is one thing that truly gives me joy and I'm grateful for the ability.

And, as always, thank YOU, dear reader, for your support.

ABOUT THE AUTHOR

 Sara Jo Cluff grew up in Yorba Linda, California, right next to the Happiest Place on Earth (aka her second home). Now, she resides in Utah with her husband, Chad, and crazy cats.

She loves creating stories from scratch and seeing where the characters take her. When she's not writing, she's hanging out with her husband, watching Netflix, reading, or doing jigsaw puzzles.

She's a proud #PepperPack #Ambassador for the Most Delicious Beverage on Earth: Dr Pepper.

Visit her author website, www.sarajocluff.com, and for merchandise, visit shop.spreadshirt.com/awkwardpepper.

ALSO BY SARA CLUFF

THE KISS LIST- When high school student Camille Collins' ex-boyfriend spreads a dirty rumor that she's a terrible kisser, Camille and her friends devise the perfect plan to prove Dylan wrong--a kiss list. Perfect kisses with a few of the hottest guys in school will leave too much evidence for anyone to deny.

FILLER FRIEND - After a catastrophic friendship, Elinora decides that having any relationship isn't worth the heartbreak. Her parents still want her to socialize, so she starts her Filler Friend operation, unbeknownst to them. She'll fill-in as a friend for anyone at school, whether it's getting a gamer out of the house or being a plus one at their parent's boring work party.

NEW HAVEN SERIES - Seventeen-year-old Emmie Woodard has lived a controlled life. The city of River Springs—run by Infinity Corp—makes all her choices for her. What to wear, what to eat, how to act, and her future in the city. She pushes back during Recruitment, refusing to be the society's puppet.

THE IMMORTAL LIFE OF COTTON WYLEY - Why be a superhero when you could be the trusty sidekick?

THE KISS LIST

Chapter 1

I needed a license plate frame that said, "I'd rather be kissing." Because, honestly, if I could be doing anything right now, it would be kissing.

Which was why I pressed my freshly glossed lips against my boyfriend's somewhat dry lips. They wouldn't be dry when I was done with him. Dylan didn't hesitate—he pulled me into his lean chest, and our lips moved in perfect harmony like Pentatonix. After being together for over a year, it all came naturally.

We were on the leather couch in the front room of my house, me in his lap, his firm arms wrapped tightly around me, holding my body close, and his warm hand cradling the back of my neck. His long fingers drummed like they wanted to move, but he knew better than to let his hands wander. He'd get a solid smack across the cheek, like every time he'd ever tried.

I drew the line at kissing. A dark, thick line that wouldn't be going away any time soon, no matter how big of an eraser Dylan tried to use.

"Break it up." At Dad's deep voice, Dylan picked me up off his lap and set me down next to him.

Dad had one of those voices that no matter what he said, he came across serious, and slightly life-threatening. Add in his short-cropped military hair and huge muscles, and a lot of people stayed clear of him.

Dad didn't really care that much about us kissing. As long as we weren't alone in my bedroom, he was okay with it. But, obviously, it wasn't his favorite thing to watch.

"Hey, Mr. Collins," Dylan said, showing his dazzling white teeth and using his charming tone that made every adult smile. Except my dad.

Dad was in his 'at ease' stance, feet shoulder width apart, arms folded, and chin tilted up. He had on his hardly worn button-down shirt and slacks. The blue paisley tie was tied like it had been an afterthought. Mom would fix it when she got the chance.

Dad exhaled loudly through his nose—his calming technique—then turned his attention to me. "Camille, your mom and I need you to watch Seth tonight."

As if on cue, my little brother bounded into the room and put his hands on his hips. "Dad, I'm ten. I can take care of myself." He had his blond hair in a short mohawk and wore his favorite Minecraft shirt that was developing a few holes since he wore it so often.

Dad broke out in a fit of laughter, the rumbly sound making Dylan and me laugh as well. With his habit of opening the door for anyone, Seth couldn't stay home by himself, but Dad loved how grown up he tried to be.

"You all suck." Seth glared, his blue eyes too adorable to take seriously.

Dad's laughter cut off, and he slapped Seth upside the head. "Language."

Seth rubbed the back of his head, the glare intensifying. "Camille says it all the time."

I leaned my arms on the back of the couch and kneeled on the cushion, my bare knees sliding on the leather so I could face them. "That's because I'm seventeen. I can get away with almost anything."

Mom rounded the corner of the hall, dressed in her typical form-fitting black dress, her blue eyes intently on her smart phone, her manicured thumb moving across it at lightning speed. She put my friends and me to shame when it came to how often she used her phone and how fast she could go. She was a teenage girl in an adult's body.

"Not true." Mom didn't take her eyes off the phone as she went into the kitchen and opened the fridge. She had a new case at her law firm that was occupying most of her time.

I held up a finger. "I said *almost*."

Dad snatched the phone from Mom's hand. She threw out her hands to retrieve it, but he just turned his back on her, a sly grin sliding onto his face. He loved to see Mom squirm.

"I was using that," Mom said with the same tone she used on Seth when he was misbehaving.

"I know," Dad said, dropping the phone into his jeans pocket. "But your clients will live until tomorrow. I promise."

Mom dropped her hands with a sigh. She opened her mouth, her eyes ready to challenge him, but instead, she grabbed a lime Diet Coke from the fridge, popped it open, and downed it.

"That's so impressive," Dylan whispered next to me.

I elbowed him, and he grunted, rubbing his stomach

where I hit him. Mom didn't like anyone commenting on her "drinking problem," as Dad called it.

Dad pointed his thick finger at us. "Dylan can't be here."

I rolled my eyes. "Yeah, I know."

He told us that every time he and Mom left me in charge. He didn't like the thought of Dylan and me being alone in the house without them there. I once tried to argue that we weren't alone since Seth would be home. The intense glare that followed, with Dad's jaw pulled tight, and veins popping out basically everywhere, forced me to never bring that up again.

Dylan kissed my cheek, leaving behind some of my lip gloss I'd given him earlier. "I gotta get home anyway. Have fun tonight, Mr. and Mrs. Collins." He jogged over to Seth and held his hand high in the air. Seth jumped up, slapping his hand against Dylan's, smiling brightly the whole time.

Normally, I hated seeing him go, and I'd beg him to stay just a little while longer. But as I watched his backside as he left the house, nothing flitted inside me—good or bad. I shook the random thought from my head. I was probably just tired.

Dad took the opportunity to come up behind me and slap the back of my head—his favorite thing to do.

"Not in my house," he mumbled.

"What? Looking at my boyfriend?"

He rubbed the top of my hair until it became a tangled mess. "Lusting after him."

I threw my head back and laughed so hard, I snorted. It took me a few seconds to calm enough that I could talk. "*Lusting*? Seriously, Dad? Gah. Will you please not use that word around me?"

Dad folded his arms, emphasizing his muscles. "If you stop lusting, then I'll have no reason to use it."

Seth had his small fingers in his ears and his eyes closed as he hummed the Star Wars theme song.

"Maybe we could grab an early dinner as a family before Dad and I leave for the party," Mom said, tossing her empty can in the recycle bin. She brushed back the blonde curls blocking part of her eye.

"Who has a party on a Thursday night anyway?" I asked.

Dad pointed his thumb at Mom. "Her weird clients."

Mom slapped his arm, and he huffed, smiling the whole time. A smile finally broke out on her face as well. Until she noticed Dad's tie, huffed, and stepped in to fix it.

When she finished, she went to Seth—still humming and plugging his ears—wrapped her arms around him, squeezed him tight, and pressed her lips close to his ear. "Food."

Seth took his fingers out of his ears, but couldn't lower his arms since Mom still had him in her grasp. He smiled wide, showing off his crooked front teeth. "Can we go to McDonald's?"

Dad scrunched his face, disgust filling every wrinkle. "No."

"You never let us go there," Seth said, flapping his hands awkwardly. Mom wouldn't release him, but he wasn't trying to get away.

"Because I'm being a responsible parent," Dad said. "I love you kids and care about your wellbeing."

I hopped over the couch, landing on the tile, shuffling closer to them and swaying my hips like a little girl. "Is that why you're going to take us to Chick-fil-A?"

Dad wiggled his eyebrows, his smile splitting wide. "You know it."

"What's the difference?" Seth asked, holding his palms up. "They both have chicken nuggets that are delicious."

"Oh, Seth." I squeezed his cheeks since Mom held him in place and he couldn't do anything about it. "One day your taste buds will develop, and you'll know the difference between gross and delicious."

Mom kissed the side of Seth's head, avoiding his Mohawk. "I personally love McDonald's chicken nuggets. Maybe we could go there, and your father and sister can go to Chick-fil-A."

Dad held up a hand. "We eat as a family." When Seth pouted, Dad sighed. "They're right next to each other. You two can bring your food over and eat with us."

Seth tried to pump his fist, but couldn't move. He grunted. "Mom, you're making it hard for me to do anything."

"I know," she said, rocking him left and right.

Dad caught my eye, and I nodded. Seth saw our interaction and squealed, trying to wiggle away from Mom. "Stay away!"

With wicked grins, Dad and I swarmed in on Seth and tickled him while Mom held him in place. Seth squirmed and giggled, his eyes closing tight.

"Stop!"

We kept on tickling, getting his sides, armpits, and stomach. When I ventured down to his feet, he kicked out his legs, smacking his foot into my cheek. It hurt a little, but it was all too funny for me to care.

"Stop!" He laughed. "I'm going to pee my pants!"

Dad immediately stepped back and threw up his hands. "I don't want to clean that up."

Seth danced where he stood, so Mom let him go and pushed him toward the hall. He took off running, his socks sliding on the tile as he neared the bathroom. He already had his pants unzipped.

I leaned over laughing, clapping my hands. Tears pricked at the corner of my eyes. It didn't take long until Mom and Dad were laughing uncontrollably like me. Seth came out of the bathroom glaring, but couldn't help laughing when he got a good look at us.

He threw his arms wide. "Glad I can entertain you guys. Can we go now? I'm starving, and those chicken nuggets aren't going to eat themselves."

Dad patted Seth's shoulder and turned him toward the front door, but then spotted Mom on her phone, probably emailing a client. He glanced at his jeans pocket, looking both annoyed and impressed that Mom had somehow wrangled it free. He opened the door, and they were about to step outside before I spoke up.

"I'm thinking Seth should probably put some shoes on," I said, pointing at his socked feet. What would they do without me?

Dad looked down at them. "Huh." He rubbed Seth's shoulders. "Hurry before I beat you to the car."

Seth plopped down in the entryway and scrambled to get his shoes on. Dad kept jerking like he was going to take off toward the car, causing Seth to whine. When he finished with the laces, Seth flew to his feet, past Dad, and out the door. Dad had to sprint to keep up.

"Mom, can I go to a concert with Dylan next weekend?" I asked. The best time to ask her for things was when she was preoccupied. Which was actually most of the time.

"Uh huh," Mom said, her eyes glued to her phone. We

walked out the front door, and I locked it since that would be another thing they'd forget to do.

I could tell her anything, and it wouldn't register. "It's one of those wild ones. Lots of drugs, clothes coming off and such."

"That sounds fun." Mom opened the passenger door of the car, her thumb moving across the screen of her phone.

"Also, I'm an assassin."

Mom pressed *send* on her phone and smiled up at me. "That's nice, dear." She got into the car and closed the door.

With a sigh, I joined my crazy family in the car and wished for once that Mom would pay attention to us during dinner. But I never liked to get my hopes up.

Made in the USA
Monee, IL
04 December 2021